PHILIP K. DICK

L I E S , I N C .

Philip K. Dick was born in Chicago in 1928 and lived most of his life in California. He briefly attended the University of California, but dropped out before completing any classes. In 1952, he began writing professionally and proceeded to write numerous novels and short story collections. He won the Hugo Award for the best novel in 1962 for *The Man in the High Castle* and the John W. Campbell Memorial Award for best novel of the year in 1974 for *Flow My Tears, the Policeman Said.* Philip K. Dick died on March 2, 1982, in Santa Ana, California, of heart failure following a stroke.

NOVELS BY PHILIP K. DICK

Clans of the Alphane Moon
Confessions of a Crap Artist
The Cosmic Puppets
Counter-Clock World
The Crack in Space
Deus Irae (with Roger Zelazny)
The Divine Invasion
Do Androids Dream of Electric Sheep?
Dr. Bloodmoney
Dr. Futurity
Eye in the Sky
Flow My Tears, the Policeman Said
Galactic Pot-Healer
The Game-Players of Titan
Lies, Inc.
The Man in the High Castle
The Man Who Japed
Martian Time-Slip
A Maze of Death
Now Wait for Last Year
Our Friends from Frolix 8
The Penultimate Truth
Radio Free Albemuth
A Scanner Darkly
The Simulacra
Solar Lottery
The Three Stigmata of Palmer Eldritch
Time Out of Joint
The Transmigration of Timothy Archer
Ubik
VALIS
Vulcan's Hammer
We Can Build You
The World Jones Made
The Zap Gun

LIES, INC.

LIES, INC.

PHILIP K. DICK

FORMERLY PUBLISHED AS
The Unteleported Man

VINTAGE BOOKS
A Division of Random House, Inc.
New York

FIRST VINTAGE BOOKS EDITION, MARCH 2004

Library of Congress Cataloging-in-Publication Data
Dick, Philip K.
Lies, Inc. / Philip K. Dick.
p. cm.
Rev. ed. of: The unteleported man. 1964. Rev. ed. under title:
Lies, Inc., originally published: London : Gollancz, 1984.
ISBN 1-4000-3008-0
1. Interplanetary voyages—Fiction. 2. Space colonies—
Fiction. 3. Spaceships—Fiction. I. Title: Lies
Incorporated. II. Dick, Philip K. Unteleported man. III. Title.
PS3554.I3L54 2004
813'.54—dc22 2003065789

www.vintagebooks.com

Printed in the United States of America
10 9 8 7 6 5 4 3 2

LIES, INC.

ONE

The SubInfo computers owned by Lies Incorporated had been caught in an unnatural act by a service mechanic. SubInfo computer Five had transmitted information which was not a lie.

It would have to be taken apart to see why. And to whom the correct information had gone.

Probably there would be no way to discern to whom the correct information had gone. But a carrier check maintained an automatic record of all subinformation transmitted by the bank of computers located here and there on Terra. The information had to do with a rat. According to the carrier check the rat lived with a colony of other rats in a garbage dump in Oakland, California.

What importance could information dealing with a rat have? Lewis Stine, the chief mechanic for Lies Incorporated, pondered this as he broke the flow of current to SubInfo computer Five and prepared to begin taking it apart. Of course he could ask the computer . . . but the computer, being programmed to lie, would of course lie—even to Lies Incorporated itself. That was an irony which Stine did not appreciate. This problem always surfaced when it came time to dismantle one of the computers.

Any other bank of computers, Stine thought, could be asked.

Just for a moment he restored power to SubInfo computer Five and punched buttons on the console of a terminal. Whom did you transmit to? he asked.

BEN APPLEBAUM, RACHMAEL

"Fine," Stine said. At least he knew that. Somebody on Terra with the name Rachmael ben Applebaum probably now knew more about rats than he cared to know, albeit on a subliminal basis.

You're probably thinking a lot about rats these days, Mr. ben Applebaum, Stine said to himself. And you are wondering why.

Again he cut the power to the computer. And began to go to work.

Standing before his bathroom mirror shaving, Rachmael ben Applebaum thought about the delicious taste of cheeseburger fragments—not a whole cheeseburger (you rarely found those) but the wonderful dried bits lying here and there among the coffee grounds, grapefruit rinds and egg shells.

I'll fly over to Bob's Big Boy, he decided, and order a cheeseburger for breakfast.

And then he thought, It's those damn dreams.

Actually it was one dream over and over again. And he always had it around three a.m.; several times he had awakened, gotten out of bed, bewildered and disturbed by the intensity of the dream, and noted the clock. The *place* he dreamed of; it was awful. And yet, for some reason, while he was actually there—actually dreaming—the place seemed great. And this was the part that bothered him the most: that he liked it so. It seemed familiar; it seemed to be a place he regarded as home.

However, so did a number of other people—

People. They hadn't looked exactly like people, although they had talked like people.

"That's mine," Fred said, holding on to an armload of dog kibble.

"The hell you say," Rachmael said angrily. "I saw it first. Give it here or I'll pop you."

He and Fred fought over the armload of dog kibble, and Rachmael finally won. But he won in an odd way: by biting Fred on the shoulder. He hadn't hit him; he had bitten him.

Strange, Rachmael thought as he continued to shave.

I'm going to have to see a psychiatrist, he said to himself. Maybe it's memories of a former life. Millions of years ago before I . . . before I had evolved into a human being. Far lower on the evolutionary scale. Biting people, or rather biting animals. Yes, he thought; Fred was an animal of some kind. But we talked English.

In his dream he kept a secret hoard of valuables which the others in the settlement knew nothing about. He thought of them now, those precious artifacts which he cherished, which he had gone to such lengths—and effort—to acquire. Mostly food, of course; nothing was more important than food. And yet—you could sometimes find string. He had a lot of string: fine brown string; he had wound it up into a heap and, during the day, he slept in the midst of it. The pile of string comforted him; it lulled him and made his dreams peaceful. All but one; there at the settlement, asleep during the day in his pile of string, he had one dreadful dream which kept coming back.

It had to do with a huge fish opening its mouth wide . . . and vast ugly teeth strove to crunch him, crunch him with avid relish.

Jeez, Rachmael said. Maybe I'm not here shaving; maybe I'm just dreaming this. Maybe I'm asleep in my pile of string, and having a good dream, not the bad one; having the dream where I'm a—

He thought, A *man*.

So then, by inference, he thought, I'm not a man when I'm at the settlement. That would explain why I bit, and why Fred bit. That son-of-a-bitch, he said to himself. He knows where a lot of dog kibble is and he won't tell any of the rest of us. I'll find it; I'll find his trove.

But then, he realized, while I'm out doing that, maybe Fred (or someone else) will find *my* trove and take away my string. My wonderful string which was so hard to drag back to my hiding place; it kept snagging and catching on things . . . I'll defend that string with my life, Rachmael said to himself. Any son-of-a-bitch who tries to steal it will wind up without his face.

He looked at his wristwatch. Got to hurry, he said to himself. It's late; I overslept again. And I can't get the dream out of my head. It was too vivid for a dream. It wasn't a dream; maybe it was involuntary telepathy of some kind. Or contact with an alternate universe. That's probably what it was: another Earth on which I was born as an animal rather than a human being.

Or a microwave transmission, using my brain as a transducer without an electronic interface. They have those, especially the police agencies.

He was very much afraid of the world-wide police agencies. Especially Lies, Incorporated, the worst police agency of them all. Even the Soviet police were afraid of them.

They're beaming psychotronic signals at me subliminally while I'm asleep, he thought. And then he realized how paranoid that was. Christ; no sane person would think that. And even if Lies, Incorporated did transmit microwave-boosted telepathic information to him in his sleep, would it have to do with rats?

With rats!

I'm a goddamn rat, he realized. When I go to sleep I abreact back millions of years to when I was once a rat, and I think rat thoughts and have rat ideas; I cherish what a rat cherishes. That explains my fighting with Fred for the dog kibble. It's simple: memories from the paleocortex, rather than the neocortex.

There's an anatomical explanation. Has to do with accretional layers of the brain; the brain has old layers which come to wakefulness during normal sleep.

That's the trouble with living in a police state, he said to himself; you think—you imagine—the police are behind everything. You get paranoid and think they're beaming information to you in your sleep, to subliminally control you. Actually the police wouldn't do that. The police are our friends.

Or was *that* idea beamed to me subliminally? he wondered suddenly. "The police are our friends." The hell they are!

He continued shaving, feeling glum about the whole thing. Maybe the dream will stop coming, he said to himself. Or—

Pausing, he thought, Maybe the dream is trying to tell me something.

For a long time he stood without moving, the razor held away from his face. Tell me what? That I'm living in a garbage dump where there's dried scraps of food, rotting food, other rats?

He trembled.

And, as best he could, continued shaving.

T W O

"Syn-cof?" the receptionist asked sympathetically. "Or Martian fnikjuice tea, while you wait?"

Rachmael ben Applebaum, getting out a genuine Tampa, Florida Garcia y Vega cigarillo, said, "I'll just sit, thanks." He lit the cigar, waited. For Miss Freya Holm. He wondered what she looked like. If she was as pretty as the receptionist—

A soft voice said, almost timidly, "Mr. ben Applebaum? I'm Miss Holm. If you'll come into my office—" She held the door open, and she was perfection; his Garcia y Vega cigarillo dwindled, neglected in the ashtray as he rose to his feet. She, no more than twenty, chitin-black long hair that hung freely down her shoulders, teeth white as the glossy bond of the expensive UN info mags . . . he stared at her, at the small girl in the gold-spray bodice and shorts and sandals, with the single camellia over her left ear, stared and thought, *And this is my police protection.*

"Sure." Numbly, he passed her, entered her small, contemporarily furnished office; in one glance he saw artifacts from the extinct cultures of six planets. "But Miss Holm," he said, then, candidly.

"Maybe your employers didn't explain; there's pressure here. I've got one of the most powerful economic syndromes in the Sol system after me. Trails of Hoffman—"

"THL," Miss Holm said, seating herself at her desk and touching the *on* of her aud-recorder, "is the owner of Dr. Sepp von Einem's teleportation construct and hence monopolistically has made obsolete the hyper-see liners and freighters of Applebaum Enterprise." On her desk before her she had a folio, which she consulted. "You see, Mr. Rachmael ben Applebaum—" She glanced up. "I wish to keep you in data-reference distinct from your father, the late Maury Applebaum. So may I call you Rachmael?"

"Y-yes," he said, nettled by her coolness, her small, firm poise—and the folio which lay before her; long before he had consulted Listening Instructional Educational Services—or, as the pop mind called it in UN-egged-on derision, Lies Incorporated—the police agency had gathered, with its many monitors, the totality of information pertaining to him and to the collapse from abrupt technological obsolescence of the once formidable Applebaum Enterprise. And—

"Your late father," Freya Holm said, "died evidently at his own instigation. Officially the UN police list it as *Selbstmort* . . . suicide. We however—" She paused, consulting the folio. "Hmmm."

Rachmael said, "I'm not satisfied, but I'm resigned." After all, he could not bring back his heavy, red-faced, near-sighted and highly over-taxed father. *Selbstmort*, in the official German of the UN, or not. "Miss Holm," he began, but she cut him off, gently.

"Rachmael, the Telpor electronic entity of Dr. Sepp von Einem, researched and paid for, developed in the several interplan labs of Trails of Hoffman, could do nothing else than bring chaos to the drayage industry. Theodoric Ferry, who is chairman of the board of THL, must have known this when he financed Dr. von Einem at his Schweinfort labs where the Telpor . . ."

Her voice faded.

Rachmael ben Applebaum sat with a circle of friends around a superior person, very wise and ancient. They called him Abba, which meant Daddy. When Abba spoke the entire settlement listened, and as best they could the individuals committed to memory what Abba told them. Because what that ancient person told them had an absolute quality to it; Abba had not originated in the settlement, but knew things which no one else knew, and he guided them all.

". . . breakthrough occurred," Abba said in his low, gentle voice. "And yet THL owned—outside of your father's—the largest single holding of the now-defunct Applebaum Enterprise. Therefore, my little ones, know this: Trails of Hoffman Limited deliberately ruined a corporation which it had major investments in . . . and this, I admit, has seemed strange to us."

The wise, elderly Abba faded out. Freya Holm glanced up alertly, tossed back her mass of black hair.

"And now they hound you for restitution; correct?"

Rachmael blinked; he managed to nod mutely.

Quietly, Miss Holm asked, "How long did it take a passenger liner of your father's corporation to reach Whale's Mouth with a load of, say, five hundred colonists, plus their personal effects?"

After a tormented pause he said, "We—never even tried. Years. Even at hyper-see."

The girl, across from him, still waited, wanting to hear him say it.

"With our flagship transport," he said, "eighteen years."

"And with Dr. von Einem's teleportation instrument—"

"Fifteen minutes," he said harshly. And Whale's Mouth, the number IX planet of the Fomalhaut system, was to date the sole planet discovered either by manned or unmanned observers which was truly habitable—truly a second Terra. Eighteen years . . . and even deep-sleep would not help, for such a prolonged period; aging, although slowed down, although consciousness was dimmed, still occurred. Alpha and Prox; that had been all right; that had been short enough. But Fomalhaut, at twenty-four light years—

"We just couldn't compete," he said. "We simply could not carry colonists that far."

"Would you have tried, without von Einem's Telpor break-through?"

Rachmael said, "My father—"

"Was thinking about it." She nodded. "But then he died and it was too late and now you've had to sell virtually all your ships to meet note-payment due-dates. Now, from us, Rachmael. You wanted . . . ?"

"I still own," he said, "our fastest, newest, biggest ship, the *Omphalos*. She's never been sold, no matter how great the pressure THL has put on me, within and outside the UN courts." He hesitated, then said it. "I want to go to Whale's Mouth. By ship. Not by Dr. von Einem's Telpor. And by my own ship, by what we meant to be our—" He broke off. "I want to take her all the way to Fomalhaut, on an eighteen-year voyage—alone. And when I arrive at Whale's Mouth I'll prove—"

"Yes?" Freya said. "Prove what, Rachmael?"

As he sat there, formulating his answer, he saw again the tender, intelligent shape of Abba; but Abba did not look human. A fur of darkness and complexity covered Abba and as the wise one spoke his voice seemed shrill and eerie. Remnants of the dream, Rachmael realized; coming back at me in my waking state.

Abba said, "There lies a wonderful place. In it lies very fine food. In it lies . . . in it lies . . . *lies*."

The last word lingered in Rachmael's mind. *Lies.*

Across from him the girl waited for him to answer.

"Lies," he said. "Something about lies."

"Oh, the name they give us." Freya laughed.

A pun, he thought. The two words sound the same, spelled the same, but mean different things.

"That we could have done it," Rachmael said. "Had von Einem not come along with that teleportation thing, that—" He gestured and felt, within him, impotent fury. And still the word lingered in his mind, traced there by Abba, who was wise but who was not human.

Lies.

Freya said, "Telpor is one of the most vital discoveries in human history, Rachmael. Teleportation, from one star-system to another. Twenty-four light-years in fifteen minutes. When you reach Whale's Mouth by the *Omphalos*, I for instance will be—" She calculated. "Forty-three years old."

He was silent.

"What," Freya asked in a soft voice, "would you accomplish by your trip?"

He thought, This is Lies Incorporated that I am sitting here talking to. The last people in the world I should be talking to. I may have been programmed by them to come here, programmed subliminally, in my sleep, my dreams . . . which explains the word *lies*.

Presently Freya said, reading from her folio, "You have, for six months now, been thoroughly checking out the *Omphalos* at a concealed—even from us—launch field and maintenance dock on Luna. She is now considered ready for the inter-system flight. Trails of Hoffman has tried, through the courts, to attach her, to claim her as their legal property; this you have managed to fight. So far. But now—"

"My lawyers tell me," Rachmael said, "that three days stand between me and THL seizing the *Omphalos*."

"You can't blast off within three days?"

"The deep-sleep equipment. It's a week from being readied." He let out his breath raggedly. "A subsidiary of THL manufactures vital components. They've been—held up."

Freya nodded. "And your coming here is to request us to pick up the *Omphalos*, with one of our veteran pilots, disappear with her for at least a week, until she's ready for the flight to Fomalhaut. Correct?"

"That's it," he said, and sat waiting.

After a pause Freya said, "You can't pilot the ship yourself?"

"I'm not good enough to lose her," Rachmael said. "They'd find me. But yours—one of your top-line pilots." He did not look directly at her; it meant too much.

"You can pay our fee of—"

"Nothing."

"'Nothing'?"

"I have absolutely no funds. Later, as I continue to liquidate the assets of the corporation, possibly I—"

Freya said, "There's a note here from my employer, Mr. Glazer-Holliday. He observes that you're poscredless. His instructions to us—" She read the note, silently. "However, we're to cooperate with you."

"Why?"

"My employer doesn't say. We have been aware of your financial helplessness for some time." Glancing up at him she said, "We will okay the dispatch of an experienced pilot who will take—"

"Then you expect me to come here."

She gazed at him.

"Did you suggest that I come here?" he said. "Because to be honest with you I do not trust Lies Incorporated."

"Well, we lie a lot." She smiled.

"But you can save the *Omphalos.*"

"Probably. Our pilot—and he will be one of our best—will take the *Omphalos* off where THL, where even the UN agents acting for the Secretary General, Herr Horst Bertold, won't find her."

"Probably," he echoed.

"This our man can do," Freya continued, "while you manage, if you can, to obtain the final components of the deep-sleep equipment. But I doubt if you'll obtain those components, Rachmael. There's an additional memo here to that effect, too. You're correct: Theodoric Ferry sits on its board of directors, too, and this is all legal, this monopoly which the firm possesses." Her smile was bitter. "UN sanctioned."

He was silent. Obviously it was hopeless; no matter how long the Lies Incorporated professional and ultra-veteran space pilot kept the huge liner the *Omphalos* lost between planets, the components would be "held up unavoidably," as the invoices, marked back-order, would read.

"I think," Freya said presently, "that your problem is not the mere obtaining of deep-sleep components. That can be handled; there are ways . . . we, for instance, can—although this will cost you a good deal of money eventually—pick them up on the black market. Your problem, Rachmael—"

"I know," he said. His problem was not *how* to get to the Fomalhaut system, to its ninth planet, Whale's Mouth which—

Again the furred body phased in, the superimposition.

"There it lies," Abba said. "Lies . . . lies . . . lies."

Damn double exposure of reality, Rachmael said to himself; he blinked. What is this, a reality dysfunction of some kind? Or something coming from his right hemisphere to his left, some vital information available to the right which it now urged on the left?

—which was Terra's sole thriving colony world. In fact his problem was not the eighteen-year voyage at all.

His problem was—

"Why go at all?" Abba intoned, the vast animal figure to whom they all looked for the dispensation of wisdom. "When Dr. von Einem's Telpor construct, available at a nominal cost through any of Trails of Hoffman's many retail outlets on Terra—"

Yes, yes, Rachmael thought irritably.

"—makes the trip a mere fifteen-minute minor journey, and within financial reach of even the most modest, income-wise speaking, Terran family?" Abba smiled his tender smile. "Consider that, dear son."

Aloud, Rachmael said, "Freya, the trip by Telpor to Whale's Mouth—it sounds fine." And forty million Terran citizens had taken advantage of it. And the aud and vid reports returning—via the Telpor construct—all told glowingly of a world not overcrowded, of tall grass, of odd but benign animals, of new and lovely cities built by robot-assists taken across at UN-expense to Whale's Mouth. "But—"

"But," Freya said, who was now combined with Abba into one tender and wise entity, huge and furry and pretty, "the peculiar fact is that it's a one-way trip."

Instantly he nodded. "Yes, that's it."

"Sure it is," Freya-Abba said as with a single voice.

"No one can come back," Rachmael said.

The double entity smiled in a cunning way, a sly way. "That is easily explained, my son. The Sol system is located at the axis of the universe."

"What the hell does that mean?" Rachmael said.

"The recession of the extra-galactic nebulae demonstrate von Einem's Theorem One that—" The voice turned into garbled noise, and the double impositions blurred, as if a locking control had gotten twisted; the entire image became warped and deformed, and then, suddenly, the double figure facing him was upside down.

"There must," Rachmael continued, as best he could, considering that he was now talking to a dual entity which was upside down, "out of those forty million people, be a few who want to return. But the TV and 'pape reports say they're all actually totally ecstatically happy. You've seen the endless TV shows, life at Newcolonized-land. It's—"

The upside-down figure belched. "Lies," it said.

"What?" Rachmael said.

"Too perfect, Rachmael?" The figure slowly rotated until it became right-side up, and then Abba faded out; only the girl remained.

"Statistically, *malcontents must exist*. Why do we never hear of them? And we can't go and take a look." Because, if you went by Telpor to Whale's Mouth and saw, you were there, as they were, *to stay*. So if you did find malcontents—what could you do for them? Because you could not take them back; you could only join them. And he had the intuition that somehow this just wouldn't be of much use. Even the UN left Newcolonizedland alone, the countless UN welfare agencies, the personnel and bureaus newly set up by the present Secretary General Horst Bertold, from New Whole

Germany: the largest political entity in Europe—even they stopped at the Telpor gates. Neues Einige Deutschland . . . NED. Far more powerful than the mangy, dwindling French Empire or the UK—they were pale remnants of the past.

And New Whole Germany—as the election to UN Secretary General of Horst Bertold showed—was the Wave of the Future . . . as the Germans themselves liked to phrase it.

"So in other words," Freya said, "you'd take an empty passenger liner to the Fomalhaut system, spend eighteen years in transit, you, the sole unteleported man, among the seven billion citizens of Terra, with the idea—or should I say, the hope?—that when you arrive finally at Whale's Mouth, in the year 2032, you'll find a passenger complement, five hundred or so unhappy souls who want out? And so you then can resume commercial operations . . . von Einem takes them there in fifteen minutes and then eighteen years later you return them to Terra, back home to the Sol system."

"Yes," he said fiercely.

"Plus another eighteen years—for them—too—for the flight back. For you thirty-six years in all. You'd return to Terra in the year—" She calculated. "2050 AD. I'd be sixty-one years old; Theodoric Ferry, even Horst Bertold, would be dead; perhaps Trails of Hoffman Limited wouldn't even exist, any more . . . certainly Dr. Sepp von Einem would be dead years ago; let's see: he's in his eighties now. No, he'd never live to see you reach Whale's Mouth, let alone return. So if all this is to make him feel bad—"

"Is it insane?" Rachmael said. "To believe, first, that *some* unhappy persons must be stuck at Whale's Mouth . . . and yet we're not hearing, via THL's monopoly of all info media, all energy, passing back this way. And second—"

"And second," Freya said, "to want to spend eighteen years of your life in getting there to rescue them." Professional, intent, she eyed him. "Is this idealism? Or is this vengeance against Dr. von Einem because of his Telpor construct that made your family's liners and commercial carriers obsolete for inter-system travel? After all, if you do manage to leave in the *Omphalos*, it'll be big news, a novelty; it'll be fully covered on TV and in the 'papes, here on Terra; even the UN won't be able to squelch the story—the first, sole, *manned* vessel to go to Fomalhaut, not just one of those old-time instrument packages. Why, you'd be a time capsule; we'd all be waiting for you to arrive first there and then, in 2050, back here."

"A time capsule," he said, "like the one fired off at Whale's Mouth. Which never arrived here on Terra."

She shrugged. "Passed Terra by, was attracted by the sun's gravitational field; was swallowed up unnoticed."

"Unnoticed by *any* tracking station? Out of over six thousand separate monitoring devices in orbit in the Sol system *none* detected the time capsule when it arrived?"

Frowning, Freya said, "What do you mean to imply, Rachmael?"

"This time capsule," Rachmael said, "from Whale's Mouth, the launching of which we watched years ago on TV—it wasn't detected by our tracking stations because it never arrived. And it never arrived, Miss Holm, because despite those crowd scenes *it was never sent.*"

"You mean what we saw on TV—"

"The vid signals, via Telpor," Rachmael said, "which showed the happy masses at Whale's Mouth cheering at the vast public launching ceremony of the time capsule—were fakes. I've run and rerun recordings of them; the crowd noise is spurious." Reaching into his cloak he brought out a seven-inch reel of iron oxide Ampex and tape; he tossed it onto her desk. "Play it back. Carefully. *There were no people cheering.* And for a good reason. Because no time capsule, containing quaint artifacts from the Fomalhaut ancient civilizations, was launched from Whale's Mouth."

"But—" She stared at him in disbelief, then picked up the aud tape, held the reel uncertainly. *"Why?"*

"I don't know," Rachmael said. "But when the *Omphalos* reaches the Fomalhaut system and Whale's Mouth and I see Newcolonizedland, I'll know." And, he thought, I don't think I'll find ten or sixty malcontents out of forty million . . . by that time, of course, it'll be something like a billion colonists. I'll find—

He ended the thought abruptly. He did not know.

But eventually he would know. In the little matter of eighteen years.

THREE

In the sybaritic living room of his villa, on his satellite as it orbited Terra, the owner of Lies, Incorporated, Matson Glazer-Holliday, sat in his human-made dressing gown smoking a prize, rare Antonio y Cleopatra cigar and listening to the aud tape of the crowd noises.

And, directly before him he watched the oscilloscope as it transformed the audio signal into a visual one.

To Freya Holm he said, "Yes, there is a cycle. You can see it, even though you can't hear it. This aud-track is continuous, running over and over again. Hence the man's right; it's a fake."

"Could Rachmael ben Applebaum have—"

"No," Matson said. "I've sequestered an aud copy from the UN info archives; it agrees. Rachmael didn't tamper with the tape; it's exactly what he claims it to be." He sat back, pondering.

Strange, he thought, that von Einem's Telpor gadget works only one way, radiating matter out . . . with no return of that matter, at least by teleportation, possible. So, rather conveniently for Trails of Hoffman, all we get via Telpor as a feedback from Whale's Mouth is an electronic signal, energy alone . . . and this one now exposed as a fake; as a research agency I should have discovered this long ago—Rachmael, with all his creditors hounding him jet-balloonwise, keeping him awake night and day, hammering at him with countless technological assists, impeding him in the normal course of conducting routine business, has detected this spuriousness, and I—damn it. Matson thought; I missed, here. He felt gloomy.

"Cutty Sark Scotch and water?" Freya asked.

He nodded absently as Fredya, who was his mistress, disappeared into the liquor antechamber of the villa to see if the 1985 bottle—worth a fortune—were empty yet.

But, on the credit side, he had been suspicious.

From the start he had doubted the so-called "Theorem One" of Dr. von Einem; it sounded too much like a cover, this one-way transmission by the technicians of THL's multitude of retail outlets. Write home from Whale's Mouth, son, when you get there, he thought acidly; tell your old mom how it is on the colony world with its fresh air, sunshine, all those cute little animals, those wondrous buildings THL robots are constructing . . . and the report-back, the letter, *as electronic signal*, had duly arrived. But the beloved son; he could not personally, directly report. Could not return to tell his story, and, as in the ancient story of the lion's den, all the footprints of guileless creatures led *in* to the den, yet none led *out*. It was the fable all over again—with something even more sinister added. That of what appeared more and more to be a thoroughly phony trail of *outgoing* tracks: the electronic message-units. By someone who is versed in sophisticated hardware, Matson thought; someone is tinkering around, and is there any reason to look beyond the figure of Dr. Sepp von Einem himself, the inventor of the Telpor, plus Neues Einige Deutschland's very efficient technicians who ran Ferry's retail machinery?

There was something he did not like about those German technicians who manned the Telpors. So business-like. As their ancestors must have been, Matson mused. Back in the twentieth century when those ancestors, with the same affectless calm, fed bodies into ovens or living humans into ersatz shower baths which turned out to be Zyklon B hydrogen cyanide gas chambers. And financed by reputable big Third Reich business, by Herr Krupp u. Söhne. Just as von Einem is financed by Trails of Hoffman, with its vast central offices in Grosser Berlinstadt—the new capital of New Whole Germany, the city in fact from which our distinguished UN Secretary General emanates.

"Get me," Matson said to Freya, "instead of Scotch and water, the file on Horst Bertold."

In the other room Freya rang up the autonomic research equipment wired into the walls of the villa . . . electronic hardware, minned—miniaturized—for the most part, of a data-sorting and receiving nature, plus the file-banks, and—

Certain useful artifacts which did *not* involve data but which involved high-velocity A-warhead darts that, were the satellite to be attacked by any of the UN's repertory of offensive weapons, would take up the fight and abolish the missiles before they reached their target.

At his villa on his Brocard ellipse satellite Matson was safe. And, as a precaution, he conducted as much business as possible from this spot; below, in New New York City, at Lies, Incorporated's offices, he always felt naked. Felt, in fact, the nearby presence of the UN and Horst Bertold's legions of "Peace Workers," whose armed, gray-faced men and women who, in the name of Pax Terrae, roamed the world, even into the pathetic moonies, the sad, failure-but-still-extant early "colony" satellites which had come before von Einem's breakthrough and the discovery by George Hoffman of Fomalhaut IX, now called Whale's Mouth and now *the* colony.

Too bad, Matson thought archly, that George Hoffman didn't discover more planets in more star systems habitable by us, the frail needs of living, sentient, mentating biochemical upright bipeds which we humans are. Hundreds and hundreds of planets, but—

Instead, temperature which melted thermo-fuses. No air. No soil. No water.

One could hardly say of such worlds—Venus had proved a typical example—that the "living was easy." The living, in fact, on such worlds was confined to homeostatic domes with their own at, wa, and self-regu temp.

Housing, per dome, perhaps three hundred somatic souls. Rather a small number, considering that as of this year Terra's population stood at seven billion.

"Here," Freya said, sliding down to seat herself, legs tucked under her, on the deep-pile *wool* carpet near Matson. "The file on H.B." She opened it at random; Lies, Incorporated field reps had done a thorough job: many data existed here that, via the UN's carefully watchdogged info media, never had reached the public, even the so-called "critical" analysts and columnists. They could, by law, criticize to their hearts' content, the character, habits, abilities and shaving-customs of Herr Bertold . . . except, however, the basic facts were denied them.

Not so, however, to Lies Incorporated—an ironic sobriquet, in view of the absolutely verified nature of the data now before its owner.

It was harsh reading. Even for him.

The year of Horst Bertold's birth: 1954. Slightly before the Space Age had begun; like Matson Glazer-Holliday, Horst was a remnant of the old world when all that had been glimpsed in the sky were "flying saucers," a misnomer for a US Air Force anti-missile weapon which had, in the brief confrontation of 1982, proved ineffectual. Horst had been born to middle-class Berlin—West Berlin, it had then been called, because, and this was difficult to remember, Germany had in those days been divided—parents: his father had owned a meat market . . . rather fitting, Matson reflected, in that Horst's father had been an SS officer and former member of an Einsatzgruppe which had murdered thousands of innocent persons of Slavic and Jewish ancestry . . . although this had not interfered with Johann Bertold's meat market business in the 1950s and '60s. And then, in 1972, at the age of eighteen, young Horst himself had entered the spotlight (needless to say, the statute of limitations had run out on his father, who had never been prosecuted by the West German legal apparatus for his crimes of the '40s, and had, in addition, evaded the commando squads from Israel who, by 1970, had closed up shop, giving up the task of tracking down the former mass-murderers). Horst, in 1972, had been a leader in the Reinholt Jugend.

Ernst Reinholt, from Hamburg, had headed a party which had striven to unify Germany once more; the deal would be that as a military and economic power she would be neutral between East and West. It had taken ten more years, but in the fracas of 1982 he had obtained from the US and the USSR what he wanted: a united, free Germany, called by its present name, and just chuck full of vim and *Macht.*

And, under Reinholt, Neues Einige Deutschland had played dirty pool from the start. But no one was really surprised; East and West were busy erecting tents where major popcens—population centers such as Chicago and Moscow—had existed, and hoping to god that the Sino-Cuban wing of the CP did not, taking advantage of the situation, move in and entrench . . .

It had been the secret protocol of Reinholt and his NWG that it would not be neutral after all. On the contrary.

New Whole Germany would take out China.

So this was the unsavory basis on which the Reich had reobtained unity. Its *Waffen* technicians had devised, as instructed, weapons which had, in 1987, dealt a terminal punch to People's China. Matson, examining the folio, very rapidly scanned this part, because the Reich had come up with some show-stoppers, and even the abominable US nerve gas had seemed like a field of daisies in comparison—he did not wish to see any mention of what Krupp u. Söhne had devised as an answer to China's thousands of millions who were spilling as far west as the Volga, and toward the US, were crossing from Siberia—taken in 1983—into Alaska. In any case the compact had been agreed on, and even Faust would have blanched at it; now the world had no People's China but a New Whole Germany to contend with.

And what a quid pro quo that had proved to be. Because, correctly and legally, Neues Einige Deutschland had obtained control of the sole planet-wide and hence Sol system-wide governing structure, the UN. They held it now. And the former member of the Reinholt Jugend, Horst Bertold, was its Secretary General. And had faced squarely, as he had promised when compaigning for election—it had become, by 1985, an elective office—that he would deal with the colonization problem; he would find a Final Solution to the tormented condition that (one) Terra was as overpopulated throughout as Japan had been in 1960 and (two) both the alternate planets of the Sol system and the moonies and the domes et al. had failed wretchedly.

Horst had found, via Dr. von Einem's Telpor teleportation construct, a habitable planet in a star system too far from Sol to be reached by the quondam drayage enterprise of Maury Applebaum. Whale's Mouth, and the Telpor mechanisms at Trails of Hoffman's retail outlets, were *the* answer.

To all appearances it was duck soup, feathers, scut included. But—

"See?" Matson said to Freya. "Here's the written transcript of Horst Bertold's speech before he was elected and before von Einem showed up with the Telpor gadget. *The promise was made before teleportation to the Fomalhaut system was technologically possible*— in fact, before the existence of Fomalhaut IX was even known to unmanned elderly relay-monitors."

"So?"

Matson said grimly, "So our UN Secretary General had a mandate before he had a solution. And to the German mind that means one thing and one thing only. The cat and rat farm solution." Or, as he now suspected, the dog food factory solution.

It had been suggested, ironically, in imitation of Swift by a fiction writer of the 1950s, that the "Negro Question" in the US be solved by the building of giant factories which made Negroes into canned dog food. Satire, of course, like Swift's *A Modest Proposal*, that the problem of starvation among the Irish be solved by the eating of the children . . . Swift himself lamenting, as a final irony, that he had no children of his own to offer to the market for consumption. Grisly. But—

This all pointed to the seriousness—not merely of the problem of overpopulation and insufficient food production—but to the insane, schizoid solutions seriously being considered. The brief World War Three—never officially called that; called instead a Pacifying Action, just as the Korean War had been a "Police Action"— had taken care of a few millions of people, but—not quite enough. As a solution it had worked to a partial extent; and was, in many influential quarters, viewed exactly as that; as a partial solution. Not as a catastrophe but as a half-answer.

And Horst Bertold had promised the balance of the answer.

Whale's Mouth was it.

"So in my opinion," Matson murmured, to himself mostly, "I've always been suspicious of Whale's Mouth. If I hadn't read Swift and C. Wright Mills and the Herman Kahn Report for Rand Corporation . . ." He glanced at Freya. "There have," he said, "always been people who would solve the problem that way." *And I think*, he thought, as he listened to the aud tape of the crowd noises, a tape which pretended to consist of a transcript from the launching, at Whale's Mouth, of the ritualistic, celebration-inspired time capsule back through hyper-space—or in some such ultra-high-velocity fashion—to Terra, *that we have those people and that solution with us again.*

We have, in other words, UN Secretary General Horst Bertold and Trails of Hoffman Limited and its economic multi-pseudopodia empire. And dear Dr. Sepp von Einem and his many Telpor outlets, his curiously *one way* teleporting machine.

"That land," Matson murmured, vaguely quoting, lord knew who, what sage of the past, "which all of us must visit one day . . . that land beyond the grave. But no one had returned to report on't. And until they do—"

Freya said perceptively, "Until they do, you're going to stay suspicious. Of the whole Newcolonizedland settlement. Aud and vid signals are not good enough to convince you—because *you* know how easily they can be faked." She gestured at the deck running the tape at this very moment.

"A client," Matson corrected her. "Who on a nonverbal level, what our Reich friends call *thinking with the blood*, suspects that if he takes his one remaining inter-stellar worthy flagship, the—" What was it called? "The *Navel*," he said. "The *Omphalos*; that's what that lofty Greek word means, by the way. Takes the *Navel* direct to Fomalhaut, that after eighteen years of weary deep-sleep which is not quite sleep, more a hypnagogic, restless tossing and turning at low temp, slowed-down metabolism, he will arrive at Whale's Mouth, and oddly it will not be beer and skittles. It will not be happy conapt dwellers, smiling children in autonomic schools, tame, exotic, native life forms. But—"

But just what would he find?

If, as he suspected, the aud and vid tracks passing from Whale's Mouth to Terra via von Einem's Telpor mechanisms were covers—what reality lay beneath?

He simply could not guess, not when forty million people were involved. The dog food factory? Are, god forbid, those forty million men, women and children *dead*? Is it a bone-yard, with no one there, no one even to extract the gold from their teeth—because now we use stainless steel?

He did not know, but—someone knew. Perhaps entire New Whole Germany, which, having cornered the lion's share of power in the UN, hence ruled throughout the nine planets of the Sol system; perhaps as a totality it, on a subrational, instinctive level, knew. As, in the 1940s, it had intuited the existence of the gas chambers beyond the cages of twittering birds and those high walls that kept out all sight and sound . . . and except for that oddly acrid smoke from chimneys all day long—

"They know," Matson said aloud. Horst Bertold knew, and so

did Theodoric Ferry, the owner of THL, and so did doddering but still crafty old Dr. von Einem. And the one hundred and thirty-five million inhabitants of Neues Einige Deutschland, to some degree; not verbally—you couldn't put an expert psych rep of Lies, Incorporated in a small room with a Munich cobbler, run a few routine drug-injections, make the standard quasi-Psionic transcripts, EEGs of his para-psychological reactions, and learn, know, the literal, exact truth.

The whole matter was, damn it, still obscured. And this time it was not cages of twittering birds or shower baths but something else—something, however, equally effective. Trails of Hoffman published 3-D, multi-color, brilliantly artistic, exciting brochures displaying the ecstatic life beyond the Telpor nexus; the TV ran ceaseless, drive-you-mad ads all day and night, of the underpopulated veldt landscape of Whale's Mouth, the balmy climate (via olfactory track), the warm the-answer-is-yes two-moon-filled nights . . . it was a land of romance, freedom, experimentation, kibbutzim without the desert: cooperative living where oranges grew *naturally*, and as large as grapefruits, which themselves resembled melons or the breasts of the women there. But.

Matson decided carefully, "I am sending a veteran field rep across, via normal Telpor, posing as an unmarried businessman who hopes to open a watch repair retail shop at Whale's Mouth. He will have grafted subderm a high-gain transmitter; it will—"

"I know," Freya said patiently; this was evening and she obviously wished for a relaxation of the grim reality of their mutual business. "It will regularly release a signal at ultra-high-frequency on a nonused band, which will ultimately be picked up here. But that'll take *weeks*."

"Okay." He had it now. The Lies, Incorporated field rep would send back a letter, via Telpor, in the customary manner encoded. It was that simple. If the letter arrived: fine. If not—

"You will wait," Freya said, "and wait. And no encoded letter will come. And then you will really begin to think that our client,

Mr. ben Applebaum, has tripped over something ominous and huge in the long darkness which is our collective life. And *then* what will you do? Go across yourself?"

"Then I'm sending you," Matson said. "As the field rep there."

"No," she said, instantly.

"So Whale's Mouth frightens you. Despite all the glossy, expensive literature available free."

"I know Rachmael is right. I knew it when he walked in the door; I knew it from your memo. I'm not going; that's that." She faced her employer-paramour calmly.

"Then I'll draw at random from the field-personnel pool." He had not been serious; why should he offer his mistress as a pawn in this? But he had proved what he wished to prove: their joint fears were not merely intellectual. At this point in their thinking neither Freya nor he would risk the crossing via Telpor to Whale's Mouth, as thousands of guileless citizens of Terra, lugging their belongings and with innocent high hopes, did daily.

I hate, he thought, to turn anyone into the goat. But—

"Pete Burnside. Rep in Detroit. We'll tell him we wish to set up a Lies Incorporated branch at Whale's Mouth under a cover name. Hardware store. Or TV fixit shop. Get his folio; see what talents he has." We'll make one of our own people, Matson thought, the victim—and it hurt, made him sick. And yet it should have been done months ago.

But it had taken bankrupt Rachmael ben Applebaum to goose them into acting, he realized. A man pursued by those monster creditor balloons that bellow all your personal defects and secrets. A man willing to undergo a *thirty-six-year trip* to prove that something is foul in the land of milk and protein on the far side of those Telpor gates through which, on receipt of five poscreds, any adult Terran can avail himself for the purpose of—

God knew.

God—and the German hierarchy dominating the UN plus THL; he had no illusions about that: *they* did not need to analyze the crowd-noise track of the time capsule ceremony at Whale's Mouth to know.

As he had. And his job was investigations; he was, he realized with spurting, burgeoning horror, possibly the only individual on Terra *really* in a position to push through and obtain an authentic glimpse of this.

Short of eighteen years of space flight . . . a time-period which would allow infinite millions, even a billion if the extrapolations were correct, to pass by way of Telpor constructs on that—to him—terrifying one-way trip to the colony world.

If you are wise, Matson said to himself grimly, you never take one-way trips. Anywhere. Even to Boise, Idaho . . . even across the street. Be certain, when you start, *that you can scramble back.*

F O U R

At one in the morning, Rachmael ben Applebaum was yanked from his sleep—this was usual, because the assorted creditor-mechanisms had been getting to him on a round-the-clock basis, now. However, this time it was no robot raptor-like creditor mechanism. This was a man. Dark, a Negro; small and shrewd-looking. Standing at Rachmael's door with i.d. papers extended.

"From Listening Instructional Educational Services," the Negro said. He added, "I hold a Class-A inter-plan vehicle pilot-license."

That woke Rachmael. "You're going to take the *Omphalos* off Luna?"

"If I can find her." The dark, small man smiled briefly. "May I come in? I'd like you to accompany me to your maintenance yard on Luna so there's no mistake: I know your employees there are armed; otherwise—" He followed Rachmael into the conapt living room—the sole room, in fact: living-conditions on Terra being what they were. "Otherwise Trails of Hoffman would be ferrying equipment to their domes on Mars with the *Omphalos* as of last month—right?"

"Right," Rachmael said as he blearily dressed.

"My name's Al Dosker. And I did you a small side-favor, Mr. ben Applebaum. I took out a creditor-construct waiting in the hall." He displayed, then, a side arm. "I suppose, if it got into litigation, it'd be called 'property destruct.' Anyhow, when you and I leave, no THL device is going to monitor our path." He added, half to himself, "That I could detect, anyhow." At his chest he patted a variety of *bug chasers*; minned electronic instruments that recorded the presence of vid and aud receptors in the vicinity.

Shortly the two men were on their way to the roof field—

And then Rachmael was back at the settlement.

"It's my food," Fred said.

Oh God, Rachmael thought. Here I am again.

"The thing is," Fred said amiably, as he dragged the turkey leg across the weed-pocked ground, "that a SubInfo computer screwed up. Subliminal information, right? They're repairing it, but meanwhile it's transmitted a lot to the right hemisphere hebesphere—I forget." He gave up trying to drag the turkey leg and extended his hand to Rachmael. "Name's Stine," he said. "Lewis Stine. I've damn near got it fixed."

Numbly, Rachmael shook hands. He wondered what had become of Dosker.

"Want to know how I'm fixing it?" Fred said.

"I'd rather know—"

"With this," Fred said, indicating the turkey leg. "It's a highly specialized piece of technogonically sophisticated—"

"You're just a goddamn rat," Rachmael said, "and you've got about four words scrambled up together. I'm living in a rat heap with other rats."

"No, I'm a highly skilled computer repairman," Fred—or Lewis

Stine—said, looking nettled. "Or am I?" He contemplated the turkey leg. "You're right. It doesn't look like something you'd fix a computer with. Maybe I should lay back for a while and think this over. The problem is, I intended to eat that turkey leg. If that's what it is. See, while I'm working on the computer—which is what I'm doing right now, although you'd never know it—my thoughts are being transmitted to you because I haven't been able to shut the computer down. I mean I *can* shut it down, but that's contravindicated."

"Indicated," Rachmael corrected him.

"Yeah; contraindicated. Thank you." Fred eyed him. "You a computer repairman, too?"

"God no," Rachmael said.

"Rats are highly telepathic," Fred said. "This was proved back in 1978 by the Russians. They took these rats, see, and shut them inside a lead enclosure which screened out all thoughts. Then they hooked up the rats to an encephalograph. And then—" Fred grinned. "Get this. They killed the rats. You know what the encephalogram showed?"

"Flat line," Rachmael said.

"Right. And then they quickly brought in a psychic. The psychic thought at the dead rats, and the encephalograph showed brainwave activity. See? Isn't that clever?"

"Fascist Russians," Rachmael said hotly. He was not amused.

"You have to admit it's a clever way to prove that rats are telepathic," Fred said.

"No," Rachmael said, "it proves that psychics are telepathic. It just showed—"

"I'll mash in your head with this crescent wrench," Fred said, grabbing up the turkey leg as best he could. "All the great scientific discoveries were made by rats—*are* made by rats."

"Made by the use of rats," Rachmael corrected. He could see that Fred would never get the turkey leg off the ground.

"Rats keep the human population down," Fred said, abandoning his attempts to pick up the turkey leg. "Abba explained that to us before he died. He also explained where we go when we die."

"I know," Rachmael said. "I was there. I heard him."

The roof field faded back in, replacing the weed-pocked settlement; Fred and his turkey leg vanished.

Dosker had parked his taxi-marked flapple off to one side. "Get in," Dosker said to him.

"Have I been here all this time?" Rachmael said.

Glancing at him, Dosker said, "I don't get you."

"Never mind," Rachmael said.

How ordinary the flapple looked. But as it arced into the night sky Rachmael blinked at its velocity; he had to accept the obvious: this was not the usual thrust which now impelled them. They had hit 3.5 Machs within nanoseconds.

As Dosker piloted the flapple he reached into the glove compartment, brought out a turkey leg and began gnawing on it. Rachmael gazed at him fixedly, stricken. "What's the matter?" Dosker said. "Haven't you ever seen a turkey leg before?"

"It's fine," Rachmael said. "Fine looking turkey leg. Damn fine." He lapsed into silence.

A computer foul-up. But being repaired. To have to be clued in by a rat . . . another rat, he realized. And the tender and wise Abba had passed on to his celestial reward. But he would be reborn; always, Abba was reborn. Every year or so. He was their—eternal leader.

"You'll direct me," Dosker was saying as he gnawed on the turkey leg. "Since even we at Lies, Incorporated don't know where you've got the *Omphalos*. You did a good job of berthing her, or perhaps we're beginning to slip . . . or both."

"Okay." At the 3-D Lunar map he took hold of the locating trailing-arm, linked the pivot in position, then swept out a route until the terminus of the arm touched the recessed locus where his technicians worked busily at . . .

I wish he'd stop gnawing on that turkey leg, Rachmael said to himself.

. . . at the *Omphalos*. Worked, while waiting for parts which would never come.

"We're off course," Dosker said abruptly. Speaking not to Rachmael but into his console mike. Shit; we've been phooed."

Phooed—a trade term. Rachmael felt fear, because the word was a condensation of PU—picked up. Picked up by a field, and this one was moving Dosker's small flapple out of its trajectory. At once Dosker fired the huge Whetstone-Milton rockets, tried to reassert with their enormous strength homeo-course . . . but the field continued to tug, even against the millions of pounds of thrust of the twin engines, as both fired in unison, acting as retro-jets against the field exerting its presence unseen. But, on a variety of console instruments, registering.

Rachmael, after an interval of strained, wordless silence, said to Dosker, "Where's it taking us?"

"From a Three to L course," Dosker said laconically. He set down his turkey leg, now.

"Not to Luna, then." They would not, the two of them, reach the *Omphalos'* place of berth; that was now clear. But—

Where instead?

"We're in T-orb," Dosker said. Orbit around the Earth, despite the push of the two W-M engines. Dosker, now, reluctantly, in a motion of admitted defeat, cut them. Fuel for them had no doubt dropped to a dangerously low level: if the field let go they would orbit anyhow, orbit without the possibility of being capable of creating a trajectory that would lead to an ultimate landing either on Luna *or* on Terra. "They've got us," Dosker said, then, half to Rachmael and half into the mike that projected from the ship's console. He recited a series of encoded instructions into the mike, listened, then cursed, said to Rachmael, "We're cut off aud and vid, all signal-contact; I'm not getting through to Matson. So that's it."

"That's what?" Rachmael demanded. "You mean we give up? We just orbit Terra forever and die when we run out of oxygen?" Was this the fight that Lies, Incorporated put up when faced by Trails of Hoffman? He, alone, had held out better; now he was disgusted, astonished and completely perplexed, and he watched without comprehension as Dosker inspected his bank of *bug chasers* at his chest. At the moment the Lies, Incorporated pilot seemed interested only in whether or not monitors were picking them up—as well as controlling, externally, the trajectory of their ship.

Dosker said, "No monitors. Look, friend ben Applebaum." He spoke swiftly. "They cut my transmission on aud by micro-relay to Matson's satellite, but of course—" His dark eyes glinted with amusement. "I have on me a dead man's throttle; if a continuous signal from me is interrupted it automatically sets off an alarm at Lies, Incorporated, at its main offices in New New York and also at Matson's satellite. So by now they know something's happened." He lowered his voice, speaking almost to himself alone. "We'll have to wait to find out if they can get to us before it doesn't matter."

The ship, without power, in orbit, glided silently.

And then, jarringly, something nosed it; Rachmael fell; sliding along the floor to the far wall he saw Dosker tumble, too, and knew that this had been the locking of another ship or similar device against them—knew and then all at once realized that at least it hadn't detonated. At least it had not been a missile. Because if it had—

"They could," Dosker said, as he got unsteadily to his feet, "have taken us out permanently." By that he, too, meant a detonating weapon. He turned toward the tri-stage entrance hatch, used for null-atmosphere penetration.

The hatch, its circular seal-controls spun from impulses emanating outside, swung open.

Three men, two of them riffraff with lasers, with the decayed eyes of those who had been bought, hamstrung, lost long ago, came first. And then a clear-faced elegant man who would never be bought because he was a great buyer in the market of men; he was a dealer, not produce for sale.

It was Theodoric Ferry, chairman of the board of Trails of Hoffman Limited. Ahead of him his two employees swung a vacuum-cleaner-like mechanism; it searched, buzzing and nosing, probing until its operators were satisfied; they nodded to Theodoric, who then addressed Rachmael.

"May I seat myself?"

After a startled pause Rachmael said, "Sure."

"Sorry, Mr. Ferry," Dosker said. "The only seat is taken." He sat at the control console in such a way that his small body had expanded at its base to fill both bucket seats; his face was hard and hating.

Shrugging, the large, white-haired man said, "All right." He eyed Dosker. "You're Lies' top pilot, aren't you? Al Dosker . . . yes, I recognize you from the clips we've made of you. On your way to the *Omphalos*. But you don't need Applebaum here to tell you where she is; *we* can tell you." Theodoric Ferry dug into his cloak, brought out a small packet which he tossed to Al Dosker. "The locus of the dry-docks where Applebaum has got her."

"Thanks, Mr. Ferry," Dosker said with sarcasm so great that his voice was almost forged into incomprehensibility.

Theodoric said, "Now look, Dosker; you sit quietly and mind your own business. While I talk to Applebaum. I've never met him personally, but I knew his very-much-missed late father." He extended his hand.

Dosker said, "If you shake with him, Rachmael, he'll deposit a virus contamination that'll produce liver toxicity within your system inside an hour."

Glowering, Theodoric said to the Negro, "I asked you to stay in your place. A pun." He then removed the membrane-like, up-to-now invisible glove of plastic which covered his hand. So Dosker had been right, Rachmael realized as he watched Theodoric carefully deposit the glove in the ship's incinerating disposal-chute. "Anyhow," Theodoric said, almost plaintively, "we could have squirted feral airborne bacteria around by now."

"And taken out yourselves," Dosker pointed out.

Theodoric shrugged. Then, speaking carefully to Rachmael, he said, "I respect what you're trying to do. Don't laugh."

"I was not," Rachmael said, "laughing. Just surprised."

"You want to keep functioning, after the economic collapse; you want to keep your legitimate creditors from attaching the few—actually sole—asset that Applebaum Enterprise still possesses—good for you, Rachmael. I'd have done the same. And you impressed Matson; that's why he's supplying you his only decent pilot."

With a mild grin, Dosker reached into his pocket for a pack of cigarillos; at once the two decayed-eyed men accompanying Theodoric caught his arm, expertly manipulated it—the harmless pack of cigarillos fell to the floor of the ship.

One after another, the cigarillos were cut open by Theodoric's men, inspected . . . the fifth one turned out to be hard; it did not yield to the sharp-bladed pocket knife, and, a moment later, a more complex analytical device showed the cigarillo to be a homeostatic cephalotropic dart.

"Whose Alpha-wave pattern?" Theodoric Ferry asked Dosker.

"Yours," Dosker said tonelessly. He watched without affect as the two decayed-eyed but very expert employees of THL crushed the dart under heel, rendering it useless.

"Then you expected me," Ferry said, looking a little nonplussed.

Dosker said, "Mr. Ferry, I *always* expect you."

Returning once more to Rachmael, Theodoric Ferry said, "I admire you and I want to terminate this conflict between you and THL. We have an inventory of your assets. Here." He extended a sheet toward Rachmael; at that, Rachmael turned toward Dosker for advice.

"Take it," Dosker said.

Accepting the sheet, Rachmael scanned it. The inventory was

accurate; these did constitute the slight totality of the remaining assets of Applebaum Enterprise. And—glaringly, as Ferry had said, the only item of any authentic value was the *Omphalos* herself, the great liner plus the repair and maintenance facilities of Luna which now, hive-like, surrounded and checked her as she waited futilely . . . he returned the inventory to Ferry, who, seeing his expression, nodded.

"We agree, then," Theodoric Ferry said. "Okay. Here's what I propose, Applebaum. You can keep the *Omphalos*. I'll instruct my legal staff to withdraw the writ to the UN courts demanding that the *Omphalos* be placed under a state of attachment."

Dosker, startled, grunted; Rachmael stared at Ferry.

"What," Rachmael said, then, "in return?"

"This. That the *Omphalos* never leave the Sol system. You can very readily develop a profitable operation transporting passengers and cargo between the nine planets and to Luna. Despite the fact—"

"Despite the fact," Rachmael said, "that the *Omphalos* was built as an inter-stellar carrier, not inter-plan. It's like using—"

"It's that," Ferry said, "or lose the *Omphalos* to us."

"So Rachmael agrees"—Dosker spoke up—"not to take the *Omphalos* to Fomalhaut. The written agreement won't mention any one particular star system, but it's not Prox and not Alpha. Right, Ferry?"

After a pause Theodoric Ferry said, "Take it or leave it."

Rachmael said, "Why, Mr. Ferry? *What's wrong at Whale's Mouth?* This deal—it proves I'm right." That was obvious; he saw it, Dosker saw it—and Ferry must have known that in making it he was ratifying their intimations. Limit the *Omphalos* to the nine planets of the Sol system? And yet—the corporation Applebaum Enterprise, as Ferry said, *would continue*; it would live on as a legal, economic entity. And Ferry would see that the UN turned a certain amount, an acceptable quantity, of commerce its way. Rachmael would wave goodbye to Lies, Incorporated, to first this small dark superior space pilot, and then, by extension, to Freya Holm, to Matson Glazer-Holliday, cut in effect himself off from the sole power which had chosen to back him.

"Go ahead," Dosker said. "Accept the idea. After all, the deep-sleep components won't arrive, but it won't matter, because you're not going into 'tween system space anyhow." He looked tired.

Theodoric Ferry said, "Your father, Rachmael; Maury would have done anything to keep the *Omphalos*. You know in two days we'll have her—and once we do, there's no chance you'll ever get her back. Think about it."

"I—know right now," Rachmael said. Lord, if he and Dosker had managed to get the *Omphalos* out tonight, lost her in space where THL couldn't find her . . . and yet that was already over; it had ended when the field had overcome the enormous futile thrust of the twin engines of Dosker's Lies, Incorporated ship: Trails of Hoffman had stepped in too soon. In time.

All along, Theodoric Ferry had pre-thought them; it was not a moral issue: it was a pragmatic one.

"I have legal forms drawn up," Ferry said. "If you'll come with me." He nodded toward the hatch. "The law requires three witnesses. On the part of THL, we have those witnesses." He smiled, because it was over and he knew it. Turning, he walked leisurely toward the hatch. The two decayed-eyed employees followed, both men relaxed . . . they passed into the open circularity of the hatch—

And then convulsed throughout, from scalp to foot, internally destroyed; as Rachmael, shocked and terrified, watched, he saw their neurological, musculature systems give out; he saw them, both men penetrated entirely so that each became, horrifying him, flopping, quivering, malfunctioning—more than malfunctioning: each unit of their bodies fought with all other portions, so that the two heaps on the floor became warring subsyndromes within themselves, as muscle strained against muscle, visceral apparatus against diaphragmatic strength, auricular and ventricular fibrillation; both men, unable to breathe, deprived even of blood-circulation, staring, fighting within their bodies which were no longer true bodies . . .

Rachmael looked away.

"Cholinesterase-destroying gas," Dosker said, behind him, and at that instant Rachmael became aware of the tube pressed to his own neck, a medical artifact which had injected into his blood stream its freight of atropine, the antidote to the vicious nerve gas of the notorious FMC Corporation, the original contractors for this, the most destructive of all anti-personnel weapons of the previous war.

"Thanks," Rachmael said to Dosker, as he saw, now, the hatch swing shut; the Trails of Hoffman satellite, with its inert field, was being detached—within it persons who were *not* THL employees pried it loose from Dosker's flapple.

The dead man's throttle signaling device—or rather null-signaling device—had done its job; Lies, Incorporated experts had arrived and at this moment were systematically dismantling the THL equipment.

Philosophically, Theodoric Ferry stood with his hands in the pockets of his cloak, saying nothing, not even noticing the spasms of his two employees on the floor near him, as if, by deteriorating in response to the gas, they had somehow proved unworthy.

"It was nice," Rachmael managed to say to Dosker, as the hatch once more swung open, this time admitting several employees of Lies Incorporated, "that your co-workers administered the atropine to Ferry as well as to me." Generally, in this business, no one was spared.

Dosker, studying Ferry, said, "He was given no atropine."

Reaching, he withdrew the empty tube with its injecting needle from his own neck, then the counterpart item from Rachmael's. "How come, Ferry?" Dosker said.

There was, from Ferry, no answer.

"Impossible," Dosker said. "Every living organism is—" Suddenly he grabbed Ferry's arm; grunting, he swung brusquely the arm back, against its normal span—and yanked.

Theodoric Ferry's arm, at the shoulder-joint, came off. Revealing trailing conduits and minned components, those of the shoulder still functioning, those of the arm, deprived of power, now inert.

"A sim," Dosker said. Seeing that Rachmael did not comprehend he said, "A simulacrum of Ferry that of course has no neurological system. So Ferry was never here." He tossed the arm away. "Naturally; why should a man of his stature risk himself? He's probably sitting in his demesne satellite orbiting Mars, viewing this through the sense-extensors of the sim." To the one-armed Ferry-construct he said harshly, "*Are* we in genuine contact with you, Ferry, through this? Or is it on homeo? I'm just curious."

The mouth of the Ferry simulacrum opened and it said, "I hear you, Dosker. Would you, as an act of humanitarian kindness, administer atropine to my two THL employees?"

"It's being done," Dosker said. He walked over to Rachmael, then. "Well, our humble ship, on acute examination, seems never to have been graced by the presence of the chairman of the board of THL." He grinned shakily. "I feel cheated."

But the offer made by Ferry via the simulacrum, Rachmael realized. *That* had been genuine.

Dosker said, "Let's go to Luna, now. As your advisor I'm telling you—" He put his hand, gripped harshly, on Rachmael's wrist. "Wake up. Those two gnugs will be all right, once the atropine is administered; they won't be killed and we'll release them in their THL vehicle—minus its field, of course. You and I will go on to Luna, to the *Omphalos*, as if nothing happened. Or if you won't I'll use the map the sim gave me; I'm taking the *Omphalos* out into 'tween space where THL can't tail her, even if you don't want me to."

"But," Rachmael said woodenly, "something did happen. An offer was made."

"That offer," Dosker said, "proves that THL is willing to sacrifice a great deal to keep you from your eighteen-year trip to Fomalhaut for a look at Whale's Mouth. And—" He eyed Rachmael. "Yet that makes you *less* interested in getting the *Omphalos* out into uncharted space between planets where Ferry's trackers can't—"

I could save the *Omphalos*, Rachmael thought. But the man beside him was correct; this meant of course that he had to go on: Ferry had removed the block, had proved the need of the eighteen-year flight.

"But the deep-sleep components," he said.

"Just get me to her," Dosker said quietly, patiently. "Okay, Rachmael ben Applebaum? Will you do that?" The controlled and very professional voice penetrated; Rachmael nodded. "I want the locus from you, not from the chart that sim gave me; I've decided I'm not touching that. I'm waiting for you, Rachmael, for you to decide."

"Yes," Rachmael said, then, and walked stiffly to the ship's 3-D Lunar map with its trailing arm; he seated himself and began to fix the locus for the hard-eyed, dark, Lies, Incorporated ultra-experienced pilot.

FIVE

At the Fox's Lair, the minute French restaurant in downtown San Diego, the maitre d' glanced at the name which Rachmael ben Applebaum had jotted down on the sheet with its fancy, undulating, pseudo-living letterhead and said, "Yes. Mr. Applebaum. It is—" He examined his wristwatch. "Now eight o'clock." A line of well-cloaked people waited; it was always this way on crowded Terra: all restaurants, even the bad ones, were overfilled each night from five o'clock on, and this was hardly a mediocre restaurant, let alone an outright bad one. "Genet," the maitre d' called to a waitress wearing the lace stockings and partial jacket-vest combination now popular; it left one breast, the right, exposed, and its nipple was elegantly capped by a Swiss ornament with many minned parts; the ornament, shaped like a large gold pencil eraser, played semi-classical music and lit up in a series of attractive shifting light-patterns which focused on the floor ahead of her, lighting her way so that she could pass among the closely placed tiny tables of the restaurant.

"Yes, Gaspar," the girl said, with a toss of her blonde, high-piled hair.

"Escort Mr. Applebaum to table twenty-two," the maitre d' told her, and ignored, with stoic, glacial indifference, the outrage among those customers lined up wearily ahead of Rachmael.

"I don't want to—" Rachmael began, but the maitre d' cut him off.

"All arranged. *She* is waiting at twenty-two." And, in the maitre d's voice, everything was conveyed: full knowledge of an intricate erotic relationship which—alas—did not, at least as yet, exist.

Rachmael followed Genet, with her light-emanating useful Swiss-made nipple-assist, through the darkness, the noise of people eating in jammed proximity, bolting their meals with the weight of guilt hunching them, getting done and aside so that those waiting could be served before the Fox's Lair, at two a.m., closed its kitchens . . . we are really pressed tight to one another, he thought, and then, all at once, Genet halted, turned; the nipple cap now radiated a soft, delightful and warm pale red aura which revealed, seated at table twenty-two, Freya Holm.

Seating himself opposite her, Rachmael said, "You don't light up."

"I could. And play the *Blue Danube* simultaneously." She smiled; in the darkness—the waitress had gone on, now—the dark-haired girl's eyes glowed. Before her rested a split of Buena Vista chablis, vintage 2002, one of the great, rare treats of the restaurant, and exceeding expensive; Rachmael wondered who would pick up the tab for this twelve-year-old California wine; lord knew he would have liked to, but—he reflexively touched his wallet. Freya noticed.

"Don't worry. Matson Glazer-Holliday owns this restaurant. There will be a tab for a mere six poscreds. For one peanut butter and grape jelly sandwich." She laughed, her dark eyes dancing in the reflected light from barely illuminated overhead Japanese lanterns. "Does this place intimidate you?" she asked him, then.

"No. I'm just generally tense." For six days now the *Omphalos* had been lost—and even to him. Perhaps even to Matson. It could well be—necessary for security purposes—that only Al Dosker, at the multi-stage console of the ship's controls, knew where she had gone. For Rachmael, however, it had been psychologically devastating to watch the *Omphalos* blast out into the limitless darkness: Ferry had been right—the *Omphalos* had been the sine qua non of Applebaum Enterprise; without her nothing remained.

But at least this way she might return; or more accurately, he eventually might be taken, by Lies, Incorporated, by high-velocity flapple to her, allowed to see, board her, again, to begin his eighteen-year trip. And, the other way—

"Don't dwell on Ferry's offer," Freya said softly. She nodded to the waitress, who placed a solidstem but chilled wine glass before Rachmael; he automatically, obediently, poured himself a trace of the 2002 Buena Vista white, tasted it; kept himself from taking more; he merely nodded in compliment to the wine, tried to make it appear that he was accustomed to such an outrageously, almost divinely penetrating bouquet and flavor. It made absurd everything he had drunk his life long.

"I'm not thinking of it," he said to Freya. Not, he thought, in view of what you have—or are supposed to have—in your purse.

Her large black leather mailpouch-style purse rested on the table beside her, within reach of his fingers.

"The components," Freya said softly, "are in the purse in a simulated gold round container, marked *Eternity of Sexual Potency Fragrance #54*, a routine continental scent; anyone going through my purse would expect to find it. There are twelve components, all super-min, of course. Beneath the inner lid. On India paper, on the reverse of the label, is a wiring diagram. I will rise to my feet in a moment and go to the powder room; after a few seconds—you must sit quietly, Rachmael, because it is about a seventy-thirty possibility that THL agents are monitoring us, either directly as patrons or by instrument—you must sit; then, when I don't return immediately, you fidget, you try to attract Genet's attention, to order some dinner for yourself or at least—and this is vital—obtain the menu."

He nodded, listening intently.

"She will notice you and give you a menu; it is quite stiff and large, since it contains the wine list. You will place it on the table so that it covers my purse."

Rachmael said, "And I accidently knock your purse to the floor, and the contents spill out, and in gathering them up I—"

"Are you insane?" Quietly she said, "You cover the purse. There is a strip of titanium within the right-hand overleaf of the menu. The container of scent has a titanium-tropic ambulation-circuit; it will within two seconds register the presence of the strip and will rotate itself out of my purse, which I've left open; it will travel across the *underside* of the menu. The strip is at the bottom, where your right hand with complete naturalness will be resting as you hold what has been deliberately made up an awkward, stiff menu. When it touches the titanium strip the container will emit a weak charge, about ten volts; you will feel this galvanization and you will then, with your four fingers, take hold of the container, detach it from the titanium strip to which it has tropically adhered, drop it from the underside of the menu onto your lap. And then, with your *other* hand, you will shift the container from your lap into your pocket." She rose. "I'll be back within six minutes. Goodbye. And good luck."

He watched her go.

And then, as he sat there, he realized that he had to rise, too; had to act—the job of transferring the deep-sleep components obtained for him from the blackmarket was difficult and delicate, because Theodoric Ferry, ever since Lies, Incorporated had taken out his satellite and its crew, its simulacrum of Ferry himself, had kept total surveillance over everything Rachmael had done; the ultimate in technological and personnel resources of Trails of Hoffman Limited had been brought into play, motivated now by Theodoric's personal animus.

What had been a remote and impersonal conflict had become once more, he reflected, that which it had always been for his father: a deeply human, immediate matter. A struggle which, at last, had brought his father's death and the disintegration of the organization.

Thinking this, Rachmael began dutifully to fidget, then rose, began hunting for the girl with the light-emanating, gay music resounding, Swiss nipple.

"A menu, sir?" Genet stood before him, holding out the great, wonderfully printed and engraved, in fact embossed, menu; he thanked her, accepted it humbly, returned to his table with the pleasant tunes of Johann Strauss in his ears.

The menu, the size of an old-fashioned antique disc record album, easily covered Freya's purse. He sat holding it open, reading the wine list, and especially the prices. Good god! It cost a fortune even for a split of good wine, here. And for a fifth of a three-year-old generic white—

All the retail establishments such as the Fox's Lair were exploiting Terra's overpopulation; people who had waited three hours to get in here to eat and drink would pay these prices—by then they had, psychologically, no choice.

A weak electric shock made his right hand quiver; the circular container of miniaturized deep-sleep components had already made physical contact with him and, with his fingers, he pried it, clamlike, loose from its grip, its tropism; he dropped it into his lap, felt its weight.

As directed, he then reached for it with his left hand, to transfer it to his cloak pocket . . .

"Sorry—oops." A busboy, a robot, carrying a loaded, chest-high tray of dishes, had bumped him, making him totter on his chair. People everywhere, those rising, those seating themselves, the robot busboys clearing, the waitresses with their lights and tunes everywhere . . . confused, Rachmael reseated himself, reached for the container on his lap.

It was gone.

Fallen to the floor? In disbelief he peered down, saw his shoes, the table legs, a discarded match folder. No round gold-like container.

They had gotten it. It was they who had sent the "busboy." And now it, too, with its load of dishes, had vanished in the general confusion.

Defeated, he sat vacantly staring. And then, at last, from the split of wine, he poured himself a second drink, lifted the glass as if in toast: a toast to the success, admitted and accepted, of the invisible extensions of THL around him that had, in the crucial instant, intervened, deprived him of what he needed essentially in order to leave the Sol system with the big *Omphalos*.

It did not matter now whether he made contact with Dosker aboard her; lacking the components it was insanity to leave.

Freya returned, seated herself across from him, smiled "All okay?"

Leadenly, he said, "They stopped us. Dead." For now, anyhow, he thought. But it's not finished yet.

He drank, his heart laboring, the delicate, expensive, delicious, and utterly superfluous wine—the wine of at least temporary utter defeat.

On the TV screen, Omar Jones, President of Newcolonizedland, highest official in residence at the great modular settlement at Whale's Mouth, said jovially, "Well, you folks back home, all bunched together there in those little boxes you live in—we greet you, wish you luck." The familiar, round, pleasant face beamed its smile of warmth. "And we're just wonderin', folks, when you all are going to team up with us and join us here at Newcolonizedland. Eh?" He cupped his ear. As if, Rachmael thought, it were a two-way transmission. But this was illusion. This was a video tape sent across in signal-form by way of von Einem's Telpor nexus at Schweinfort, New Whole Germany. By, through, the good offices of the UN's network of Earth satellites, relayed to TV sets throughout Terra.

Aloud, Rachmael said, "Sorry, President Omar Jones, of New-colonizedland, Whale's Mouth." I'll visit you, he thought, but my own way. Not by a von Einem Telpor operating for five poscreds at one of Trails of Hoffman's retail outlets . . . so it'll be a little while; in fact, he thought, I'd guess you, President Jones, will be dead by the time I arrive.

Although after the defeat at the Fox's Lair—

They, the opposition, had in effect severed him from his source of support, from Lies, Incorporated. He had sat across from their rep, pretty, dark-haired Freya Holm, drunk vintage wine with her, chatted, laughed. But when it came time to transfer vital components from Lies, Incorporated across a five-inch space to him . . .

The vidphone in the minuscule bedroom-cubby of his conapt said *Pwannnnnnk!* Indicating that someone desired to contact him.

Shutting off the jolly face of President Omar Jones of Newcolonizedland, Whale's Mouth, he went to the vidphone, lifted the receiver.

On its gray, undersized screen there formed the features of Matson Glazer-Holliday. "Mr. ben Applebaum," Matson said.

"What can we do?" Rachmael said, feeling the weight of their loss. "In fact those people are probably monitoring this—"

"Oh yes; we register a tap on this vidline." Matson nodded, but he did not seem nonplussed. "We know they're not only monitoring this call but recording it, both aud and vid. However, my message to you is brief, and they're welcome to it. Contact the master circuit of your local public Xerox-spool library."

"And then?" Rachmael asked.

"Do research," Matson Glazer-Holliday said carefully. "Into the original discovery of Whale's Mouth. The first unmanned data-receptors, recorders and transmitters which were traveled from the Sol system, years ago, to the Fomalhaut system; in fact, back in the twentieth century."

Rachmael said, "But why—"

"And we'll be in touch," Matson said briskly. "Goodbye. And glad to have—" He eyed Rachmael. "Don't let that little incident at the restaurant get to you. It's routine. I assure you." He mock-saluted, and then the image on the tiny colorless—the Vidphone Corporation of Wes-Dem provided minimal service, and, as a public utility licensed by the UN, got away with it—the image died.

Rachmael, bewildered, hung up the aud receiver.

The records of the original unmanned monitors which had been dispatched to the Fomalhaut system years ago were public records; what could exist there that would be of value? Nevertheless he dialed the local branch of the New New York Xerox-spool public library.

"Send to my apt," he said, "the abstract, the comprehensive material available, on the initial scouting of the Fomalhaut system." By those now old-fashioned constructs which George Hoffman had utilized—by which the habitable planet Whale's Mouth had been discovered.

Presently a robot runner appeared at his door with a variety of spools. Rachmael seated himself at his scanner, inserted the first spool, noting that it was marked *A General Survey of the Fomalhaut Unmanned Inter-system Vehicle Reports, Shorter Version*, by some-one named G. S. Purdy.

For two hours he ran the spool. It showed that sun coming nearer and nearer, then the planets, one by one and disappointing, bitterly so, until now number nine bloomed into view; and all at once—

No more barren rocks, unblunted mountains. No airless, germ-less, hygienic void with methane as gas or crystallized at greater astronomical units from the sun. Suddenly he saw a swaying and undulating, blue-green frieze, and this had caused Dr. von Einem to trot out his Telpor equipment, to set up the direct link between this world and Terra. This plum-ripe landscape had gotten Trails of Hoffman interested commercially—and had written *mene, mene* for Applebaum Enterprise.

The last vid monitor-reading was fifteen years old. Since then direct contact via teleportation gear had made such ancient hardware obsolete. And hence the original unmanned monitors, in orbit around Fomalhaut—

Had what? Been *abandoned*, according to author Purdy. Their batteries turned off by remote instruct; they still, presumably, circled the sun within the orbit of Whale's Mouth.

They were still there.

And their batteries, having been off all these years, had conserved, not expended energy. And they were of the advanced liquid-helium III type.

Was *this* what Matson had wanted to know?

Returning to the reference spool he ran it, ran it, again and again, until he had the datum at last. The most sophisticated vid monitor belonged to Vidphone Corporation of Wes-Dem. *They* would know if it, called Prince Albert B-y, was still in orbit around Fomalhaut.

He started toward his vidphone, then stopped. After all, it was tapped. So instead he left his conapt, left the huge building entirely, joined a ped-runnel until he spied a public phonebooth.

There, he called the Vidphone Corporation, its central offices in Detroit, open on a twenty-four-hour-a-day basis.

"Give me your archives," he instructed the robot switchboard.

Presently a human, wizened but efficient-looking, gnome-like official in a gray jacket, like a bookkeeper, appeared. "Yeah?"

"I'm inquiring," Rachmael said, "as to the Prince Albert B-y mon-sat put in orb around Fomalhaut seventeen years ago. I'd like you to check as to whether it's still in orb and if it is, how it can be activated so—"

The signal went dead. At the other end the Vidphone Corporation official had hung up. He waited. The Vidphone switchboard did not come onto the wire, nor did the regular, local robot.

I'll be darned, Rachmael thought. Shaken, he left the phonebooth.

He continued on aboard the runnel until at last he reached a second public phonebooth.

Entering he this time dialed Matson Glazer-Holliday's satellite. Presently he had the owner of Lies, Incorporated again facing him from the screen.

Carefully, Rachmael said, "Sorry to bother you. But I've been running info spools on the original unmanned monitors of the Fomalhaut system."

"Learn anything?"

"I asked," Rachmael said, "the Vidphone Corporation of Wes-Dem if its Prince Albert B-y—"

"And they said?"

Rachmael said, "They immediately cut the con."

"It," Matson said, "is still up. Still in orb."

"And sending out signals?"

"Not for fifteen years. At hyper-see it takes its signals one week to cross the twenty-four light-year gap to the Sol system. Rather shorter than it would require for the *Omphalos* to reach the Fomalhaut system."

"Is there any way to once more activate the satellite?"

"Vidphone Corp could contact it direct, through a Telpor," Matson said. "If they wanted to."

"Do they?"

After a pause Matson said, "Did they cut you off just now?"

Pondering, Rachmael said, "Can someone else give the impulse to the satellite?"

"No. Only the Vidphone Corp knows the sequence which would cause it to respond."

"Is this what you wanted me to find out?" Rachmael asked.

Smiling, Matson Glazer-Holliday said, "Goodbye, Mr. ben Apple-baum. And good luck, as you continue your research." He then hung up, and once more Rachmael faced a dead screen.

At his villa, Matson turned away from the vidset to Freya Holm, who perched on the couch, legs tucked under her, wearing a high-fashion transparent spidersilk blue blouse and meter-reader's pants. "He found it," Matson said. "Right away. That about the PA B-y sat." Pacing, Matson scowled. "All right." He had decided. "Our rep, under the cover-name Bergen Phillips, will be sent to Whale's Mouth six hours from now. By way of the THL outlet at Paris. As soon as he's at Whale's Mouth he'll transmit to us, through the Telpor, an encoded document describing the true conditions." But probably THL's people would have nabbed "Bergen Phillips" by then, and, through techniques well-known in the trade, have learned all that the Lies, Incorporated veteran knew; they would then send a faked encoded message, assuring Matson that all was well—and he would never know, on receipt of such a message, whether it truly emanated from "Bergen Phillips" or from THL. However—

Freya saw it, too. "Have this rep, once he's across, give the activating sequence to the PA B-y sat. So it'll start transmitting data to the Sol system direct, once again."

"*If,*" Matson said. "*If* it still will function after fifteen years. And *if* the Vidphone Corp does not countermand the instruct the moment data starts to flow in." However, he could tap the Vidphone Corp's lines and pick up even that initial meager data. What he might obtain before the flow ceased coming in might be a graphic pan-shot of Whale's Mouth—and then so what if the sat was shut off once more.

As naturally it would be, since THL controlled the Vidphone Corp.

"Just one good vid shot," Matson said. "And we'll know."

"Know what?" She reached to set down her drink glass on the nearby antique genuine glass-topped coffee table.

Matson said, "I'll tell you that, dear, when I see the shot." He went to the comboard, sent out the already implemented request for the field rep who was to cross over to Whale's Mouth to be brought to his satellite. These instructs had to be given orally and *not* over lines; to line it was to howl it broadcast.

In fact perhaps he had already communicated too much to Rachmael. But—in such a business one took risks. And he could assume that Rachmael's callback had emanated from a public booth; the man, although an amateur, was at least cautious. And these days such caution was not paranoid; it was practical.

On the TV screen in 3-D color with olfactory track the round, jovial features of President Omar Jones of Newcolonizedland said, "You folks there on good old overcrowded Terra"—and, behind him, faded in a scene of miles of open veldt-like park—"you amaze us. We hear you're going to send a ship here, by hyper-see, and it'll arrive . . . let's see." He pretended to be contemplating.

Before the set (not quite paid for) Jack McElhatten, a hard-working, easy-going, good-natured guy, said to his wife, "Chrissakes, look at that open land." It reminded him of his sweet, fragile childhood, of years ago and now gone, the Oregon Trail part of Wyoming west of Cheyenne. And the desire, the yearning, grew in him. "We have to emigrate," he said to Ruth then. "We owe it to our kids. They can grow up as—"

"Shh," Ruth said.

On the screen President Omar Jones of Newcolonizedland said, "In just about eighteen years, folks, that ship will arrive this way and park down. So here's what we've done; we've set aside November 24, 2032, as Flying Dutchman Day. The day that ship reaches us." He chuckled. "I'll be, um, ninety-four and, sorry to say, probably not here to participate in Flying Dutchman Day. But maybe posterity, including some of you young folks—"

"You hear that?" McElhatten said to his wife, incredulous.

"Some nut is going to go the old way. Eighteen years in 'tween space! When all you have to do—"

"BE QUIET," Ruth said, furiously, trying to listen.

"—be here to greet this Mr. Applebaum," President Omar Jones intoned in clowning solemnity. "Banners, vox-pop streamers . . . we should have a population of between, well, say, one billion then, but still plenty of land. We can take up to *two* billion, you know, and still leave plenty of room. So come on and join us; cross over and be here to celebrate Flying Dutchman Day, folks." He waved, and, it seemed to Jack McElhatten, this man at Whale's Mouth was waving directly to him. And, within him, the yearning grew.

The frontier, he thought. Their neighbors in the tiny cramped conapt with which they shared a bathroom . . . or had, up until last month, at which point the Pattersons had emigrated to Whale's Mouth. The vid-sig letters from Jerome Patterson; god, they had raved about conditions across on the other side. If anything, the info spots—ads, to be exact—had understated the beauty of the real-sit over there. The beauty—and the opportunity.

"We need *men*," President Omar Jones was declaring. "Good strong men who can do any kind of work. Are you that man? Able, willing, and get-up-and-go, over eighteen years of age? Willing to start a new life, using your mind and your hands, the skills God gave you? Think about it. What are you doing with those hands, those skills, *right now*?"

Doing quality-control on an autofac line, McElhatten thought to himself bitterly; a job which a pigeon could do better; fact was, a pigeon did do so, to check *his* work.

"Can you imagine," he said to his wife, "holding down a job where a pigeon has a better eye than you for mis-tolerances?" And that was exactly his situation; he ejected parts which were not properly aligned, and, when he missed, the pigeon noted the miss, the defective part allowed to pass; it picked out the misaligned part, pecked a reject-button which kicked the part from the moving belt.

And, as they quit and emigrated, the quality control men at Krino Associates were, one by one, replaced by pigeons.

He stayed on now, really, only because the union to which he belonged was strong enough to insist that his seniority made it mandatory for Krino to keep him on. But once he quit, once he left—

"Then," he said to Ruth, "the pigeon moves in. Okay, let it; we're going across to Whale's Mouth, and from then on I won't be competing with birds." Competing, he thought, and losing. Offering my employers the poorer showing. "And Krino will be glad," he said, with misery.

"I just wish," Ruth said, "that you had a *particular* job lined up over there at Newcolonizedland. I mean, they talk about 'all the jobs,' but you can't take 'all the jobs.' What one job are you—" She hesitated. "Skilled for?" After all, he had worked for Krino Associates for ten years.

"I'm going to farm."

She stared at him.

"They'll *give* us twenty acres. We'll buy sheep here, those black-faced ones. Suffolk. Take six across, five ewes and a ram, put up fences, build ourselves a house out of prefab sections—" He knew he could do it. Others had, as they had described—not in impersonal ads—but in letters vid-signaled back and then transcribed by Vidphone Corporation and posted on the bulletin board of the conapt building.

"But if we don't like it," Ruth murmured apprehensively, "we won't be able to come back; I mean, that seems so strange. Those teleportation machines . . . working one way only."

"The extra-galactic nebulae," he said patiently. "The recession of matter outward; the universe is exploding, growing; the Telpor relates your molecules as energy configurations in this outflow—"

"I don't understand," Ruth said. "But I do know this," she said, and, from her purse, brought a leaflet.

Studying the leaflet, McElhatten scowled. "Cranks. This is hate literature, Ruth. Don't accept it." He began to crumple it up.

"They don't call themselves by a hating name. 'Friends of a United People.' They're a small group of worried, dedicated people, opposed to—"

"I know what they're opposed to," McElhatten said. Several of them worked at Krino Associates. "They say we Terrans should stay within the Sol system. Stick together. Listen." He crumpled up the leaflet. "The history of man has been one vast migration. This to Whale's Mouth; it's the greatest yet—twenty-four light-years! We ought to be proud." But naturally there'd be a few idiots and cranks opposing history.

Yes, it was history and he wanted to be part of it. First it had been New England, then Australia, Alaska, and then the try—and failure—on Luna, then on Mars and Venus, and now—success. At last. And if he waited too long he would be too old and there would be too many expatriates so free land would no longer be available; the government at Newcolonizedland might withdraw its land offer any time, because after all, every day people streamed over. The Telpor offices were swamped.

"You want me to go?" he asked Ruth. "Go first—and send a message back, once I have the land and am ready to begin building? And then you and the kids can come?"

Nervously, she said, "I hate to be parted from you."

"Make up your mind."

"I guess," she said, "we should go together. If we go at all. But these—letters. They're just impulses onto energy lines."

"Like telephone or vidphone or telegraph or TV messages. Has been for one hundred years."

"If only *real letters* came back."

"You have," he said derisively, "a superstitious fear."

"Maybe so," Ruth admitted. But it was a real fear nonetheless. A deep and abiding fear of a one-way trip from which they could never return, except, she thought, eighteen years from now, when that ship reaches the Fomalhaut system.

She picked up the evening 'pape, examined the article, jeering in tone, about this ship, the *Omphalos*. Capable of transporting five hundred, but this time carrying one sole man: the ship's owner. And, the article said, he was fleeing to escape his creditors; that was his motive.

But, she thought, *he* can come back from Whale's Mouth.

She envied—without understanding why—that man. Rachmael ben Applebaum, the 'pape said. If we could cross over now with you, she thought, if we asked—

Her husband said quietly, "If you won't go, Ruth, *I'm going alone*. I'm not going to sit there day after day at that quality-control station, feeling that pigeon breathing down the back of my neck."

She sighed. And wandered into the common kitchen which they shared with their right-hand neighbors, the Shorts, to see if there was anything left of their monthly ration of what the bill of lading called cof-bz. Synthetic coffee beans.

There was not. So, instead, she morosely fixed herself a cup of synthetic tea. Meanwhile, the Shorts—who were noisy—came and went, in and out of the kitchen. And, in her living room, her husband sat before the TV set, an enraptured child, listening to, following with devout and absorbed full attention the nightly report from Whale's Mouth. Watching the new, the next, world.

I guess, she thought, he's right.

But something deep and instinctive within her still objected. And she wondered queerly why. And she thought, then, once more of Rachmael ben Applebaum, who, the 'pape said, was attempting the eighteen-year trip *without* deep-sleep equipment; he had tried and failed to obtain it, the 'pape said gleefully; the guy was so marginal an operator, such a fly-by-nighter, that he had no credit, pos or otherwise. The poor man, she thought. Conscious and alone for eighteen whole years; couldn't the company that makes those deep-sleep units *donate* the equipment he needs?

The TV set in the living room declared, "Remember, folks, it's Old Mother Hubbard there on Terra, and the Old Woman who lived in a shoe; you've got so many children, folks, and just what do you plan to do?"

Emigrate, Ruth decided, without enthusiasm. Apparently. And—soon.

SIX

Against Rachmael ben Applebaum's tiny flapple the great hull of his one asset of economic value—and that attached through the courts—bumped in the darkness, and at once automatic mechanisms came into operation. A hatch whined open; inner locks shut and then retired as air passed into vacuum and replaced it, and, on his console, a green light lit. A good one.

He could safely pass from his meager rented flapple into the *Omphalos*, as it hung in powerless orbit around Mars at .003 astronomical units.

Directly he had crossed through the lock-series—without use of a pressure suit or oxygen gear—Al Dosker said to him, eyeing him and with laser pistol in hand, "I thought it might be a simulacrum, supplied by THL. But the EEG and EKG machines say you're not." He held out his hand; and Rachmael shook. "So you're making the trip anyhow, without the deep-sleep components. And you think, after eighteen years, you'll be sane? I wouldn't be." His dark, sharp-cut face was filled with compassion. "Can't you induce some fray to come along? One other person, and what a difference, especially if she's—"

"And quarrel," Rachmael said, "and wind up with one corpse. I'm taking an enormous edu-tape library; by the time I reach Fomalhaut I'll be speaking Attic Greek, Latin, Russian, Italian—I'll be reading alchemical texts from the Middle Ages and Chinese classics in the original from the sixth century." He smiled, but it was an empty, frozen smile; he was not fooling Dosker, who knew what it was like to try an inter-system run without deep-sleep. Because Dosker had made the three-year trip to Proxima. And, on the journey back, had insisted, from his experience, on deep-sleep.

"What gets me," Rachmael said, "is that THL has gotten to the black market. That they're even able to dry up illegal supplies of minned parts." But—the chance had been missed in the restaurant; the components had been within reach, five thousand poscreds' worth. And—that was that.

"You know," Dosker said slowly, "that one of Lies, Incorporated's experienced field reps is crossing, using a regular Telpor terminal, like the average fella. So we may be contacting the *Omphalos* within the next week; you may be able to turn back; we may save you the eighteen years going, and, or have you forgotten, the eighteen years returning?"

"I'm not sure," Rachmael said, "if I make it I'll come back." He was not fooling himself; after the trip to Fomalhaut he might be physically unable to start back—whatever conditions obtained at Whale's Mouth he might stay there because he *had* to. The body had its limits. So did the mind.

Anyhow they now had more to go on. Not only the failure of the old time capsule ever to reach the Sol system—and conveniently forgotten by the media—but the Vidphone Corporation of Wes-Dem's absolute refusal, under direct, legal request by Matson Glazer-Holliday, to reactivate its Prince Albert B-y satellite orbiting Fomalhaut. This one fact alone, Rachmael reflected, should have frightened the rational citizen. But—

The people did not know. The media had not reported it.

Matson, however, had leaked the info to the small, militant, anti-emigration org, the Friends of a United People. Mostly they were old-fashioned, elderly and fearful, whose distrust of emigration by means of Telpor was based on neurotic reasons. But—they did print pamphlets. And Vidphone Corp's refusal had duly been noted immediately in one of their Terra-wide broad-sheets.

But how many persons had seen it—that Rachmael did not know. He had the intuition, however, that very few people had. And—emigration continued.

As Matson said, the footprints leading into the predator's lair continued to increase in number. And still none led out.

Dosker said, "All right, I am now officially, formally surrendering the *Omphalos* back to you. She appears to check out through every system, so you should have nothing to fear." His dark eyes glinted. "I tell you what, ben Applebaum. During your eighteen years of null-deep-sleep you can amuse yourself as I've been, during the last week." He reached to a table, picked up a leather-backed book. "You can," he said quietly, "keep a diary."

"Of what?"

"Of a mind," Dosker said, "deteriorating. It'll be of psychiatric interest." Now he did not seem to be joking.

"So even you," Rachmael said, "consider me—"

"Without deep-sleep equipment to drop your metabolism you're making a terrible mistake to go. So maybe the diary won't be a transcript of human deterioration; maybe that's already taken place."

Wordlessly, Rachmael watched the dark, lithe man step through the lock, disappear, out of the *Omphalos* and into the tiny rented flapple.

The lock clanged shut. A red light flicked on above it and he was alone, here in this, his giant passenger liner, as he would be for eighteen years and maybe, he thought, maybe Dosker is right.

But still he intended to make the trip.

At three o'clock a.m. Matson Glazer-Holliday was awakened by one of his staff of automatic villa servants. "Your lord, a message from a Mr. Bergen Phillips. From Newcolonizedland. Just received. And you asked—"

"Yes." Matson sat up, spilling the covers from Freya, who slept on; he grabbed his robe, slippers. "Let's have it."

The message, typed out by routine printers of the Vidphone Corp, read:

BOUGHT MY FIRST ORANGE TREE. LOOKS LIKE A BIG CROP.
COME ON JOIN MOLLY AND ME.

Now Freya stirred, sat up; her spidersilk nightgown, one strap of it, slipped from her bare, pale shoulder. "What is it?" she murmured.

"The first encoded note from B.P.," Matson said; he absently tap-tapped the folded message against his knee, pondering.

She sat up fully, reached for her pack of Bering cigarillos. "What does he report, Mat?"

Matson said, "The message is version six."

"That—things are exactly as depicted." She was wide-awake, now; she sat lighting her cigarillo, watching him intently.

"Yes. But—THL psychologists, waiting on the far side, could have nabbed the field rep. Washed his brain, gotten everything and then sent this; so it meant nothing. Only a transmission of one of the odd-numbered codes—indicating in various degrees that conditions at Whale's Mouth were not as depicted—would have been worth anything. Because of course THL psychologists would have no motive to fake *those*."

"So," Freya said, "you know nothing."

"But maybe he can activate the Prince Albert B-y sat." One week; it would not be long, and the *Omphalos* could easily be contacted by then. And, since its solo pilot did not lie in deep-sleep, he could be informed.

However, if after a week—

"If no data came from the sat," Matson said thoughtfully, "it still proves nothing. Because then Bergen will transmit message *n*, meaning that the sat has proved inoperative. *They* will do all that, too, if they have him. So still nothing!" He paced about the bedroom, then took the burning cigarillo from the girl in the rumpled bed, inhaled from it violently, until it heated up and scorched his fingers. "I," he said, "will not live out eighteen years." I will never live to know the truth about Whale's Mouth, he realized. That time-period; it was just too long to wait.

"You'll be seventy-nine," Freya said practically. "So you'll still be alive. But a *jerry* with artiforgs for natural organs."

But—I'm just not that patient, Matson realized. A newborn baby grows virtually to adulthood in that time!

Freya retrieved the cigarillo, winced at its temperature. "Well, possibly you can send over—"

"I'm going over," Matson said.

Staring at him, after a moment she said, "Oh god. God."

"I won't be alone. I'll have a 'family.' At every outlet of Trails of Hoffman a Lies, Incorporated commando team—" He possessed two thousand of them, many veterans of the war; they would pass over at the same moment as he, would link up at Whale's Mouth. And, in their "personal" gear, they would convey enough detection, relay, recording and monitoring equipment to reestablish the private police agency. "So you're in charge here on Terra," he told Freya. "Until I get back." Which would be thirty-six years from now, he thought acidly. When I'm ninety-seven years old . . . no, that's right: we can obtain deep-sleep mechanisms at Whale's Mouth because I remember them taking it across; that's one reason why it's so short of supply, here. Originally it was thought that if colonization didn't work they could vacate—*roanoke*, they called it— they could roanoke back to the Sol system in deep-sleep by ship . . . from giant liners manufactured at Whale's Mouth from prefab sections passed across by Dr. von Einem's Telpor teleportation gates.

"A coup," Freya said, then. "In fact—a *coup d'etat*."

Startled, he said, "What? God no; I never—"

"If you take two thousand top reps," Freya said, "Lies, Incorporated won't exist here; it'll be a shade. But over there—it'll be formidable. And the UN has no army at Whale's Mouth, Matson. You're aware of that, at least on an unconscious level. Who could oppose you? Let's see. The President of Newcolonizedland, Omar Jones, is up for reelection in two years; you'd possibly want to wait—"

"At the first call from Whale's Mouth," Matson said harshly, "Omar Jones could have UN troops trotting through every Telpor instrument in the world. And their tactical weapons with them, everything up to cephalotropic missiles." And he hated—and feared—those.

"*If* a call came from Whale's Mouth. But once you're on the other side, you could handle that. *You could be sure no such emergency announcement was sent out.* Isn't that what we've been discussing all this time? Isn't this really why you bought Rachmael's idea—your knowledge that all communication from the other side can be—*managed*?" She waited, smoking, watching him with a feminine vigil of intensity and acuity.

Presently he said tightly, "Yes. We could do that. They may have THL psychologists armed and ready for individuals. But not for two thousand trained police. We'd have control in half an hour—probably. Unless, unknown to us, Horst Bertold has been sending troops across." And, he pondered, why should he? All they face—up to now—is bewildered citizens, expatriates who want jobs, homes, new roots . . . in a world they can't leave.

"And remember this, too," Freya said. She lifted the strap of her nightgown once more, then, covering her faintly freckled shoulder. "The receiving portion of the teleportation rig has to be spacially installed; every one of those over there had to be sent originally by inter-stellar hyper-see ship, and that took years. So you can stop the UN and Bertold just by rendering the receiving stations of the Telpors inoperative—*if they suspect.*"

"And *if* I can move quickly enough."

"But you," she said calmly, "can. Taking your best men, with their equipment . . . unless—" She paused, licked her lip, as if puzzling out a purely academic problem.

Maddened, he said, "Unless what, goddamn it?"

"They may identify your reps as they cross. And you. They may be ready. I can see it now." She laughed merrily. "You pay your poscreds, smile at the nice THL bald-headed, gargoyle-like New Whole Germany technicians who run those Telpors, you stand there while they subject your body to the field of the equipment . . . keep standing there innocently, fade away, reappear twenty-four light-years away at Whale's Mouth . . . and are lasered dead before you're even fully formed. It takes fifteen minutes. For fifteen minutes, Mat, you would be helpless, half materialized both here and there. And all your field reps. And all their gear."

He glared at her.

"Thus," she said, "goes *hubris*."

"What's that?"

"The Greek word for 'pride.' For trying to rise above the station the gods have allocated you. Maybe the gods don't want you to seize control of Whale's Mouth, Matty darling. Maybe the gods don't want you to overreach yourself."

"Hell," he said, "as long as I have to go across anyhow—"

"Sure; then why *not* take control? Push jovial, insipid Omar Jones aside? After all . . ." She stubbed out her cigarillo. "You'd be doomed to stay there anyhow; why live the ordinary life with the ordinary *hoi polloi*? Here, you're strong . . . but Horst Bertold and the UN, with Trails of Hoffman as their economic support, *are stronger*. Over there—" She shrugged, as if made weary by human aspirations—or human vanity. Over there it was simply a different situation.

No one, he realized, could compete if he managed to move, in one sudden swoop, his entire entourage and weaponry across . . . using, ironically, von Einem's own official retail stations themselves. He grinned at that; it amused him to think that THL would personally see to it that he and his veteran reps reached Newcolonizedland.

"And then in 2032," Freya said, "when Rachmael ben Apple-baum, probably an unwashed, bearded, mumbling hebephrenic schizophrenic by then, shows up in his great and good ship the *Omphalos*, he'll discover it's a hell, there, exactly as he antici-pated . . . but it'll be *you* who'll be running it. And I'll bet *that* will surprise him more than a little."

Nettled, he said, "I can't think about it any more. I'm going back to sleep." He removed his robe and slippers, got wearily into the bed, aware of his years; he felt old. Wasn't he too decrepit for something like this? Not getting into bed; lord, he wasn't too old to clamber in beside Freya Holm, not yet, anyhow. But too old for what Freya had proposed—what she had correctly, possibly even telepathically, ascertained from his unconscious mind. Yes, it was actually true.

He had, from Rachmael's initial vidphone call, at the back levels of his cognition-processes, pondered this, from the very beginning.

And *this* was his reason for assisting—or rather trying to assist—the morose, creditor-balloon-hounded Rachmael ben Applebaum.

He thought, according to published info there is a home army, so-called, at Whale's Mouth, of three hundred volunteer citizens. For use as a sort of national guard in case of a riot. Three hundred! And none of them professionals, with experience. It was a pastoral land, the ads explained. A G. of E. lacking a snake; since there was a super-abundance of everything for everyone, what was an army needed for? What have-not existed to envy what have? And what reason to try, by force, to seize his holdings?

I'll tell you, Matson Glazer-Holliday thought. The have-nots are here on this side. Myself and those who work for me; we're gradu-ally, over the years, being ground down and overpowered by the true titans, by the UN and THL and—

The haves are across twenty-four light-years in the Fomalhaut system, at its ninth planet.

Mr. ben Applebaum, he thought to himself as he lay supine,

drew, from reflex, Freya Holm against him, you will have quite a surprise when you get to Whale's Mouth.

It was a pity that he himself—and he intuited this with certitude—would not be alive at that date.

As to *why* not, however, his near-Psionic intuition told him nothing.

Beside him Freya moaned in her half-sleep, settled close to him, relaxed.

He, however, lay awake, staring into the nothingness. Deep in a new, hard thought. The like of which he had never experienced before.

SEVEN

The monitoring and recording-transmitting satellite, Prince Albert B-y, creaked out its first video signal, a transcript of the first video telescopic records which it had taken of the surface beneath it in over a decade. Portions of the long-inert network of minned parts failed; backup systems, however, took over, and some of these failed, too. But the signal, directed toward the Sol system twenty-four light-years away, was sent out.

And, on the surface of Fomalhaut IX, an eye winked. And from it a ground-to-air missile rose and in a period so slight that only the finest measuring-devices could have detected a lapse-period at all, arrived at its target, the groaning carrot-shaped monitoring satellite which had, inoperative, silently existed—and hence harmlessly. Up to now.

The warhead of the missile detonated. And the Prince Albert B-y ceased to exist, soundlessly, because at its altitude there was no atmosphere to transmit the event in the dimension of noise.

And, at the same time on the surface below, a powerful transmitter accepted a tape run at enormous velocity; the signal, amplified by a row of cold, superbly built surgegates, reached transmission level and was released; oddly, its frequency coincided with that of the signal just emitted by the now nonexistent satellite.

What would radiate from the two separate transmitters would blend in a cacaphony of meaningless garble. Satisfied, the technicians operating the ground transmitter switched to more customary channels—and tasks.

The deliberately deranged combined signal sped across space toward the Sol system, beamed, in its mad confusion, at a planet which, when it received this, would possess nothing but a catfight of noise.

And the satellite, reduced to its molecular level by the warhead, would emit no more signals; its life was over.

The event, the first transmission by the satellite up into the final scramble by the far more powerful surface transmitter, had consumed five minutes, including the flight—and demolition—of the missile: the missile and its priceless, elaborate, never-to-be-duplicated target.

—A target which, certain circles had long ago agreed in formal session, could be readily sacrificed, were the need to arise.

That need had arisen.

And the satellite was duly gone.

At the site of the missile-launching a helmeted soldier leisurely fitted a second g.-to-a. missile into the barn, attached both its anode and cathode terminals, made sure that the activating board was relocked—by the same key through which he had obtained official entry—and then he, too, returned to his customary chores.

Time lapse: perhaps six minutes in all.

And the planet, Fomalhaut IX, revolved on.

———

Deep in thought as she sat in the comfortable leather, padded seat of the luxury taxi flapple, Freya Holm was startled by the sudden mechanical voice of the vehicle's articulation-circuit. "Sir or madam, I request your pardon, but a deterioration of my meta-battery forces me without choice to land for a quick-charge without delay. Please give me oral permission as an acknowledgment of your willingness otherwise we will glide to destruct."

Looking down she saw the high-rise spires of New New York, the ring of city outside the inner, old kremlin of New York itself. Late for work, she said to herself, damn it. But—the flapple was correct; if its meta-battery, its sole power supply, were failing, to get out of the sky and on the surface at a repair station was mandatory; a long powerless glide would mean death in the form of collision with one of the tall commercial buildings below. "Yes," she agreed, resignedly, and groaned. And today was the day.

"Thank you, sir or madam." With sputtering power the flapple spiraled down until at last, under adequate control, it coasted to a rather rough but at least not dangerous halt at one of New New York's infinite flapple service stations.

A moment later uniformed service station men swarmed over the parked flapple, searching for—as one explained courteously to her—for the short which had depleted the meta-battery, good normally, the attendant told her cheerfully, for twenty years.

Opening the flapple door the attendant said, "May I check under the passenger's console, please? The wiring there; those circuits take a lot of hard use—the insulation may be rubbed off." He, a Negro, seemed to her pleasant and alert and without hesitation she moved to the far side of the cab.

The Negro attendant slid in, closed, then, the flapple door. "Moon and cow," he said, the current—and highly temporary—ident-code phrase of members of the police organization Lies, Incorporated.

Taken by surprise Freya murmured, "Jack Horner. Who are you? I never ran into you before." He did not look like a field rep to her.

"A 'tween space pilot. I'm Al Dosker; I know you—you're Freya Holm." He was not smiling now; he was quiet, serious, and, as he sat beside her, perfunctorily running his fingers over the wiring of the passenger's control console he said, half chantingly, "I have no time, Freya, for small talk; I have five minutes at the most; I know where the short is because I sent this particular flapple taxi to pick you up. See?"

"I see," she said, and, within her mouth, bit on a false tooth; the tooth split and she tasted the bitter out-layer of a plastic pill: a container of Prussic acid, enough to kill her if this man proved to be from their antagonists. And, at her wrist, she wound her watch—actually winding a low-velocity homeostatic, cyanide-tipped dart which she would control by the "watch" controls; it could either take out this man or, if others showed up, herself, in case of a failure of the oral poison. In any case she sat back rigid, waiting.

"You," the Negro said, "are Matson's mistress; you have access to him at any time; this I know—this is why I've approached you. Tonight, at six p.m. New New York time, Matson Glazer-Holliday will arrive at an outlet of Trails of Hoffman; carrying two heavy suitcases he will request permission to emigrate. He will pay his six poscreds, or seven, if his luggage is overweight, and then be teleported to Whale's Mouth. And at the same time, at every Telpor outlet throughout Terra, a total aggregate of roughly two thousand of his toughest veteran field reps will do the same."

She said nothing; she stared straight ahead. Within her purse an aud recorder captured all this, but heaven only knew for what.

The Negro said, "On the far side he, by deploying his veterans and the wep-equipment which they will assemble from components carried in their suitcases as 'personal articles,' will attempt a coup. Will halt emigration, make at once inoperative the Telpors, toss President Omar Jones—"

"So?" she said. "If I know this, why tell me?"

"Because," Dosker said, "I am going to Horst Bertold two hours before six. I believe that is usually considered four o'clock." His voice was icy, harsh. "I am an employee of Lies, Incorporated but I did not join the organization to participate in a power play like this. On Terra, Matson G.-H. stands about where he ought to be: third in the pecking order. On Whale's Mouth—"

"And you want me," Freya said, "to do exactly what between now and four o'clock? Seven hours."

"Inform Matson that when he and the two thousand LI field reps arrive at the retail outlets of THL they will not be teleported but will be arrested and undoubtedly painlessly murdered. In the German manner."

"This," she said, "is what you want? Matson dead and them, those—" She gestured, gripping, clawing the air. "Bertold and Ferry and von Einem to run the corporate Terran–Whale's Mouth political-economic entity with no one to—"

"I don't want him to try."

"Listen," Freya said bitingly. "The coup that Matson expects to carry out at Whale's Mouth is based on his assumption that a home army of three hundred ignorant volunteers exists over there. I don't think you have to worry; the problem is that Mat actually *believes* the lies he sees on TV; he's actually incredibly primitive and naive. Do *you* think it's a Promised Land over there, with a tiny volunteer army, waiting for someone to come along with *real* force, aided by modern wep-technology, such as Mat possesses, to harvest for the asking? If this were so, do you honestly believe Bertold and Ferry *would not have done it already?"*

Dosker, disconcerted, eyed her hesitantly.

"I think," she said, "that Mat is making a mistake. Not because it's immoral but because he's going to discover that, once he's over there, he and his two thousand veterans, he'll be facing—" She broke off. "I don't know. But he won't succeed in any *coup d'etat.* Whoever runs Newcolonizedland will handle Mat; that's what terrifies me. Sure, I'd like him to stop; I'd be glad to tell him that one of his top employees who knows all the inside details about the coup is going to, at four p.m., tip off the authorities. I'll do everything in my power, Dosker, to get him to abandon the idea, to face the fact that he's wandering idiotically into a terminal trap. My reasons and yours may not—"

"What do you think," Dosker said, "is over there, Freya?"

"Death."

"For—everybody?" He stared at her. "Forty million? Why?"

"The days," she said, "of Gilbert and Sullivan and Jerome Kern are over. We're on a planet of seven billion. Whale's Mouth could do the job, but slowly, and there's a more efficient way, and every one of those in key posts in the UN, put in by Herr Horst Bertold, knows that way."

"No," Dosker said, his face an ugly, putty-colored gray. "That went out in 1945."

"Are you sure? Would *you* want to emigrate?"

He was silent. And then, stunning her, he said, "Yes."

"What? Why?"

Dosker said, "I will emigrate. Tonight at six, New New York time. With laser pistol in my left hand, and I'll kick them in the groin; I want to get at them, if that's what they're doing; I can't wait."

"You won't be able to do a thing. As soon as you emerge—"

"With my bare hands. I'll get *one* of them. Any one will do."

"Start here. Start with Horst Bertold."

He stared at her, then.

"We have the wep-techs," Freya said, and then ceased speaking as the flapple door was opened by another—cheerful—attendant.

"Found the short, Al?" he asked.

"Yes," Al Dosker said. He fooled, fumbled, under the dashboard, his face concealed. "Should be okay now. Recharge the meta-bat, stick it back in, and she can take off."

The other attendant, satisfied, departed. Freya and Al Dosker were alone once more, briefly, with the flapple door hanging open.

"You—may be wrong," Dosker said.

Freya said, "It's got to be something like that. It can't be three hundred assorted-shape volunteer army privates, because Ferry and Bertold or at least *one* of them would have moved in, and that's the one fact we know: *we know what they're like.* There just cannot, Dosker, be a power vacuum at Whale's Mouth."

"All ready to go, miss," one of the other attendants called.

The flapple's articulation-circuit asserted, "I feel a million times better; I'm now prepared to depart for your original destination, sir or madam, as soon as the superfluous individual has disemflappled."

Dosker, trembling said, "I—don't know what to do."

"Don't go to Ferry or Bertold. Begin at that."

He nodded. Evidently she had reached him; that part was over.

"Mat will need all the help he can get," she said, "from six o'clock on. From the moment his first field rep hits Whale's Mouth. Dosker, why don't you go? Even if you're a pilot, not a rep. Maybe you can help him."

The flapple started its motor up irritably. "Please, sir or madam, if you will request—"

"Are you teleporting?" Dosker asked her. "With them?"

Freya said, "I'm scheduled to cross at five. To rent living quarters for Mat and me. I'll be—remember this so you can find us—Mrs. Silvia Trent. And Mat will be Stuart Trent. Okay?"

"Okay," Dosker mumbled, backed out, shut the flapple door.

The flapple began to ascend, at once.

And she relaxed. And spat out the capsule of Prussic acid, dropped it into the disposal chute of the flapple, then reset her "watch."

What she had said to Dosker, god knew, was the truth. She knew it—knew it and could do nothing to dissuade Matson. On the far side professionals would be in wait, and even if they didn't anticipate the coup, even if there had been no leak and they saw no connection between the two thousand male individuals scattered all over the world, applying at every Telpor outlet on Terra . . . even so, she knew they would be able to handle Mat. He was just not that big and they *could* handle him.

But *he* did not believe it. Because Mat saw the possibility of power; it was a gaff that had hooked deep in his side and the wound spilled with the blood of yearning. Suppose it was true; suppose only a three-hundred-man army existed. *Suppose.* The hope and possibility enflamed him.

And babies, she thought, as the flapple carried her toward the New New York offices of Lies, Incorporated, are discovered under cabbages.

Sure, Mat; you keep on believing.

EIGHT

To the pleasant, rather overextensively bosomed young female receptionist, Rachmael ben Applebaum said, "My name is Stuart Trent. My wife was teleported earlier today, so I'm anxious to slip in under the wire; I know you're about to close your office."

He had planned this for some time. It was his top card, to be played—hopefully to the surprise of everyone.

The girl glanced searchingly at him. "You're certain, Mr. Trent, that you desire to—"

"My wife," he repeatedly harshly. "She's already over. She left at five." He added, "I have two suitcases. A leady is bringing them." And into the office of Trails of Hoffman, strode the robot-like machine, bearing the two imitation cowhide bulging suitcases.

The consummately nubile receptionist said, "Please fill out these forms, Mr. Trent. I'll make certain that the Telpor techs are ready to receive one more, because as you say, we are about to close."

The entrance gate, in fact, was now locked.

He made out the forms, feeling only a coldness, an empty mindless—fear. Lord, it really was fear! He actually, at this late moment, when Freya had already been teleported across to Whale's Mouth, felt his autonomic nervous system secrete its hormones of cringing panic; he wanted to back out.

But this was too well-planned. If they were expecting anyone they would be expecting Matson Glazer-Holliday. No one would expect him.

However, despite his panic, he managed to fill out the forms. Because, higher than the autonomic nervous system, was the frontal lobe's awareness that the moment Freya crossed over, it was decided.

In fact, that was the reason for sending her in advance; he knew his own irresolution. Freya had been made the cat's paw of that irresolution; by having her go he forced himself to complete this.

And, he thought, for the best; we must find some way, in life, to overcome ourselves . . . we're our own worst enemies.

"Your shots, Mr. Trent." A THL nurse stood by with needles. "Will you please remove your outer garments?" The nurse pointed to a small and hygienic back chamber; he entered, began removing his clothing.

Presently he had received his shots; his arms ached and he wondered dully if they had done it already. Had this been something fatal, administered over the cover of prophylactic shots?

Two elderly German technicians, both as bald as doorknobs, all at once manifested themselves, wearing the goggles of Telpor operators. The field itself, if viewed too long, caused permanent destruction of the retina. "Mein Herr," the first technician said briskly, "kindly, sir, remove the balance of your garb. *Sie sollen ganz unbedeckt sein.* We wish not material, no sort, to impede the Stärke of the field. All objects, including your parcels, will follow you within minutes."

Rachmael finished undressing, and terrified, followed them down a tiled hall to what suddenly loomed as a mammoth chamber, almost barren. He saw in it no elaborate Dr. Frankenstein hodgepodge of retorts and bubbling cauldrons, only the twin perpendicular poles, like the concrete walls of a good tennis court, covered with circular cup-like terminals. Between the poles he would stand, a mute ox, and the surge of the field would pass from pole to pole, engulfing him. And he would either die—if they knew who he was—or if not, then he would be gone from Terra for the balance of his life, or at least thirty-six years.

Lord God, he thought. I hope Freya got by all right. Anyhow the short encoded message signifying everything all right had arrived from her. He knew that.

Abba had told him. Abba reborn—in Rachmael's own mind. Abba immortal and discorporate, to bond with one of the believers.

"Mr. Trent," a technician said (he could not discern which one it was; they looked the same), fitting his goggles in place. "Bitte; please look down so that your eyes do not perceive the field-emanations; Sie versteh'n the retinal hazard."

"Okay," he said, nodding, and looked down, then, in almost a gesture of modesty. He raised one arm, touched his bare chest with one hand, as if concealing himself—protecting himself against what suddenly became a stunning, blinding ram-head which butted him simultaneously from both sides.

The forces, absolutely equal, made him freeze, as if poured as a polyester as he stood. Anyone watching would have thought him free to move. But he was ensnared for good by the surge passing from anode to cathode, with himself as—what, the ion ring? His body attracted the field; he felt it infuse him as a dissolving agent.

And then the left surge stopped. He staggered, glanced up involuntarily. And thought, Abba, are you with me?

No answer from within his mind.

The two bald, goggled Reich technicians were gone. He was in a far smaller chamber, and one elderly man sat at a desk, an old-fashioned desk, carefully logging from numbered tags a huge mound of suitcases and wrapped, tied parcels.

"Your clothing," the official said, "lies in a metal basket to your right marked 121628. And if you're faint, there's a cot; you may lie down."

"I'm—all right," Rachmael said. Abba! he thought in panic. Did they destroy you within me? Are you gone? Do I have to face this alone, now?

Silence within him.

He made his way unsteadily to his clothing. Hands shaking, he dressed, then stood uncertainly.

"Here are your two items of luggage," the bureaucrat at the desk said, without looking up. He seemed like some ancient nodding sheep, drowsing away at his chores. "Numbers 39485 and 39486. Please arrange to remove them from the premises." He then brought out an old golden pocket watch on a fob, flipped it open to read the dial. "No, excuse me. No one will be following you from the New New York nexus. Take your time."

"Thanks." Rachmael picked up the heavy suitcases, walked toward a large double door. "Is this," he asked, "the right direction?"

"That will indeed take you out on Laughing Willow Tree Avenue," the clerk informed him.

"I want a hotel or a motel."

"Any surface vehicle can transport you." The clerk returned to his work, broke contact. He had no more info to offer.

Pushing the door open, Rachmael stepped out onto the sidewalk. And stopped dead in his tracks.

Acrid smoke billowed about him, stinging his nostrils. He bent in a reflexive half-crouch. Then, here now on the far side, on the ninth planet of Fomalhaut, Rachmael ben Applebaum fingered relentlessly the meager flat tin, the container in his trouser pocket: this was the wep-x that the Advance-weapons Archives had at last provided him—radically disguised as well as radically beyond anything in the standard arsenals of the UN. The camouflage of the hyper-miniaturized time-warping construct had seemed to him, when he first viewed it, the sine quo non of misleading packages: the weapon appeared to be a bootlegged tin of prophoz from Yucatán, fully automated, helium-battery powered, guaranteed for five-year operation and gynetropic.

Briefly, he huddled in the safe shadow of a wall, the weapon out, now, visible in the palm of his hand. Even the gaily painted half witted slogan of the Central American factory had been duplicated, and, at a time like this, on a stranger-planet in another system, he read the quixotic words familiar to him since adolescence:

MORE FUN
AFTER DONE!

And with this, he thought, I'm going to get Freya back. In its witless, gaily colored way the camouflage-package of the weapon seemed more of an insult, a quasi-obscene commentary on the situation confronting him. However, he returned it to his pocket; sliding upward to an erect position he once again viewed the nebulous rolls of particles in suspension, the cloud masses derived from the molecularization of the nearby buildings. He saw, too, dim human shapes that sped at ludicrously accelerated speed, each in its own direction, as if some central control usually in operation had, at this dangerous time, where so much was at stake, clicked off, leaving each of the sprinting figures on its own.

And yet they all seemed to understand what they were doing; their activities were not undirected, not random. To his right a cluster had gathered to assemble a complex weapon; with industrious, ant-busy fingers they snapped one component after another into position in expert progression: they knew their business, and he wondered—he could not, in the erratic light, make out their uniforms—which faction they represented. Probably, he decided, better to conclude they belonged to THL; safer, he realized. And he would have to assume this, until otherwise proved, about each and every person whom he encountered here on this side, this Newcolonizedland which was no—

Directly before him a soldier appeared whose eyes glowed huge and unwinking, owl eyes which fixed on him and would never, now that they had perceived him, again look away.

Diving to the ground, Rachmael fumbled numbly for the prophoz tin; it had happened too soon, too unexpectedly—he was not ready and the weapon which he had brought here to use for Freya was not even positioned to protect him, let alone her. His hand touched it, buried deep within his pocket . . . and at that moment a muffled *pop* burst near his face as, above him, the THL soldier twisted to re-aim and fire once more.

A high-velocity dart waggled its directing fins as it spun at him. It was, he realized as he watched it descend toward him, an LSD-tipped dart; the hallucinogenic ergotic alkaloid derivative constituted—had constituted ever since its introduction into the field of weapons of war—a unique instrument for reducing the enemy to a condition in which he was absolutely neutralized: instead of destroying him, the LSD, injected intravenously by the dart, destroyed his *world*.

Sharp, quick pain snuffed at his arm; the dart had plunged into him, had embedded itself successfully.

The LSD had entered his circulatory system. He had, now, only a few minutes ahead; that realization alone generally took the target out: to know, under conditions such as these, that very shortly the entire self-system, the structure of world-character which had developed stage by stage over the years from birth on—

His thoughts ceased. The LSD had reached the cortical tissue of his frontal lobe and all abstract mentational processes had instantly shut down. He still saw the world, saw the THL soldier leisurely reloading the dart-releasing gun, the rolling clouds of A-warhead-contaminated ash, the half-ruined buildings, the ant-like scampering figures here and there. He could recognize them and understand what each was. But beyond that—nothing.

Color, Rachmael thought as he saw the transformation in the THL soldier's face; the color-transformation—it had already set in. Swiftly, the drug moved him to ruin; in his bloodstream it rushed him toward the end of his existence in the shared world. For me, he knew, this—but he could not even think it, carry out the steps of a logical thought. Awareness was there, knowledge of what was happening. He watched the lips of the THL soldier become bright, phosphorescent, shiny-pink pure luminosity; the lips, forming a perfect bow, then floated off, detached themselves from the soldier's face, leaving behind the ordinary colorless lips: one hemisphere of Rachmael's brain had received the LSD and succumbed, undoubtedly the right, he being right-handed, the hemisphere on that side therefore being the undifferentiated of the two. The left still held out, still saw the mundane world; even now, deprived of abstract reasoning, no longer capable of adult cerebral processes, the higher centers of the left hemisphere of his brain fought to stabilize the picture of the world as he knew it, fought knowing that within seconds, now, that picture would give way, would collapse and let in, like some endless flood, the entirety of raw percept-data, uncontrolled, unstructured, without meaning or order, each datum unrelated to the others: the portion of his brain which imposed the framework of space and time onto incoming data would not be able to carry out its task. And, with the ringing in of that instant, he would plunge back decades. Back to the initial interval after birth— entry into a world utterly unfamiliar, utterly incomprehensible.

He had lived through that once. Each human, at the moment of birth, had. But now. Now he possessed memory, retention of the disappearing usual world. That and language; that and realization of what ordinary and expected experience would presently become.

And how long, subjectively, it would last. How long it would be before he regained—if he did regain—his customary world once more.

The THL soldier, his weapon reloaded, started away, already searching for the next target; he did not bother to notice Rachmael, now. He, too, knew what lay ahead. Rachmael could be forgotten; even now he no longer lived in the shared world, no longer existed.

Without thought, prompted by a brain-area silent but still functioning, Rachmael raced after the THL soldier; with no lapse of time, without a sense of having crossed intervening space, he clutched the soldier, dragged him aside and took possession of the long-bladed throwing knife holstered at the man's waist. Choking him with his left arm Rachmael yanked the blade backward in an arc that reversed itself: the blade returned, and the THL soldier followed its reverse trajectory as it approached his stomach. He struggled; in Rachmael's grip he strained, and his eyes dulled as if baked, dried out, without fluid and old, mummified by a thousand years. And, in Rachmael's hand, the knife became something he did not know.

The thing which he held ceased its horizontal motion. It moved, but in another direction which was neither up nor forward; he had never seen this direction and its weirdness appalled him, because the thing in his hand moved without moving; it progressed and yet stayed where it was, so that he did not have to change the direction of his eye focus. His gaze fixed, he watched the shining, brittle, transparent thing elaborate itself, produce from its central column slender branches like glass stalagmites; in a series of lurches, of jumps forward into the nonspacial dimension of altered movement, the tree-thing developed until its complexity terrified him. It was all over the world, now; from his hand it had jerked out into stage after stage so that, he knew, it was everywhere, and nothing else had room to exist: the tree-thing had taken up all space and crowded reality-as-it-usually-was out.

And still it grew.

He decided, then, to look away from it. In his mind he recalled in distinctness, with labored, painstaking concentration, the THL soldier; he noted the direction, in relation to the enormous, world-filling tree-thing, along which the soldier could be found. He made his head turn, his eyes focus that way.

A small circle, like some far end of a declining tube, opened up and unveiled for him a minute portion of reality-as-it-usually-was. Within that circle he made out the face of the THL soldier, unchanged; it stabilized in normal luminosity and shape. And, meanwhile, throughout the endless area which was not the distant circle of the world, a multitude of noiseless, sparklike configurations flicked on and achieved form with such magnitude of brightness that even without focussing on them he experienced pain; they appalled the optic portion of his percept-system, and yet did not halt the transfer of their impressions: despite the unendurable brilliance the configurations continued to flow into him, and he knew that they had come to stay. Never, he knew. They would *never* leave.

For an almost unmeasurable fraction of an instant he ventured to look directly at one unusually compelling light-configuration; its furious activity attracted his gaze.

Below it, the circle which contained unaltered reality changed. At once he forced his attention back. Too late?

The THL soldier's face. Swollen eyes. Pale. The man returned Rachmael's gaze; their eyes met and each perceived the other, and then the physiognomic properties of the reality-landscape swiftly underwent a crumbling new alteration; the eyes became rocks that immediately were engulfed by a freezing wind which obliterated them with dense snow. The jaw, the cheeks and mouth and chin, even the nose disappeared as they became lesser mountains of barren, uninhabited rock that also succumbed to the snow. Only the tip of the nose projected, a peak presiding alone above a ten-thousand-mile waste that supported no life nor anything that moved. Rachmael watched, and years lapsed by, recorded by the internal clock of his perceiving mind; he knew the duration and knew the meaning of the landscape's perpetual refusal to live: he knew where he was and he recognized this which he saw. It was beyond his ability *not* to recognize it.

This was the hellscape.

No, he thought. It has to stop. Because now he saw tiny distant figures sprouting everywhere to populate the hellscape, and as they formed they continued the dancing, frenzied activities familiar to them—and familiar to him, as if he were back once more and again witnessing this, and knowing with certitude that he would, within the next thousand years, be forced to scrutinize.

His fear, concentrated and directed in this one field, superimposed like a dissolving beam over the hellscape, rolled back the snow, made its thousand-year-old depth fade into thinness; the rocks once more appeared and then retreated backward into time to resume their function as features of a face. The hellscape reverted with awful obedience to what it had been, as if almost no force were needed to push it out of existence, away from the stronghold of reality in which it had a moment before entrenched itself. And this appalled him the most of all: this told him dreadful news. The merest presence of life, even the smallest possible quantity of volition, desire and intent was enough to reverse the process by which the eternal landscape of hell made itself known. And this meant that not long ago, when the hellscape first formed, he had been without *any* life, any at all. Not an enormous force from outside breaking in—that was not what confronted him. There was no adversary. These, the terrible transmutations of world in every direction, had spontaneously entered as his own life had dwindled, faded, and at last—for a moment, anyhow—entirely shut down.

He had died.

But he was now again alive.

Where, then? Not where he had lived before.

The THL soldier's face, customary and natural, hung within the diminished, constricted aperture through which reality showed, a face relieved of the intrusion of hell-attributes. As long, Rachmael realized, as I keep that face in front of me, I'm okay. And if he talks. That would do it; that would get me through.

But he won't, he realized. He tried to kill me; he wants me dead. He *did* kill me. This man—this sole link with outside—is my murderer.

He stared at the face; in return, the eyes glared unwinkingly back, the owl eyes of cruelty that loathed him and wanted him dead, wanted him to suffer. And the THL soldier said nothing; Rachmael waited and heard no sound, even after years—a decade had passed and another began and still no word was spoken. Or if it was he failed to hear it.

"Goddamn you," Rachmael said. His own voice did not reach him; he felt his throat tremble with the sound, but his ears detected no change, nothing. "Do something," Rachmael said. "Please."

The soldier smiled.

"Then you can hear me," Rachmael said. "Even after this long." It was amazing that this man still lived, after so many centuries. But he did not bother to reflect on that; all that mattered was the uninterrupted realness of the face before him. "Say something," Rachmael said, "or I'll break you." His words weren't right, he realized. Meaningful, familiar, but somehow not correct; he was bewildered. "Like a rod of iron," he said. "I will dash you in pieces. Like a potter's vessel. For I am like a refiner's fire." Horrified, he tried to comprehend the warpage of his language; where had the conventional, everyday—

Within him all his language disappeared; all words were gone. Some scanning agency of his brain, some organic searching device, swept out mile after mile of emptiness, finding no stored words, nothing to draw on: he felt it sweeping wider and wider, extending its oscillations into every dark reach, overlooking nothing; it wanted, would accept, anything, now; it was desperate. And still, year after year, the empty bins where words, many of them, had once been but were not now.

He said, then, *"Tremens factus sum ego et timeo."* Because out of the periphery of his vision he had obtained a clear glimpse of the progress of the brilliant light-based drama unfolding silently. *"Libere me,"* he said, and repeated it, once, twice, then on and on, without cease. *"Libere me Domini,"* he said, and for a hundred years he listened, watched the events projected soundlessly before him, witnessed forever.

"Let go of me, you bastard," the THL soldier said. His hands grasped Rachmael's neck and the pain was vast beyond compare; Rachmael let go and the face mocked him in leering hate. "And enjoy your expanded consciousness," the soldier said with malice so overwhelming that Rachmael felt throughout him unendurable somatic torment which came and then stayed.

"Mors scribitum," Rachmael said, appealing to the THL soldier. He repeated it, but there was no response. *"Misere me,"* he said, then; he had nothing else available, nothing more to draw on. *"Dies Irae,"* he said, trying to explain what was happening inside him. *"Dies Illa."* He waited hopefully; he waited years, but no help, no sound, came. I won't make it, he realized then. *Time has stopped. There is no answer.*

"Lots of luck," the face said, then. And began to recede, to move away. The soldier was leaving.

Rachmael hit him. Crushed the mouth. Teeth flew; bits of broken white escaped and vanished, and blood that shone with dazzling flame, like a flow of new, clear fire, exposed itself and filled his vision; the power of illumination emanating from the blood overwhelmed everything, and he saw only that—its intensity stifled everything else and for the first time since the dart had approached him he felt wonder, not fear; this was good. This captivated and pleased him, and he contemplated it with joy.

In five centuries the blood by degrees faded. The flame lessened. Once more, drifting dimly behind the breathing color, the lusterless face of the THL soldier could be made out, uninteresting and unimportant, of no value because it had no light. It was a dreary and tiresome specter, long known, infinitely boring; he experienced excruciating disappointment to see the fire decrease and the THL soldier's features regather. How long, he asked himself, do I have to keep seeing this same unlit scene?

The face, however, was not the same. He had broken it. Split it open with his fist. Opened it up, let out the precious, blinding blood; the face, a ruined husk, gaped disrobed of its shell: he saw, not the mere outside, but into its genuine works.

Another face, concealed before, wriggled and squeezed out, as if wishing to escape. As if, Rachmael thought, it knows I can see it, and it can't stand that. That's the one thing it can't endure.

The inner face, emerging from the cracked-open gray-chitin mask, now tried to fold up within itself, attempted vigorously to wrap itself in its own semi-fluid tissue. A wet, limp face, made of the sea, dripping, and at the same time stinking; he smelled its salty, acrid scent and felt sick.

The oceanic face possessed a single multi-lensed eye. Beneath the beak. And when it opened its toothless mouth the wideness of the cavity divided the face entirely; the mouth separated the face into two unconnected equal parts.

"*Esse homo bonus est,*" Rachmael said, and wondered numbly why such a simple statement as *To be a man is good* sounded so peculiar to his ears. "*Non homo,*" he said, then, to the squashed, divided sea-face, "*video. Atque malus et timeo; libere me Domini.*" What he saw before him was not a man, not a man's face, and it was bad and it frightened him. And he could do nothing about it; he could not stop seeing it, he could not leave, and it did not go away, it would never go because there was no time at work, no possibility of change; what confronted him would peer at him forever, and his knowledge of it would dwell inside him for an equal duration, passed on by him to no one because there was no one. "*Exe,*" he said, helplessly; he spoke pointlessly, knowing it would do no good to tell the creature to go away, since there was no way by which it could; it was as trapped as he, and probably just as terrified. "*Amicus sum,*" he said to it, and wondered if it understood him. "*Sumus amici,*" he said, then, even though he knew it was not so; he and the thing of water were not friends, did not even know what the other consisted of or where it had come from, and he himself, in the dull,

sinking dark red expiration of decaying time, time at its wasted and
entropic final phase, would stay grafted in this spot confronted by
this unfamiliar thing for a million years ticked away by the ponder-
ous moribund clock within him. And never in all that great interval
would he obtain any news as to what this ugly deformed creature
signified.

It means something, he realized. This thing's ocean-face; its
presence at the far end of the tube, at the outer opening where I'm
not, that isn't a hallucinated event inside me—it's here for a reason;
it drips and wads itself into glued-together folds and stares without
winking at me and wants to keep me dead, keep me from ever getting back. *Not my friend,* he thought. Or rather knew. It was not an
idea; it was a concrete piece of observed reality outside: when he
looked at the thing he saw this fact as part of it: the non-friend
attribute came along inseparably. The thing oozed; it oozed and
hated together. Hated him, and with absolute contempt; in its over-
splattering liquid eye he perceived its derision: not only did it not
like him, it did not respect him. He wondered why.

My god, he realized. It must know something about me. Probably it has seen me before, even though I haven't seen it. He knew,
then, what this meant.

It had been here all this time.

N I N E

In a pleasant living room he sat, and across from him a stout man
with good-intentioned features gnawed on a toothpick, eyed him
with a compound of tolerant amusement and sympathy, then turned
to grunt at a thin-faced middle-aged dapper man wearing gold-
rimmed glasses who also watched Rachmael, but with a severe, virtually reproving frown.

"Finally coming back for a couple of breaths of real air," the stout man observed, nodding toward Rachmael.

"There's no such thing as real air," a woman seated across from the two of them said; dark-skinned, tall, with acutely penetrating chitin-black eyes, she scrutinized Rachmael and he imagined for an instant that he was seeing Freya. "All air is real; it's either that or no air at all. Unless you think there's something called *false* air."

The stout man chuckled, nudged his companion. "Listen to that; you hear that? I guess everything you see is real, then; there's no fake nothing." To Rachmael he said, "Everything including dying and being in—"

"Can't you discuss all those sorts of things later?" a blond curly-haired youth at the far end of the room said irritably. "This is a most particularly important summation he's making, and after all, he is our elected president; we owe him our undivided attention, every one of us." His gaze traveled around the tastefully furnished room, taking all of the people in, including Rachmael. Eleven persons in addition to himself, he realized; eleven and me, but what is me? Am I what? His mind, clouded, dwelt in some strange overcast gloom, an obscuring mist that impeded his ability to think or to understand; he could see the people, the room also. But he could not identify this place, these people, and he wondered if the breach with that which had been familiar was so complete as to include himself; had his own physical identity, his customary self, been eradicated too, and some new gathering of matter set in its place? He examined his hands, then. Just hands; he could learn nothing from them, only that he did have hands and that he could see them—he could see everything, with no difficulty. Colors did not rise out of the walls, drapes, prints, the dresses of the seated, casual women; nothing distorted and magnified floated as a median world between this clearly tangible environment and his own lifelong established percept-system.

Beside him suddenly an attractive tall girl bent and said close to his ear, "What about a cup of syn-cof? You should drink something hot. I'll fix it for you." She added, "Actually it's imitation syn-cof, but I know you know we don't have the genuine product here, except in April."

An authoritative-looking middle-aged man, bony, hard-eyed with an intensity that implied a ceaseless judging of everyone and everything, said, "This is worse than 'real air.' Now we're talking about genuine synthetic coffee. I wonder what a syn-cof plant would look like growing in a field. Yes, that's the crop Whale's Mouth ought to invest in; we'd be rich in a week." To the woman beside him, a white-oak blonde, he said, "After all, Gretch, it's a cold hard fact that every goddamn syn-cof plant or shrub or however the dratted stuff grows back on Terra got—how's it go? Sing it for me, Gretch." He jerked his head toward Rachmael. "Him, too; he's never heard your quaint attempts to blat out authentic Terran folk songs."

The white-oak blonde, in a listless, bored voice, murmured half to herself, half to Rachmael, whom she was now eyeing, " 'The little boy that held the bowl/Was washed away in the flood.' " She continued to contemplate Rachmael, now with an expression which he could not read. "Flood," she repeated, then, her light blue eyes watchful, alert for his reaction. "See anything resembling—"

"Shut up and listen," the curly-haired youth said loudly. "Nobody expects you to grovel, but at least show the proper respect; this man—" He indicated the TV screen, on which Omar Jones, in the fashion long-familiar to Rachmael, boomed cheerily away; the President of Newcolonizedland at this moment was dilating on the rapture of one's first experience at seeing a high-grade rexeroid ingot slide from the backyard atomic furnace, which, for a nominal sum, could be included in the purchase of a home at the colony—and at virtually no money down. The usual pitch, Rachmael thought caustically; Terra and its inhabitants had listened to this, watched this dogged PR tirade in all its many variants, its multiple adaptations to suit every occasion. "This man," the curly-haired youth finished, "is speaking for *us*; it's everyone here in this room up there on that screen, and as President Jones himself said in that press release last week, to deny him is for us to repudiate our own selves." He turned to a large-nosed dour individual hunched over beside him, a mildly ugly unmasculine personage who merely grimaced and continued his state of absorption in Omar Jones' monolog.

The familiar tirade—but to these people here?

And—Freya. Where was she? Here, too . . . wherever *here* was?

Not now, he realized with utter hopelessness. I won't find her now.

Appealing to everyone in the room the curly-haired youth said, "I don't intend to be a weevil for the whole damn balance of my life. That's one thing I can tell you." In abrupt restless anger, a spasm of anger that convulsed his features, he strode toward the large image on the TV screen.

Rachmael said thickly, "Omar Jones. Where is he speaking from?" *This could not be Whale's Mouth.* This speech, these people listening—all of this, everything he saw and heard, ran contrary to reason, was in fact just plain impossible. At least was if Omar Jones consisted of a manufactured fake. And he was; there lay the entire point.

If this were Whale's Mouth, these people had to know that as well as he did. But—possibly the THL soldier, after shooting him with the LSD-tipped dart, had carted him to a Telpor station and dumped him back to the Sol System and Earth, the planetary system out of which he—grasping his time-warping construct cammed as a tin of Yucatán helium-powered bootlegged prophoz—had so recently emerged. And Freya. Back on Earth? Or dead at Whale's Mouth, dead here, if this was actually the colony . . . but it was not. Because this and only this explained the credulous participation by the people in this room in the hypnotic, droning oration of the man on the TV screen. They simply did not know. So he was not on the ninth planet of the Fomalhaut system any longer; no doubt of it at all. The invasion by the two thousand seasoned field reps from Lies, Incorporated had failed; even with UN assistance, with UN control of all Telpor stations, UN troops and advanced weapons—Rachmael closed his eyes wearily as acceptance of the terrible obvious fact ate out of existence any illusion that he might have held that THL could be overturned, that Sepp von Einem could be neutralized. Theodoric Ferry had handled the situation successfully. Faced with the exposure of the Whale's Mouth hoax, Ferry had reacted swiftly and expertly and now it had all been decided; for one single, limited episode the curtain had been lifted, the people of Terra had received via the UN's planet-wide communications media a picture of the actuality underlying the elaborate, complicated myth . . .

Then he was not on Terra either. Because, even though THL had in the sudden great showdown toppled the combined probe constellated out of the resources of its two immense opponents, the citizens of Terra had already been briefed fully, had already been exposed systematically to the entire truth—and nothing, short of planet-wide genocide, could reverse that.

It made no sense. Bewildered, he made his way across the room, to the window; if he could see out, find a landscape familiar or at least some aspect which linked to a comprehensible theory—any comprehensible theory—that would serve to reorient him in space and time . . . he peered out.

Below, streets wide, with trees blossoming in pink-hued splendor; a pattern of arranged public buildings, an aesthetically satisfying syndrome clearly planned by master builders who had had at their disposal a virtually unlimited variety of materials. These streets, these impressive, durable buildings, none of the constructs beyond the window had come into existence haphazardly. And none seemed destined to crumble away.

He could not recall any urban area on Terra so free of harsh functional autofacs; either the industrial combines here were subsurface, or cammed into the overall design somehow, disguised so effectively that they blended even under his own expert scrutiny. And no creditor jet-balloons. Instinctively, he searched for sign of one; flapples cranked back and forth in their eccentric fashion—

this much was familiar. And on the ped-runnels crowds roamed busily, fragmenting at junctions and streaming beyond the range of his vision intent (this, too, was customary; this was eternal and everywhere, a verity of his life on Terra) on their errands. Life and motion: activity of a dedicated, almost obsessive seriousness; the momentum of the city told him that what he saw below had not popped obligingly into existence in response to his scrutiny. Life here had gone on for a long time before him. There was too much of it and far too much kinetic force, to be explained away as a projection of his own psyche; this which he saw was not delusional, an oscillation of the LSD injected into his blood stream by the THL soldier.

Beside him, the white-oak blonde deftly appeared, said softly in his ear, "A cup of hot syn-cof?" She paused. Still numbed, Rachmael failed to answer; he heard her, but his bewilderment stifled even a reflexive response. "It will really make you feel better," the girl continued, after a time. "I know how you feel; I know very well what you're going through because I remember going through the same experience myself when I first found myself here. I thought I had gone out of my mind." She patted him, then, on the arm. "Come on. We'll go into the kitchen."

Trustingly, he found himself accepting her small warm hand; she led him silently through the living room of people intent on the image of Omar Jones enlarged to godlike proportions on the TV screen, and presently he and the girl were seated opposite each other at a small brightly decorated plastic-surfaced table. She smiled at him, encouragingly; still unable to speak he found himself hopefully smiling back, an echo resonating in response to her relaxed friendliness. Her life, the proximity of her dynamism, her body warmth, awoke him minutely but nevertheless critically from his shock-induced apathy. Once again, for the first time since the LSD dart had plunged into him, he felt himself gain vigor; he felt alive.

He discovered, all at once, a cup of syn-cof in his hand; he sipped and as he did so he tried, against the weight of the still-formidable apathy that pervaded him, to frame a remark calculated to convey his thanks. It seemed to require a million years and all the energy available, but the task edified him: whatever had happened to him and wherever in the name of god he was, the havoc of the mind-obliterating hallucinogen had by no means truly left his system. It might well be days, even weeks, before he found himself entirely rid of it; to that he was already stoically resigned.

"Thanks," he managed, finally.

The girl said, "What did you experience?"

Haltingly, with painstaking care, he answered, "I—got an LSD dart in me. Can't tell how long I was under." Thousands of years, he thought. From the days of Rome to present. Evolution through centuries, and each hour a year. But there was no point in communicating that; he would not be telling the girl something new. Undoubtedly, when she had lived on Terra, she had been exposed—like everyone else at one time or another—to at least a residual dose of the chemical lingering in one of the major population centers' water supply: the still-lethal legacy inherited from the war of '92, so taken for granted that it had become a part of nature, not desired but silently endured.

"I asked," the girl repeated, with quiet, almost professional persuasiveness, fixing the focus of his attention on her and what she was asking, "what you experienced. What did you see? Better to tell someone now, before it gets dim; later it's very difficult to recall."

"The garrison state," he said hoarsely. "Barracks. I was there. Not long; they got to me fairly fast. But I did see it."

"Anything else?" The girl did not seem perturbed. But she listened tensely, obviously determined to miss nothing. "What about the soldier who fired the dart at you? Was there anything about him? Anything odd? Weird or unexplainable?"

He hesitated. "Christ," he said, "the hallucinations; you know lysergic acid—you're familiar with what it does. My god—I was inundated by every kind of perception. You want to hear about the Day of Judgment again, in addition to having gone through it yourself? Or the—"

"The soldier," the white-oak-haired girl said patiently.

With a ragged, sharp-pained exhalation, Rachmael said, "Okay. I hallucinated a cyclops, of the cephalopodan variety." For an interval he became silent; the effort of putting his recollection into words exhausted his precariously limited strength. "Is that enough?" he said, then, feeling anger.

"Aquatic?" Her luminous, intelligent eyes bored steadily at him; she did not let him evade her. "Requiring, or evidently requiring—"

"A saline envelope. I could see—" He made himself breathe with regularity, halting his sentence midway. "Signs of dehydration, cracking, of the dermatoid folds. From the effluvium I'd assumed a rapid evaporation of epithelial moisture. Probably indicates a homeostatic breakdown." He looked away, at that point, no longer able to meet her steady, critical gaze; the strain was too much for his vitiated powers, his ability to collect and maintain his attention. Five years old, he said to himself. The abreaction of the drug period; regression to the space-time axis of early childhood, along with the limited range of consciousness, the minute faculties of a preschoolage kid, and this is the topic that has to be dealt with; this is just too much. And it would be, he thought, even if I could pull out and function as an adult again, with an adult's ability to reason. He rubbed his forehead, feeling the ache, the constriction; like a deep, chronic sinusitis which had flared to its most malignant stage. A pain-threshold alteration, he speculated dully. Due to the drug. Routine common discomfort, ordinary somatic promptings, everything enlarged to the point of unbearability, and signifying nothing, nothing at all.

Conscious of his grim, introverted silence, the girl said, "Under LSD before, did you ever experience a physiognomic alteration of this sort? Think back to the initial mandatory episode during your grammar-school days. Can you remember back that far?"

"That was under a control," Rachmael said. "One of those Wes-Dem Board of Education psychologists, those middle-age do-gooding ladies in blue smocks who—what the hell did they use to call themselves?—something like psycheleticians. Or psychedelictrix; I forget which. I guess both groups got to me at one time or another. And then of course under the McLean Mental Health Act I took it again at sixteen and again at twenty-three." But the control, he thought; that made all the difference. Someone there all the time, trained, able to do and say the right thing: able to maintain contact with the stable objective *koinos kosmos* so that I never forgot that what I was seeing emanated from my own psyche, type-basics, or as Jung once called them, archetypes rising out of the unconscious and swamping the personal conscious. Out of the collective, suprapersonal inner space, the great sea of non-individual life.

The sea, he thought. And that physiognomic transformation of the THL soldier; my perception of him became transmuted along those lines. So I did see a type-basic, as in the previous times; not the same one, of course, because each episode under the drug is unique.

"What would you say," the girl said, "if I told you that what you saw was not mysticomimetic at all?"

"What I saw," Rachmael said, "could not have been psycheletic; it wasn't an expansion of consciousness or a rise in the sensitivity of my percept-system."

"Why not?" The girl regarded him keenly. Now two others from the living room, having left the TV set with its booming image of never-failing President Omar Jones, appeared, the thin, severe man with gold-rimmed glasses and an elderly woman with collapsed, corrugated flesh which hung in dismal wattles, with obviously dyed black, lusterless hair and far too ornate bracelets on her flabby wrists. Both seemed aware of the direction of conversation which had come before; they listened silently, almost raptly, and now a third person joined them, a dramatically colored, heavy-lidded woman in evidently her early thirties, wearing a blue-cotton Mexican-style shirt tied at the waist and open to expose effectively shaded smooth bare skin; her richly dyed, extremely tight jeans, plus the unbuttoned top of her blouse beneath the Mexican shirt, caused to be manifest a stunning, supple body—Rachmael found himself fixedly contemplating her, no longer aware of the conversation in progress.

"This is Miss de Rungs," the thin, severe-featured man with the gold-rimmed glasses said, nodding at the impressive, deeply hued woman in the Mexican shirt. "And this is Sheila Quam." He indicated the white-oak-haired girl who had prepared hot syn-cof for Rachmael.

The stout man, still poking at his mouth with his toothpick, appeared at the door of the kitchen, smiled a warped but friendly smile composed of jagged and irregular teeth and said, "I'm Hank Szantho." He held out his hand and Rachmael shook. "We're all weevils," he explained to Rachmael. "Like you. You're a weevil; didn't you know it? What paraworld did you tie into? Not a really bad one; huh?" He eyed Rachmael searchingly, his jaw working, his face coarse with shrewd but in no way malicious interest.

"We're all in the class together," the curly-haired youth said in a bellicose but oddly agitated voice, speaking directly to Rachmael as if challenging him, as if some hidden dispute, beyond Rachmael's perception, somehow had become involved. "We all have the illness; we all have to get well." He physically propelled a slender, short-haired, smartly dressed girl with sharply delineated delicate features; she gazed at Rachmael with a wild, vague anxiety which was almost an appeal—he did not know in regard to what, since the curly-haired youth—whose shoulders and musculature Rachmael noticed for the first time, appeared unusually escalated in use-value—had released her. "Right, Gretch?" the youth demanded.

To Rachmael, in a low but entirely controlled voice, the girl said, "I'm Gretchen Borbman." She held out her hand; reflexively, he shook, and found her skin smooth and lightly cool. "Welcome to our little revolutionary organization, Mr.—" She paused politely.

He gave his name.

"Arab-Israeli?" Gretchen Borbman said. "From the Federation of Semitic Peoples? Or from that drayage firm that used to be so big and now's disappeared . . . Applebaum Enterprise, wasn't it called? Any relation? What ever happened to it and to that lovely new liner, that *Omphalos* . . . wasn't that your flagship?"

It was beyond belief that she did not know; the news media had made a cause célèbre of such magnitude out of the *Omphalos'* flight to the Fomalhaut system that no one could fail to know, at least no one on Terra. But this was not Terra; already, the agreeable, normal milieu of humans in proximity to him, here, had washed into paleness the grotesque apparition of gummy seaweed slime that, caked to the steaming, drying cyclops-face, had stunk so acridly, rinsed in foulness: the degeneration into hydrokinetically maintained organic tissue of what had once been—or convincingly appeared to be—a human being, even if it was a killer-commando mercenary of Trails of Hoffman Limited.

"Yes," he said cautiously, and, deep within the appropriate section of his mentational apparatus, a conduit carried a warning signal; some sensitized mechanism woke and became thoroughly alert. And did not cease its picket-duty; it would remain in go-position until otherwise instructed; his control over it was virtually nil. "That was—still is—the sole valid asset of our firm. With the *Omphalos* we're something; without her we're not." With utmost caution he surveyed the group of people, the weevils, as they called themselves, to see if any appeared aware of the achingly recent abortive flight to Fomalhaut. None of them showed any indication; none of them spoke up or even registered a meaningful facial expression. Their joint lack of response, second by second, plunged him into alarmed, accelerated confusion. And he experienced, weirdly and as frighteningly as each time before, an unannounced oscillation of the drug-state; he felt his time-sense fluctuate radically, and everything, all objects and persons in the room, became changed. The LSD, at least briefly, had returned; this did not surprise him, but it was the wrong time; this, of all possibilities, he could do without at this palpably crucial moment.

"We get damn near no news from Terra," the stout man with the toothpick, Hank Szantho, said to him . . . the voice sounded close by, but the man's shape: it had warped into a lurid color collage, the textures of his flesh and clothes exaggerated, now rapidly becoming grotesque as the light factor doubled and then doubled again until Rachmael looked into a formless blur of heated metal, red so molten and ominous that he moved his chair back, away from the sliding slag-like sheet which had replaced the man; behind it Hank Szantho bobbed, the balloon-head capriciously located, as if by whim, in the vicinity of the collage of torch-shaped fire which had a moment ago been the body and clothing and flesh of the man.

And yet the man's face, diminished in vigor and solidity as it now was, had undergone no physiognomic disfiguration; it remained the balanced countenance of a somewhat crude but amiable, tolerant, heavy-set human.

Astutely, the white-oak-haired girl Sheila Quam said to him, "I see apprehension in your eyes, Mr. ben Applebaum. Is it the hallucinogen?" To the others she said, "I think it's rephasing within his brain-metabolism once more; obviously it hasn't as yet been excreted. Give it time. Drink your cup of syn-cof." Sympathetically, she held it up, between his line of vision and Hank Szantho's nimbus of radiant color; he managed to fix his attention, make out the cup, accept it and sip. "Just wait; it'll go away. It always does, and we're very familiar with the illness, both subjectively in ourselves and objectively in each other. We help each other." She moved her chair closer, to sit beside him; even in his condition he made note of that, and in addition the fact that this superficially slight maneuver effectively placed her between him and the dramatic, dark-complexioned woman, Miss de Rungs, and the willowy, attractive Gretchen Borbman with her springy, near-bobbed chic hair. At this loss he felt sad; a dismal awareness of his powerlessness burgeoned within him, realization that, in the drug-state, he could not fashion in any manner whatsoever a change in the flow of sense-data flowing in on him; the authority of the data, their absoluteness and degree, again reduced him to a passive device which merely registered the stimuli without responding.

Sheila Quam patted, then took gentle hold of his right hand.

"The illness," Gretchen Borbman said, "is called the Telpor Syndrome. Disjunction of the percept-system and substitution of a delusional world. It manifests itself—when it does at all—shortly after teleportation. No one knows why. Only a few get it, a very few. Ourselves, at this present time. We get cured one by one, get released . . . but there always are new ones, such as yourself, showing up. Don't be worried, Mr. ben Applebaum; it is generally reversible. Time, rest, and of course therapy."

"Sorcerer's apprentice therapy," Hank Szantho said, from some vector of space not within Rachmael's range of sight. "S.A.T., they call it. The cephalic 'wash head-benders; they're in and out of here, even Dr. Lupov—the big man from Bergholzlei in Switzerland. God, I hate those fnidgwizers; poking and messing around like we're a bunch of animals."

"'Paraworld,'" Rachmael said, after what seemed to him an almost unendurably protracted interval, due to the drug. "What is that?"

"That's what a weevil sees," the older woman with the dough-like folded face-rolls said in a cross, nagging, fretful voice, as if discussing the subject made her suffer the reoccurrence of some hated osteogenetic twinge. "Some are just dreadful; it's a terrible, terrible crime that they're allowed to get away with it, programming us with that as we're on our way over here. And of course, we are *assured* by those Telpor technicians that nothing, absolutely nothing of this sort could possibly happen." Her voice, shrill and accusing, tormented Rachmael's brain, amplified by the drug; the auditory pain became a fire-sheet, white, brittle, cutting, whirling like a circular saw and he put his hands up to shield his ears.

"For chrissakes," Hank Szantho said angrily, and his voice, also, reverberated hideously, but at a low pitch, like the shifting of the earth below during a major H-head excavation detonation catastrophically close. "Don't blame the Telpor people; blame the fruggin' Mazdasts—it's their fault. Right?" He glowered around at all of them, no longer amiable and easy-going but instead harsh, threatening them with his suspicious, wrathful attention. "Go cut the eyelens out of a Mazdast. If you can find one. If you can get close enough." His gaze, rotating from person to person, fell on Rachmael, stopped; for an interval he contemplated him, with a mixture of scorn, outrage, and—compassion. By degrees his indignation ebbed, then was entirely gone. "It's tough, isn't it, Applebaum? It's no joke. Tell all these people; you saw it, didn't you? I heard you telling Sheila. Yeah." He sighed noisily, the wind escaping from him as if the knot of life which regulated the retention of vital oxygen had all at once unraveled itself out of existence. "Some get a mechanical-construct mysticomimetism; we call that The Clock."

"The Clock," Gretchen Borbman murmured, nodding somberly. "That one really isn't there; I don't believe that ever existed, and anyhow it'd just be like encountering a simulacrum, only hypnagogic in origin. A balanced person ought to recover from that without having to go through the class." She added, obviously to herself, "The goddamn class. The goddamn unending pointless disgusting class; jesus, I hate it." She glared swiftly, furiously, around the room. "Who's the control, today? You, Sheila? I'll bet it's you." Her tone was withering, and, in Rachmael's auditory percept-system, the ferocity of it created for a moment a visual hellscape, mercifully fitful in stability; it hovered, superimposed across the surface of the plastic kitchen table, involving the syn-cof cups, the shaker of sweetex and small simulated silver pitcher of reconstituted organic butter fat in suspension—he witnessed impotently the fusion of the harmless panorama of conventional artifacts into a tabular scene of dwarfed obscenity, of shriveled and deranged indecent entanglement among the various innocent things. And then it passed. And he relaxed, his heart under a load of nausea-like difficulty; what he had, in that fragment of time, been forced to observe appalled his biochemical substructure. Even though the drug still clung to his mind and perverted it, his body remained free—and outraged. Already it had had enough.

"Our control," Hank Szantho said, with sardonic sentimentality, then a wink to Rachmael. "Yes, we have that, too. Let's see, Applebaum; your paraworld, the one the Mazdasts—if they exist—allegedly programmed you for—all this, of course, took place during teleportation while you were demolecularized—is listed codewise by the authorities here as the Aquatic Horror-shape version. Damn rare. Reserved, I suppose, for people who cut up their maternal grandmothers in a former life and fed them to the family cat." He beamed at Rachmael, showing huge gold-capped teeth, which, in the churning froth of excitement induced by the lysergic acid in his brain metabolism, Rachmael experienced as a display of revolting enormity, a disfigurement that made him clutch his cup of syncof and shut his eyes; the gold-capped teeth triggered off spasm after spasm within him, motion sickness to degree that he had never considered possible: it was recognizable but enlarged to the magnitude of a terminal convulsion. He hung onto the table, hunched over, waited for the waves of hyperperistalsis to abate. No one spoke. In the darkness of his unlit private hellscape he writhed and fought, coped as best he could with random somatic abominations, unable even to begin to speculate on the meaning of what had been *said*.

"The stuff hitting you bad?" a girl's voice sounded, gently, close to his ear. Sheila Quam, he knew. He nodded.

Her hand, on the upper part of his neck, rubbing lightly with empathic concern, soothed the demented fluctuations within control of his malfunctioning, panic-dominated autonomic nervous system; he underwent a soothing, infinitely longed-for diminution of muscular contraction; her touch had started the process, the prolonged recovery-period of someone making his way out of the drug-state back to normal somatic-sensation and time. He opened his eyes, gratefully exchanged a silent glance with her. She smiled, and the rubbing, regular contact of her hand increased in sureness; seated close to him, the smell of her hair and skin enveloping him, she steadily increased the vital tactile bridge between them alive; she made it more profound, more convincing. And, gradually, the remoteness of the reality around him shifted in degree; once again the people and objects compressed in the small yellow-lit kitchen became solid. He ceased being afraid even as insight into just how fragmenting this new onrush of the drug-oscillation had been reached the again-functioning higher centers of his brain.

" 'The Aquatic Horror-shape version,' " he said shakily; he took hold of Sheila Quam's obliging hand, stopped its motion—it had done its task—and enfolded it in his own. She did not draw away; the cool, small hand, capable of such restorative powers, such love-inspired healing, was by a frightening irony almost unbelievably fragile. It was vulnerable, he realized, to almost everything; without his immediate protection it seemed totally at the mercy of whatever malign, distorted into ominous and unnatural shape destructive entity that blossomed.

He wondered what, within that category, would manifest itself next. For himself—and the rest of them.

And—had this happened to Freya, too? He hoped to god not. But intuitively he knew that it had. And was still confronting her . . . perhaps even more so than it did him.

TEN

Around him in the room the faces of the people became, as he listened to the emphatic, virtually strident pitch of the discussion, suddenly flat and lurid. Like cartoon colors, he thought, and that struck him wrenchingly, as very sobering and very chilling; he sat stiffly, unwilling to move, because even the slightest body motion augmented the oppressive garishness of the crudely painted only quasi-human faces surrounding him.

The discussion had become a vicious, ear-splitting dispute.

Two opposing explanations of the paraworlds, he realized at last, were competing like live things; the proponents of each were more and more with each passing instant becoming manic and bitter, and abruptly he had a complete understanding of the inordinate, murderous tenacity of each person in the room, in fact all of them . . . now no one, even those who had decided to remain in the living room to admire the jerky, twitching image of President Omar Jones drone out his harangue, had managed to avoid being sucked in.

Their faces, as Rachmael glanced about, stunned him. Terrible in their animation, their mechanical, horrifyingly relentless single-mindedness, the people around him battled with one another in a meaningless, formless muck of words; he listened with dread, felt terror at what he perceived; he cringed—and felt himself cringe—from them, and the desire to hop up and run without destination or the most vague spacial orientation that might help him locate himself, learn where he was, who these envenomed antagonists were—men and women who, a few intervals ago—seconds, days; under the LSD it was impossible to be even remotedly accurate—had lounged idly before the TV set, listening to a man who he knew was synthetic, who did not exist, except in the professional brains of THL's sim-elec designs technicians, probably working out of von Einem's Schweinfort labs.

That had satisfied them. And now—

"It wasn't a programming," the fold-fleshed dyed-haired older woman insisted, blasting the air of the room with the shivering, ear-crushing shrill of her near-hysterical voice. "It was a *lack* of programming."

"She's right," the thin, severe man with gold-rimmed glasses said in a squeaky, emotion-drenched falsetto; he waved, flapped his arms in excitement, trying to make himself heard. "We were all supposed to be falsely programmed so we'd see a paradise, as they promised. But somehow it didn't take with us, the few of us here in the room; we're the exceptions, and now those bastard 'wash psychiatrists come in and do the job right."

In vitriolic weariness Miss de Rungs said, to no one in particular, "The hell with it. Leave it up to our control; let the control worry." She leaned toward Rachmael, unlit cigarillo between her dark lips. "A match, Mr. ben Applebaum?"

"Who's our control?" he asked as he got out a folder of matches.

Miss de Rungs, with contempt and rasping animosity, jerked her head at Sheila Quam. "Her. This week. And she likes it. Don't you, Sheila? You just love to make everybody jump. Squirm, squirm, when you come into the room." She continued to eye Sheila Quam with hateful vindictiveness, then turned away, sinking into a voiceless interior brooding, cut off from everyone and all verbal interaction in the room with deliberate and hostile aversion; her dark eyes filmed with loathing.

"What I saw," Rachmael said to Sheila Quam. "Under the LSD—that cephalopod. That you called—Hank Szantho called—the Aquatic Horror-shape. Was that psychedelic? Under the condition of expanded consciousness did I pick up an actual essence and penetrate a hypnoidal screening-field of some kind? And if that—"

"Oh yes; it was real," Sheila Quam said levelly; her tone was as matter-of-fact as if this was a technical, professional discussion, something of academic interest only. "The cephalops of that sort seem to be, or anyhow it's conjectured by anthropologists in the area to be—anyhow it's the most reasonable working hypothesis, which they'll probably have to go on whether they like it or not—is that the cephalopodan life-form experienced as what we refer to as Paraworld Blue, its dominant species, is the indigenous race that dwelt here before THL showed up with—" She paused, now no longer composed; her face was hardened and when she again spoke her voice was brisk and sharp. "Good big a-thought-for-this week advance weapons. Old papa von Einem's clever monstrosities. The output of Krupp and Söhne and N.E.D. filth like that." She abruptly smashed into a repellent chaos the remains of her cigarillo. "During the Telpor transfer to Whale's Mouth you were fed the routine mandatory crap, but as with the rest of us weevils it failed to take. So as soon as the LSD dart got you you started intuiting within your new environment, the illusory outer husk rigged up became transparent and you saw within, and of course when you got a good clear dose of that—"

"What about the other paraworlds?" he said.

"Well? What about them? They're real, too. Just as real. The Clock; that's a common one. Paraworld Silver; that comes up again and again." She added, "I've been here a long time; I've seen that one again and again . . . I guess it's not so hard to take as Paraworld Blue. Yours is the worst. Everybody seems to agree with that. Whether they've seen it or not. When you've gone through Computer Day and fed your experience into the fniggling thing's banks so that everybody in the class can—"

Rachmael said carefully, "Why different psychedelic worlds? Why not the same one, again and again?"

Sheila Quam raised a thin, expertly drawn eyebrow. "For everyone? The whole class, as long as it exists?"

"Yes."

After a pause she said, "I don't really know. I've wondered a whole lot of times. So have plenty of other people who know about it. The 'wash psychiatrists, for instance. Dr. Lupov himself; I heard a lecture he gave on the subject. He's as no-darn-place as anybody else, and that's what—"

"Why did Miss de Rungs say everyone squirms when you come into the room?" He waited for her answer; he did not let her off the hook.

Smoking a newly lit cigarillo placidly, Sheila Quam said, "A control, whoever he is—it varies from one month to the next; we take turns—has the power to order the euth-x of someone he thinks a menace to Newcolonizedland. There's no board of appeal, any more; that didn't work. It's a very simple form, now; I fill it out, get the person's signature, and that's it. Is that cruel?" She eyed him searchingly; evidently the query was sincere. "Next month, in fact sixteen days from now, it'll be someone else's turn and I'll be squirming."

Rachmael said, "What's the purpose of the killing? Why has the control been given such power? Such drastic authority to arbitrarily—"

"There are eleven paraworlds." Sheila said. She had lowered her voice; in the crowded kitchen the infuriated, hip-and-thigh argument had terminated by dwindling swiftly away and everyone was mutely listening to Sheila Quam. Even the de Rungs girl was listening. And her expression of malice had one; only a stricken, anticipatory dread showed. The same expression that pervaded the features of each person in the room. "Twelve," Sheila continued; the presence of the stony, voiceless audience did not seem either to nonplus her nor to goad her; she continued in the same detached, reasonable fashion. "If you count this." She gestured, taking in the kitchen and its people and then she tossed her head, indicating the booming TV set in the living room with the we-bring-you-live-on-tape voice of President of Newcolonizedland, Omar Jones. "I do," she said. "In some ways it's the most bug-built of all of them."

"But the legal, sanctioned murders," Rachmael said, staring at the girl with her glorious white-shiny hair, her immense guileless blue eyes, and, beneath her turtle-neck sweater, her small, articulated breasts. It did not seem congruent with her, this capacity, this office; it was impossible to imagine her signing death decrees. "What's the basis? Or is there a basis?" He heard his voice rise and become almost a snarl. "I guess there doesn't have to be, not if everyone is locked in." Without consultation with anyone in the class he had come to that self-evident conclusion; the huddled, resigned air about all of them showed that. He felt it in himself already, and it was a noxious, almost physically poisonous sensation, to find himself drawn gradually into this demoralized milieu. Waiting for the control to act, and for whatever reason served. "You consider these people enemies of *that* state?" He gestured convulsively toward the yammering TV set in the living room, then turned, set down his syn-cof cup with a sharp clatter; across from him Sheila Quam jumped, blinked—he seized her by the shoulders and half-lifted her to her feet. Wide-eyed, startled, she returned his gaze fixedly, peering into him, penetrating him back as he focussed with compassionless, ruthless harshness; she was not afraid, but his grip hurt her; she set her jaw in an effort to keep still, but he saw, in her eyes, the wince of physical suffering. Suffering and surprise; she had not expected this, and he could guess why: this was not what one did to the pro tem control. Pragmatically it was suicidal if not insane.

Sheila, gratingly, said, "All right; possibly someday we'll have to admit—classify—Omar Jones and the colony we've built up here as just one more paraworld. I admit it. But until then this remains the reference point. Are you satisfied? And until then any alternate distorted subreality perceived by anyone arriving is judged prima facie evidence that he's in need of a 'wash. And if psychiatric help doesn't bring him around to the point that you're at now, sharing *this* reality instead of—"

Hank Szantho said brusquely, "Tell him what the paraworlds are."

The room, then, was silent.

"Good question," the middle-aged, bony, hard-eyed man said presently.

To Rachmael, Szantho said, "It's von Einem's doing."

"You don't know that," Sheila said quietly.

"He's got some razzle-dazzle gadget he's been playing around with at the Schweinfort labs," Szantho continued. "Undoubtedly stolen from the UN, from where it tests its new top-secret weapons. Okay, I don't *know* that, not like I saw it in action or a schematic or something. But I know that's what's behind all this damn paraworld stuff; the UN invented that time-warping device recently and then Gregory Floch—"

"Ploch," Miss de Rungs corrected.

"Gloch," Sheila said bitingly. "Gregory Arnold Gloch. Anyhow, Gloch, Floch, Ploch; what does it matter?" To Rachmael she said, "That freak who switched sides. Possibly you remember, although all the news media because of really incredible UN pressure more or less squelched it, right down the line."

"Yes," he said, remembering. "Five or six years ago." Greg Gloch, the peculiar UN progeny prodigy, at that time beyond doubt the sole genuinely promising new wep-x designer at the Advance-weapons Archives, had, obviously for financial reasons, defected to a private industrial concern which could pay considerably better: Trails of Hoffman. And from there had beyond question passed directly to Schweinfort and its mammoth research facilities.

"From that time-warpage wingding," Hank Szantho continued, appealing to each of them with jerky, rapid gesticulations. "What else *could* it be? I guess nobody can say because there isn't nothing; it has to be that." He tapped his forehead, nodding profoundly.

"Nonsense," Miss de Rungs retorted. "A variety of alternate explanations come to mind. Its resemblance to the UN's time-warpage device may be merely—"

"To be fair about this," the middle-aged, hard-eyed man said in a quiet but effective monotone, "we must acquaint this newcomer with each of the major logical alternatives to Mr. Szantho's stoutly defended but only theoretically possible explanation. Most plausible of course—Szantho's theory. Second—in my opinion, at least—the UN itself, since they are the primary utilizers of the device . . . and it is, as Mr. Szantho pointed out, their invention, merely pirated by Gloch and von Einem. Assuming it was obtained by von Einem at all, and proof of this either way is unfortunately not available to us. Third—"

"From here on," Sheila said to Rachmael, "the plausibility

swiftly diminishes. He will not recount the stale possibility that the Mazdasts are responsible, a frightening boogyman we've had to live with but which no one seriously believes, despite what's said again and again. This particular possible explanation properly belongs in the category of the very neurotic, if not psychotic."

"And in addition," Miss de Rungs said, "it may be Ferry alone, with no help from anyone; from von Einem or Gloch. It may be that von Einem is absolutely unaware of paraworlds per se. But no theory can hold water if it assumes that Ferry is ignorant."

"According to you," Hank Szantho muttered.

"Well," Sheila said, "we *are* here, Hank. This pathetic colony of weevils. Theo Ferry put us here and you know it. THL is the underlying principle governing the dynamics of this world, whatever category this world falls into: pseudo-para or real or full para." She smiled grimacingly at Hank Szantho, who returned her brilliant, cold glare dully.

"But if the paraworlds are derived via the UN's time-warpage gadget," the hard-faced middle-aged man said, "then they would constitute a spectrum of equally real alternative presents, all of which split off at some disputed episode in the past, some antediluvian but critical juncture which someone—whoever it is—tinkered with through the damn gadget we're discussing. And so in no sense are they merely 'para.' Let's face that honestly; if the time-warpage gadget is involved then we might as well end all speculation as to which world is real and which are not, because the term becomes meaningless."

"Meaningless theoretically," Miss de Rungs answered, "but not to anyone here in this room. Or in fact anyone in the world." She corrected herself, "Anyone in *this* world. We have a massive stake in seeing to it that the other worlds, para nor not, stay as they are, since all are so very much worse than this one."

"I'm not even certain about that," the middle-aged man said, half to himself. "Do we know them that thoroughly? We're so traumatized about them. Maybe there's one that's better, to be preferred."

He gestured in the direction of the living room with its logorrheic flow of TV noise, the pompous, unending, empty spouting-forth of jejune trash by the nonreal president of what Rachmael—as well as everyone else on Terra—knew to be a nonreal, deliberately contrived and touted hoax-colony.

"But this world can't be para," Gretchen Borbman said, "because we all share it, and that's still our sole criterion, the one point we can hang onto." To Rachmael she said, "That's so important. Because what no one has laid on you yet, mercifully, is the fact that if two of us ever agree at the same time—" She lapsed into abrupt silence, then. And regarded Sheila with a mixture of aversion and fear. "Then out come the proper forms," she went on, at last, with labored difficulty. "Form 47-B in particular."

"Good old 47-B," the curly-haired youth said gratingly, and instantly grimaced, his face contorted. "Yes, we just love it when that's trotted out, when they run their routine check of us."

"The control," Gretchen continued, "signs 47-B after he or she—she, right now—feeds someone's paraworld gestalt in on Computer Day, which is generally late Wednesday. So after that it becomes public property; it isn't simply a subjective delusional realm or a subjective anything; it's like an exhibit of antique potsherds under glass in a museum; the entire damn public can file past and inspect it, right down to the last detail. So there would hardly be any doubt if ever two individual paraworlds agreed simultaneously."

"That's what we dread," the fold-fleshed older woman with lifeless dyed hair said in a toneless, mechanical voice, to no one in particular.

"That's the one thing," Gretchen said, "that really does scare us, Mr. ben Applebaum; it really does." She smiled, emptily, the expression of acute, unvarying apprehension calcified into sterile hopelessness over all her features, a mask of utter despair closing up into immobility her petite, clear-hewn face—clear-hewn, and frozen with the specter of total defeat, as if what she and the rest of them dreaded had crept recently close by, far too close; it was no longer theoretical.

"I don't see why a bi-personal view of the same paraworld would—" Rachmael began, then hesitated, appraising Sheila. He could not, however, for the life of him fathom her contrived, cool poise; he made out nothing at all and at last gave up. "Why is this regarded as so—injurious?"

"Injurious," Hank Szantho said, "not to us; hell no—not to us weevils. On the contrary; we'd be better able to communicate among each other. But who gives a grufg about that . . . yeah, who cares about a little minuscule paltry matter like that—a validation that might keep us sane."

Sheila said, remotely, " 'Sane.' "

"Yes, sane," Hank Szantho snarled at her.

"Folie à deux," Sheila said mildly. To Rachmael she said, "No, not injurious to us, of course. To them." She once more indicated the empty living room—empty except for the din of Omar Jones' recorded unending monolog. "But you see," she explained to Rachmael, raising her head and confronting him tranquilly, "it wouldn't just be real; that is, real in the experiential sense, the way all LSD and similar psycheletic drug-experiences are . . . they're real, but if one of the experiences is common to more than a single individual the implications are quite great; being able to talk about it and be completely understood is—" She gestured faintly, as if her meaning at this point was obvious, scarcely worth articulating.

"It would be coming true," Miss de Rungs said in a stifled, unsteady voice. "Replacing *this.*" She ejected the end word violently, then swiftly once again sank into her withdrawn brooding.

The room, now, was tomb-like still.

"I wonder which one," Hank Szantho said, half-idly, to himself but audibly. "The Blue, ben Applebaum? Yours? Or Paraworld Green, or White, or god knows which. Blue," he added, "is about the worst. Yeah, no doubt of that; it's been established for some time. Blue is the pit."

No one spoke. They all, wordlessly, looked toward Rachmael. Waiting.

Rachmael said, "Has any of the rest of you—"

"None of us, obviously," Miss de Rungs said, with rigid, clipped firmness, "has undergone Paraworld Blue. But before us—several, I believe, and fairly recently. Or so the 'wash psychiatrists say, anyhow, if you can believe them."

"But not all of us," Gretchen Borbman said, "have been before the computer, yet. I haven't, for instance. It takes time; the entire memory area of the cerebral cortex has to be tapped cell by cell, and most of the retention in stored form of the experience is subliminal. Repressed from consciousness, especially in the case of—less favorable paraworlds. In fact the episode in its entirety can be split off from the self-system within minutes after the person regains contact with reality, in which case he has absolutely no knowledge—available, conscious knowledge, that is—of what happened to him."

"And a pseudo-memory," Hank Szantho added, rubbing his massive jaw and scowling. "Substituted automatically. Also a function beyond conscious control. Paraworld Blue . . . who in his right mind, who wants to *keep* his frugging right mind, *would* recall it?"

Gretchen Borbman, impassive, drained and pale, went to pour herself a fresh cup of the still-warm syn-cof; the cup clattered as she maneuvered it clumsily. With iron-rigid fixity all of them maintained a state of contrived obliviousness toward her, pretended not to hear the tremor of her nervous hands as she carried her cup step by step back to the table, and, with painstaking caution, seated herself beside Rachmael. None of the other weevils showed any sign whatever of perceiving her existence in their midst, now; they fixedly kept their eyes averted from her halting movement across the small, densely occupied kitchen, as if she—and Rachmael—did not exist. And the emotion, he realized, was stricken terror. And not the same amorphous uneasiness of before; this was new, far more acute, and beyond dispute directed absolutely at her.

Because of what she had said? Obviously that; the ice-hard suspension of the normal sense of well-being had set in the moment Gretchen Borbman had said what seemed to him, on the surface, to be routine: that she, among others in this group, had not presented the contents of their minds, their delusional—or expanded-consciousness-derived—paraworld involvement. The fear had been there, but it had not focussed on Gretchen until she had admitted openly, called attention to the fact, that she in particular viewed a paraworld which might conform thoroughly to that of someone else in the group. And therefore would, as Miss de Rungs had said, would then be coming true; coming true and replacing the environment in which they now lived . . . an environment which enormously powerful agencies intended for extremely vital reasons to maintain.

—Agencies, Rachmael thought caustically, which I've already come up against head-on. Trails of Hoffman Limited, with Sepp von Einem and his Telpor device, and his Schweinfort labs. I wonder, he thought, what has come out of those labs lately. What has Gregory Gloch, the renegade UN wep-x sensation, thrashed together for his employers' use? *And is it already available to them?* If it was, they had no need for it as yet; their mainstays, their conventional constructs, seemed to serve adequately; the necessity for some bizarre, quasi-genius, quasi-psychotic, if that fairly delineated Gloch, did not appear to be yet at hand . . . but, he realized somberly, it had to be presumed that Gloch's contribution had long ago evolved to the stage of tactical utility: when needed, it would be available.

"It would seem to me," Gretchen Borbman said to him, evidently more calm, now, more composed, "that this rather dubious 'reality' which we as a body share—I'm speaking in particular, of course, of that obnoxious Omar Jones creature, that caricature of a political leader—has damn little to recommend it. Do you feel loyalty to it, Mr. ben Applebaum?" She surveyed him critically, her eyes wise and searching. "If it did yield to a different framework—" Now she was speaking to all of them, the entire class crowded into the kitchen. "Would that be so bad? The paraworld you saw, Paraworld Blue. Was that so much worse, really?"

"Yes," Rachmael said. It was unnecessary to comment further, certainly no one else in the tense, overpacked room needed to be convinced—the expressions on their strained faces ratified his recognition. And he saw, now, why their unified apprehension and animosity toward Gretchen Borbman signified an overwhelming, ominous approaching entity: her exposure before the all-absorbing scanner of the computer in no sense represented one more repetition of the mind-analysis which had taken place routinely with the others in the past. *Gretchen already knew the contents of her paraworld.* Her reaction had come long ago, and in her manner now consisted, for the others in the group, a clear index of what that paraworld represented, which of the designated categories it fell into. Obviously, it was a decidedly familiar one—to her and to the group as a whole.

"Perhaps," the curly-haired youth said acidly, "Gretch might be less entranced with Paraworld Blue if she had undergone a period stuck in it, like you did, Mr. ben Applebaum; what do you say to that?" He watched Rachmael closely, scrutinizing him in anticipation of his response; he obviously expected to see it, rather than hear it uttered. "Or could she have already done that, Mr. ben Applebaum? Do you think you could tell if she had? By that I mean, would there be any indication, a permanent—" He searched for the words he wanted, his face working.

"Alteration," Hank Szantho said.

Gretchen Borbman said, "I'm quite satisfactorily anchored in reality, Szantho; take my word for it. Are you? Every person in this room is just as involved in an involuntary subjective psychotic fantasy-superimposition over the normal frame of reference as I am; some of you possibly even more so. I don't know. Who knows what takes place in other people's minds? I frankly don't care to judge; I don't think I can." She deliberately and with superbly controlled unflinching dispassion returned the remorseless animosity of the ring of persons around her. "Maybe," she said, "you ought to re-examine the structure of the 'reality' you think's in jeopardy. Yes, the TV set." Her voice, now, was harsh, overwhelming in its caustic vigor. "Go in there, look at it; look at that dreadful parody of a president—is that what you prefer to—"

"At least," Hank Szantho said, "it's real."

Eyeing him, Gretchen said, "Is it?" Sardonically, she smiled; it was a totally inhumane smile, and it was directed to all of them; he saw it sweep the room, withering into dryness the accusing circle of her group-members—he saw them palpably retreat. It did not include him, however; conspicuously, Gretchen exempted him, and he felt the potency, the meaning of her decision to leave him out: he was not like the others and she knew it and so did he, and it meant something, a great deal. And he thought, I know what it means. She does, too.

Just the two of us, he thought; Gretchen Borbman and I—and for a good reason. *Alteration,* he thought. Hank Szantho is right.

Tilting Gretchen Borbman's fat face he contemplated her eyes, the expression in them; he studied her for an unmeasured time, during which she did not stir: she returned, silently, without blinking, his steady, probing, analytical penetration of her interior universe . . . neither of them stirred, and it began to appear to him, gradually, as if a melting, opening entrance had replaced the unyielding and opaque coloration of her pupils; all at once the variegated luminous matrices within which her substance seemed to lodge expanded to receive him—dizzy, he half-fell, caught himself, then blinked and righted himself; no words had passed between them, and yet he understood, now; he had been right. It was true.

He rose, walked unsteadily away; he found himself entering the living room with its untended blaring TV set—the thing dominated the room with its howls and shrieks, warping the window drapes, walls and carpets, the once-attractive ceramic lamps . . . he sensed and witnessed the deformity imposed by the crushing din of the TV set with its compulsively hypomanic dwarfed and stunted figure, now gesticulating in a speeded-up frenzy, as if the video technicians had allowed—or induced—the tape to seek its maximum velocity.

At sight of him the image, the Omar Jones thing, stopped. Warily, as if surprised, it regarded him—at least seemed to; impossibly, the TV replica of the colony president fixed its attention as rigidly on him as he in return found himself doing. Both of them, caught in an instinctive, fully alert vigil, neither able to look away even for a fraction of an instant . . . as if, Rachmael thought, our lives, the physical preservation of both of us, has cataclysmically and without warning become jeopardized.

And neither of us, he realized as he stared unwinkingly at the TV image of Omar Jones, can escape; we're both snared. Until or unless one of us can—*can do what?*

Blurred, now, as he felt himself sink into numbed fatigue, the two remorseless eyes of the TV figure began to blend. The eyes shifted, came together, superimposed until all at once, locked, they became a clearly defined single eye the intensity of which appalled him; a wet, smoldering greatness that attracted light from every source, drew illumination and authority from every direction and dimension, confronted him, and any possibility of looking away now was gone.

From behind him, Gretchen Borbman's voice sounded. "You see, don't you? Some of the paraworlds are—" She hesitated, perhaps wanting to tell him in such a manner as to spare him; she wanted him to know, but with the least pain possible. "—hard to detect at first," she finished, gently. Her hand, soothing, comforting, rested on his shoulder; she was drawing him away from the image on the TV screen, the oozing cyclopean entity that had ceased its speeded-up harangue and, in silence, emanated in his direction its diseased malevolence.

"This one," Rachmael managed to say hoarsely, "has a description, too? A code-identification?"

"This," Gretchen said, "is reality."

"Paraworld Blue—"

Turning him around by physical force to face her, Gretchen said, stricken, "'Paraworld Blue'"? Is that what you see? On the TV *screen?* I don't believe it—the aquatic cephalopod with one working eye? No; I just don't believe it."

Incredulous, Rachmael said, "I . . . thought you saw it. Too."

"No!" She shook her head violently; her face now hardened, masklike; the change in her features came to him initially, in the first particle of a second, as a mere idea—and then the actual jagged carving of old, shredding wood replaced the traditional, expected flesh, wood burned, carbonized as if seared both to injure it and to create fright in him, the beholder; an exaggerated travesty of organic physiognomy that grimaced in a fluidity, a mercury-like flux so that the irreal emotions revealed within the mask altered without cease, sometimes, as he watched, several manifesting themselves at once and merging into a configuration of affect which could not exist in any human—nor could it be read.

Her actual—or rather her normally perceived—features, by a slow process, gradually re-emerged. The mask sank down, hidden, behind. It remained, of course, still there, but at least no longer directly confronting him. He was glad of that; relief passed through him, but then it, too, like the sight of the scorched-wood mask, sank out of range and he could no longer recall it.

"Whatever gave you the idea," Gretchen was saying, "that I saw anything like *that?* No, not in the slightest." Her hand, withdrawn from his shoulder, convulsed; she moved away from him, as if retreating down a narrowing tube, farther and fatally, syphoned off from his presence like a drained insect, back toward the kitchen and the dense pack of others.

"Type-basics," he said to her, appealing to her, trying to catch onto her and hold her. But she continued to shrink away anyhow. "Isn't it still possible that only a projection from the unconscious—"

"But your projection," Gretchen said, in a voice raptor-like, sawing, "is unacceptable. To me and to everybody else."

"What do you see?" he asked, finally. There was almost no sight of her now.

Gretchen said, "I'm scarcely likely to tell you, Mr. ben Applebaum; you can't actually expect that, now, after what you've said."

There was silence. And then, by labored, unnaturally retarded degrees, a groaning noise came from the speaker of the television set; the noise at last became intelligible speech, at the proper pitch and rate: his categories of perception had again achieved a functioning parallel with the space-time axis of the image of Omar Jones. Or had the progression of the image resumed as before? Time had stopped or the image had stopped, or perhaps both . . . or was there such a thing as time at all? He tried to remember, but found himself unable to; the falling off of his capacity for abstract thought—was—what—was—

He did not know.

Something looked at him. With its mouth.

It had eaten most of its own eyes.

ELEVEN

People who are out of phase in time, Sepp von Einem thought caustically to himself, ought to be dead. Not preserved like bugs in amber. He glanced up from the encoded intel-repo and watched with distaste his mysteriously—and rather repellently—gifted proleptic co-worker, Gregory Gloch, in his clanking, whirring anti-prolepsis chamber; at the moment, the thin, tall, improperly hunched youth talked silently into the audio receptor of his sealed chamber, his mouth twisting as if composed of some obsolete plastic, not convincingly flesh-like. The mouth-motions, too, lacked authenticity; far too slow, von Einem observed, even for Gloch. The fool was slowing down. However, the memory spools of the chamber would still collect everything said by Gloch, at whatever rate. And the transmission subsequently would of course be at proper time . . . although, of course, the frequency would be abysmal, probably doubled. At the thought of the screeching which lay ahead, von Einem groaned.

His groan, received by the sensitive input audio system of the anti-prolepsis chamber, became processed: recorded at twenty inches of iron oxide audio tape a second it whipped in retrograde to rewind, then released itself at six inches a second to be carried to the earphones well fixed to Gloch's bony head. Presently Gloch responded to his reception of his superior's groan with characteristic eccentricity. His cheeks puffed out; his face turned red as he held his breath. And at the same time he grinned vacuously, his head lolling, turning himself into a parody of a brain-damaged defective—a double parody, because it was of course his own fantastic mentational processes which constituted the actual target of his lampoon. Disgusted, von Einem looked away, gritted his near-priceless custom-fashioned teeth, returned to his scrutiny of the intel-repo material which had newly been made available to him.

"I'm Bill Behren," the tinny mechanical voice of the intel-repo transport announced cheerfully. "Operator of fly 33408. Now, as you may or may not remember fly 33408 is a real winner. I mean it really gets in there and tackles its job and really gathers up the stuff, the real hot stuff. I've personally been operator for, say, fifty flies . . . but in all this time, none has really performed true-blue like this little fella. I think he—or it, whatever they are these days—deserves a vote of thanks from us all involved in this highly delicate work we do. Right, Herr von Einem?" Operator of housefly 33408 Bill Behren paused hopefully.

"The vote of thanks," von Einem said, "goes to you, Mr. Behren, for your compound eyes."

"How about that," operator Behren rambled on oozingly. "Well, I think we're all inspired by—"

"The data," von Einem said. "As to the activity at the UN Advance-weapons Archives. What specifically is meant by their code number *variation three* of that time-warping construct they're so devoted to?" Queer for, he thought to himself; the UN wep-x personnel probably take turns going to bed with it.

"Well, sir," operator Bill Behren of fly 33408 answered vigorously, "variation three appears to be a handy-dandy little portable pack unit in the ingenious shape of a tin of chocolate-flavored psychic energizers."

On the video portion of the intel-repo playback system a wide-angle shot of the portable pack appeared; von Einem glanced toward Gloch in his whirring anti-prolepsis chamber to see if the hunched, grimacing youth was receiving this transmission. Gloch, however, obviously lagged at least fifteen minutes behind, now; it would be some time before his synchronizing gear brought this video image to him. And no way to speed it up; that would defeat the chamber's purpose.

"Did I say 'chocolate-flavored'?" Behren droned on, in agitation. "I intended to say 'chocolate-*covered*.'"

And with such weapons artifacts as this, von Einem reflected, the UN expects to survive. Of course, this assumed that the intel-repo were accurate.

His inquiry into the certainty of fly 33408's information brought an immediate reaction from operator Behren.

"There are just plain virtually no houseflies as intelligent as this; I give you no niddy, Herr von Einem, no niddy at all. And here's the real substance of what 33408 has captured via his multipartis receptors: I suggest you prepare for this, as it's overwhelming." Behren cleared his throat importantly. "Ever hear of ol' Charley Falks?"

"No," von Einem said.

"Think back to your childhood. When you were, say, eight years old or maybe a little more. Recall a backyard and you playing, and ol' Charley Falks leaning over the fence and—"

"This is what your *verfluchte* fly brought back from the UN Advance-weapons Archives?" Time for a replacement of both Behren and his dipterous insect, both of them with one arboreal, American orthopterous katydid; it could carry twice the minned receptors and recording spools of 33408 and probably would possess the same brain-convolutions as Behren and his housefly put together. Von Einem felt gloomy; in fact his depression bordered on despair. At least Theo Ferry managed to handle the tricky situation at Whale's Mouth effectively—in contrast to this. And that, more than anything else, counted.

Effectively except for the unhappy weevils and their destroyed, ridiculous crypto-perceptions. The old comrades back in 1945 would have known how to dispatch those *Unmänner,* von Einem thought to himself with irritable satisfaction. It's a clear sign of genetic decay to be possessed by such subrealities, he brooded. Inferior type-basics overwhelming weak, unstable character-structures; degenerate idioplasm involved casually, beyond doubt.

"Ol' Charley Falks," operator Behren said, "is the individual back in your childhood days who more than any other human being formed your ontological nature. What you have been throughout your adult life depends absolutely, in total essence, on what ol' Charley—

"Then," von Einem said witheringly, "why is it that I fail to recall his existence?"

"The UN wep-x tacticians," operator Behren said, "have not as yet placed him there."

Within his anti-prolepsis membrane—the environment manufactured by Krupp und Söhne years ago which permitted him to collaborate with the conventionally time-oriented personalities linked indirectly to him—the warped, inspired protégé of Sepp von Einem contemplated the message-packets discharged at intervals by the data-storing houses of his intricate mechanism. As always, he felt weary; the release of stimuli came too frequently for his overtaxed metabolism . . . the adjusting of periodic discharge control gate lay unfortunately outside his manual reach.

What reached him, at the moment, consisted of what seemed the most miserable idiocy he had ever encountered; bewildered, he attempted to focus his depleted attention on it, but only ill-formed fragments of the intel-repo material constellated for his mentational scrutiny.

"... fettered fetus of homemade apples lurching ... searching ... something like pataradical outfits of lace. Iron beds of red hot sabratondea flashes just jib FRIB—"

Resignedly, Gregory Gloch listened on helplessly, wondering what transistorized turret-control of the chamber had gone astray this time.

"... medicine ice

"man.

"cone-shaped melting dripping

"away—away—"

As apathy began to seep over him an interval of almost startling meaning abruptly caught his ear; he awoke, paid rapt attention.

"Operator Behren, here, with really thrilling data on ol' Charley Falks, who, you'll remember, was placed in the formative years of Herr von Einem on an alternate time-path by the UN wep-x tacticians in order to deflect Herr von Einem from his chosen—and militarily significant—profession to a relatively harmless vocation, that of—" And then, to his chagrin, the lucid segment of verbal data faded and the meaningless chatter—with which he had, over the years, become so familiar—resumed.

"... fiber-glassed. Windows

"stained with grease

"Off a polyhemispheric double-overhead-cam
        "EXTERNAL compulsion engine
    "floating out
"into the vast gigantic money-thing-making machine
    ". . . diaperashis phenomenon disintegrating
"into foul fierce
"pressure
    "spinning spinning
"lifting harsh
        "harsh—a breath, a beat—a being still present
"—thank god . . ."

And, in the midst of this, the steady but interrupted by the far stronger signal-strength of the babble, the authentic intel-repo continued to make its vital point; he brought his internal attention to bear on it and managed to follow its thread of meaning.

Evidently fly-technician Behren had gathered at last the crucial material as to the UN's disposition of its near-absolute device. With vigorous, virtually relentless logic, Jaimé Weiss, the top-strategist now working under Horst Bertold—he who at one time had been von Einem's most brilliant and promising new discovery in the field of weapons inventiveness, but who had turned: gone over to the better-paying other side—this renegade had come up with the correct answer to the UN's strategic needs.

To kill off Sepp von Einem was now pointless; Telpor existed. But to abolish von Einem sometime in the past, before his discovery of the basic mechanism of teleportation . . .

A less skilled manipulation of past-time factors would have sought as its objective cheap outright murder—the total physical elimination of Sepp von Einem. But this, of course, would simply have left the field open to others, and if one man could locate the principle on which teleportation could be effectively based, then so, eventually, given enough time, could someone else. Telpor, not Sepp von Einem, had to be blocked—and it would require the presence of a uniquely strong personality to block it. Jaimé Weiss and Bertold could not do it; they were not that formidable. In fact, probably only one man in the world could manage it . . . successfully.

Sepp von Einem himself.

To himself Gregory Gloch thought, It's a good idea. This, his professional, official appraisal of the tactical plan which the UN had put in motion to abort the evolution of the Telpor instrument, had now to be said aloud; Gloch, selecting his words carefully, spoke into the recording microphone permanently placed before his lips, simultaneously activating the tape-transport.

"They want for their disposal," he declared, "the use of yourself, Herr von Einem—nothing else is adequate. A compliment . . . but one which you could no doubt do without." He paused, considered. Meanwhile, the tape-reel moved inexorably, but it was dead tape; he felt the pressure on him to produce a counter-tactic in response to what those opposed to his superior had so artfully—and skillfully—advanced. "Umm," he murmured, half to himself. He felt, now, even more truly out of phase in the time-dimension: he felt the gulf between himself and those, everyone else in the universe of sentient life, beyond his anti-prolepsis chamber. "In my estimate," he continued, "Your most profitable avenue of action—" And then abruptly he ceased. Because once again the random word-salad noise had burbled into seeming spontaneous existence in his ears.

This, however, appeared to be a radically different—startling so—interference than was customary.

Rubbish that it was it nonetheless made sense . . . sense, but it had obliterated—for the time being, at least—his counter-tactical idea.

Could this be a UN electronic signal deliberately beamed so as to disrupt the orderly functioning of his chamber?

The thought, theoretical as it was, chilled him as he involuntarily, without the possibility of evasion, listened to the curious mixture of nonsense and—meaning. Of the highest order.

". . . I think, though, I see why Zoobko lards, butters, marginates and otherwise fattens up the word 'spore' into the rather sinister *male* spore slogan. Their house brochure in Move-E 3-D kul-R is directed (heh-heh) at women consumers, to fumble lewdly a metaphor, ahem, no offense meant (gak). More fully articulated, it would read, 'The male spore, my dears, is as we well know tireless in its half-crazed struggle—against all sanity and moral restraint— to reach the female egg. That's the way men are. Right? We all realize it. Give a male (sic) spore half an inch and he'll take seventy-two-and-a-sixth miles. BE PREPARED! ALWAYS READY! A HUGE, SLIMY, SLANT-EYED YELLOW-SKINNED MALE SPORE MAY BE WATCHING YOU THIS VERY MINUTE! And, considering his almost demonic ability to wiggle for miles upon miles, you may at this moment be in dire, severe danger! To quote Dryden: 'The trumpet's loud clamor doth call us to arms,' etc. (And don't forget, ladies, the handsome prize awarded yearly by Zoobko Products, Incorporated for the greatest number of dead male (sic) spores mailed (pun) to our Callisto factory in an old Irish linen pillow case, attesting to (one) your tenacity in balking the evil damned things and (two) the fact that you're buying our lather-like goo in one-hundred-pound squirt cans. Also remember: if you are unable to adequately prepare yourself with a generous, expensive portion of Zoobko patented goo in the proper place, ahem, in advance of marital lawful pawing, then merely squirt the spray can with nozzle directed *directly* into the grimacing fungiform's ugly face as it hovers six feet high in the air above you. Best range—"

"Best range," Gregory Gloch said aloud, against the din of the obsessive noise in his ears, "approximately two inches."

"—'two inches,'" the tinny, mechanical racket reeled off, accompanying him, "'from his eyes. Zoobko's patented goo is not only—'"

"—'a top-drawer killer of male spores,'" Gloch murmured,

" 'but it also blasts the tear-ducts out of existence. Too bad, fella.' "
End brochure, he thought. End monolog. End sex. End of Zoobko,
or zoob of Endko. Is this an ad or a contemplation of a squandered
life? Check one. I know this discourse, he thought. By heart. Why?
How? It's as if, he thought, I said it; as if it's happening inside my
brain—not coming to me from the outside. *What does this mean? I
have to know.*

"Always bear in mind," the inexorable din continued, "that
male spores have an almost appalling capacity to progress under
their own power. If, ladies, you constantly ponder that—"

"Appalling, yes," Gloch said, "But FIVE MILES?" I said all
that, he realized. A long time ago. When I was a child. But no, he
thought; I didn't *say* all that—I thought it, worked it out in my
mind, a prank, a lampoon, when I was a kid in school. What's being
piped to me now here in this goddamn chamber, what's supposed to
be rephased sensory-data from the outside world—it's my own goddamn former thoughts returning to me, a loop from my brain to my
brain, with a ten-year lag.

"Splub gnog furb SQUAZ," the aud input circuit rattled away,
into his passive ears. Relentlessly.

My counter-weapon, Gloch thought. They've blocked my
counter-weapon with a counter-weapon, their own. Who—

"Yes sir, gnog furb," the aud input circuit declared in a hearty
but garbled voice, "this is good ol' Charley Falks' little boy Martha
signing off for now, but I'll be back with you soon and with me a
few more chuckles to lighten the day and make things SQUAZ!
cheery and bright. Toodeloo!" The voice, then, ceased. There was
only distant background static, not even a carrier wave.

I don't know any little boy named Martha, Gloch thought. And,
he realized, there's more wrong; the a-ending is out of the first Latin
declension, so "Martha" *can't* be a boy's name. Logically, it would
have to be Marthus. Or maybe they didn't know that; Charley Falks
didn't know that. Probably not well-read. As I recall, from what I
saw of Charley he was one of those self-educated simps ignorant

as hell on the inside but lathered over on the outside with a thin layer of bits of cultural, scientific, odd, dubious half-facts which he always liked to drone out for hours on end to whoever was listening or if not listening then anyhow in the vicinity and so at least potentially within earshot. And then when he got older you could practically walk off and he'd still be talking, to no one. But then of course I didn't have my chamber in those days, so my own time-sense was so faulty that what actually lasted only minutes seemed like years; at least that's what they told me, those 'wash psychiatrists, back in the early days, when they were testing me and setting me up so I could function, getting this chamber designed and built.

I wish for chrissake's, he thought mournfully, I could remember the concept for the counter-weapon I had in mind or almost had in mind or anyhow think I almost had in mind, before that garbage started coming in over the conduit.

It would have been one hell of a counter-weapon to use against Horst Bertold and the UN. He was sure of *that.*

Maybe it'll come back to me later, he reflected. Anyhow strictly speaking it was merely the nucleus of the counter-tactic idea; hardly had begun to grow. Takes time. If I'm not interrupted any further . . . if that dratted rubbish doesn't start up again promptly the second I begin to really fatten up the original notion into something Herr von Einem can put to use functionally, right out into the field to see action in the overall struggle we're bogged so darn down in at Whale's Mouth and wherever else they're all tangling . . . probably all over the universe by now; I'm probably six weeks behind, with data stored up ready to be fed to me from for instance last Thursday if not last year.

Martha, he thought. Let's see: "The Last Rose of Summer" is from that. Who wrote it? Flotow? Lehár? One of those light opera composers.

"Hummel," the aud input circuit suddenly stated, startling him; it was a familiar, dry, aged male voice. "Johann Nepomuk Hummel."

"You're a goldmine of misinformation," Gloch said irritably, in response, automatically, to one more of garrulous ol' Charley Falks' typical tidbits of wrong knowledge. He was so used to it, so darn, wearily resigned out of long experience. All the way back to his childhood, back throughout the dreary procession of years.

It's enough to make you wish you were a carpenter, Gloch mused grimly. And didn't have to think, just measure boards, saw and pound, all that purely physical activity. Then it wouldn't matter what ol' Charley Falks blabbled out, or what his pest of a kid Martha chimed in with in addition, for that matter; it didn't matter who said anything, or what.

Damn nice, he thought, if you could go back and live your life over again from the start. Only this time making it different; getting on the right track for once. A second chance, and with what I know now—

But exactly what did he know now?

For the life of him he couldn't remember.

"Pun, there," the voice from the aud circuit commented. "Life of you, life lived over . . . see?" It chuckled.

T W E L V E

Within its bow-shaped mouth the half-chewed eyes lay, rolling on the surface of its greedy, licking tongue. Those not completely eaten, those which still shone with luster, regarded him as they rolled slightly; they continued to function, although no longer fixed to the bulbed, oozing exterior surface of the head. New eyes, like tiny pale eggs, had already begun to form, he perceived. They clung in clusters.

He was seeing it. Not a deformed, half-hallucinated, pseudo-image, but the actual presence of the underlying substrate-entity which inhabited or somehow managed to lodge itself in this para-world for long periods of time—possibly forever, he realized with a shudder. Possibly for the total, absolute duration of its existence.

That might be a time-span of such magnitude as to smother any rational insight; he intuited that. The thing was old. And it had learned to feed on itself. He wondered how many centuries had passed before it had encountered that method of survival. He wondered what else it had tried first—and what it still resorted to, when necessary.

There were undoubtedly a number of techniques which it could make use of, when pressed. This act of consuming its own sensory-apparatus . . . it appeared to be a reflex act, not even consciously done. By now a mere habit; the creature chewed monotonously, and the luster within the still-watching half-consumed eyes was extinguished. But already the new ones expanding in clusters against the outer surface of the head had begun to acquire animation; several, more advanced in development than the others, had in a dim way discovered him and were with each passing second becoming more alert. Their initial interchange with reality involved him, and the realization of this made him sick with disgust. To be the first object sighted by such semi-autonomous entities—

Hoarsely, its voice thickened by the mouthful which it still continued to chew, the creature said, "Good morning. I have your book for you. Sign here." One of its pseudopodia convulsed and its tip lathered in a spasm which, after an interval, fumbled forth a bulky old-style bound-in-boards volume which it placed on a small plastic table before Rachmael.

"What—book is this?" he demanded, presently. His mind, numbed, refused to interfere as his fingers poked haphazardly at the handsome gold-stamped book which the creature had presented him.

"The fundamental reference source in this survey instruction," the cephalopodic organism answered as it laboriously filled out a long printed form; it made use of two pseudopodia and two writing instruments simultaneously, enormously speeding up the intricate task. "Dr. Bloode's great primary work, in the seventeenth edition." It swiveled the book, to show him the ornate spine. *"The True and Complete Economic and Political History of Newcolonizedland,"* it informed him, in a severe, dignified tone of voice, as if reproving him for his unfamiliarity with the volume. Or rather, he realized suddenly, as if it assumed that the title would have overpowering influences alone, without additional aid.

"Hmm," he said, then, still nonplussed—to say the least. And he thought, It can't be, but it is. Paraworld—*which?* Not precisely as it had manifested itself before; this was not Blue, because his glimpse of that, ratified by the other weevils, had contained a cyclopsic organism. And this, for all its similarity to the Aquatic Horror-shape, had by reason of its compound multi-eye system a fundamentally different aspect.

Could this actually be the authentic underlying reality? he wondered. This macro-abomination that resembled nothing ever witnessed by him before? A grotesque monstrosity which seemed, as he watched it devour and consume—to its evident satisfaction—the remainder of its eyes, almost a parody of the Aquatic Horror-shape?

"This book," the creature intoned, "demonstrates beyond any doubt whatsoever that the plan to colonize the ninth planet of the Fomalhaut system is foolish. No such colony as the projected New-colonizedland can possibly be established. We owe a great debt to Dr. Bloode for his complete elucidation of this complex topic." It giggled, then. A wet, slurred, wobbly giggle of delighted mirth.

"But the title," he said. "It says—"

"Irony," the creature tittered. "Of course. After all, no such colony exists." It paused, then, contemplatively. "Or does it?"

He was silent. For some ill-disclosed reason he felt a deep, abiding ominousness in the query.

"I wonder," the creature said speculatively, "why you don't speak. Is it so difficult a question? There is, of course, that small group of insane fanatics who allege that such a colony in some weird manner or other actually—" It halted as an ominous shape began—to both its surprise and Rachmael's—to materialize above its head. "A thing," the creature said, with resigned weariness. "And the worst style of thing in the known universe. I detest them. Do you not also, Mr. ben Applebaum?"

"Yes," Rachmael admitted. Because the detested object forming was equally familiar—and loathsome—to him also.

A creditor balloon.

"Oh, there you are!" the balloon piped at the amorphous mass of living tissue confronting Rachmael; it descended, tropic to the eye-eating creature. Obviously, it had located its target.

"Ugh," the eye-eater mumbled in disgust; with its pseudopodia it batted irritably at the invader.

"You must keep your credit-standing up and in good repute!" the balloon squealed as it bobbed and descended. "Your entire—"

"Get out of here," the eye-eater muttered angrily.

"Mr. Trent," the balloon shrilled, "your debts are odious! A great variety of small businessmen will go into bankruptcy immediately unless you honor your obligations! Don't you have the decency to do so? Everyone took you for a person who honored his obligations, an honorable man who could be trusted. Your assets will be attached through the courts, Mr. Trent; prepare for legal action to be instigated starting immediately! If you don't make at least a token attempt to pay, the entire net worth of Lies, Incorporated—"

"I don't own Lies, Incorporated any more," the eye-eater broke in gloomily. "It belongs to Mrs. Trent, now. Mrs. Silvia Trent. I suggest you go and bother her."

"There is no such person as 'Mrs. Silvia Trent,'" the creditor balloon said, with wrathful condemnation. "And you know it. Her real name is Freya Holm, and she's your mistress."

"A lie," the eye-eater rumbled ominously; again its pseudopodia whipped viciously, seeking out the agile creditor balloon, which dipped and bobbed barely beyond the flailing reach of the several sucker-impregnated arms. "As a matter of fact, this gentleman here—". It indicated Rachmael. "My understanding is that the lady and this individual are emotionally involved. Miss Holm is—was, whatever—a friend of mine, a very close friend. But hardly my mistress." The eye-eater looked embarrassed.

Rachmael said to it, "You're Matson Glazer-Holliday."

"Yes," the eye-eater admitted.

"He took this evil manifestation," the creditor balloon shouted, "to evade us. But as you can see, Mr.—" It regarded Rachmael as it bobbed and drifted. "I believe you are familiar to us, too," it declared then. "Are you one of those who has shirked his moral and legal duty, who has failed to honor his financial obligations? As a matter of fact . . ." It drifted very slowly toward Rachmael. "I think I *personally* hounded you not too long ago, sir. You are—" It considered as, within, electronic circuits linked it to its agency's central computer banks. "ben Applebaum!" it shrilled in triumph. "Zounds! I've caught two deadbeats AT THE SAME TIME!"

"I'm getting out of here," the eye-eater who was—or once had been—Matson Glazer-Holliday declared; it began to flow off, uniped-wise, getting free of the situation as quickly as possible . . . and at Rachmael's expense.

"Hey," he protested weakly. "Don't you go scuttling off, Matson. This is all too damn much; wait, for god's sake!"

"Your late father," the creditor balloon boomed at him, its voice now amplified by the background data supplied it by the central computer upon which it depended, "as of Friday, November tenth, 2014, owed four and one-third million poscreds to the noble firm Trails of Hoffman Limited, and as his heir, you, sir, must appear before the Superior Court of Marin County, California, and show just cause as to why you have failed (or if you by a miracle have *not* failed but possess the due sum in toto) and if by your failure you hope to—"

Its resonant voice ceased. Because, in approaching Rachmael the better to harass him, it had forgotten about the finely probing pseudopodia of the eye-eater.

One of the pseudopodia had whipped about the body of the creditor balloon. And squeezed.

"Gleeb!" the creditor balloon squeaked. "Gak!" it whooshed as its frail structure crumbled. "Glarg!" it sighed, and then wheezed into final silence as the pseudopodium crushed it. Fragments rained down, then. A gentle pat-pat of terminal sound.

And after that—silence.

"Thanks," Rachmael said, gratefully.

"Don't thank me," the eye-eater said in a gloomy voice. "After all, you've got a lot more troubles than that pitiful object. For instance, Rachmael, you've got the illness. Telpor Syndrome. Right?"

"Right," he admitted.

"So it's S.A.T. for you. Good old therapy by Lupov's psychiatrists, probably some second-string hick we never ought to have voted money to pay for. Some fnigging quab; right?" The eye-eater chuckled, in a philosophic fashion. "Well, so it goes. Anyhow— what's with you, Rachmael? Lately you've been, um, a weevil; part of that class and seeing Paraworld Blue . . . is that correct? Yes, correct." The eye-eater nodded sagely. "And it's just ever so much fun . . . right? With that Sheila Quam as the control, these days. And form 47-B hanging around, ready to be utilized as soon as two of you experience the same delusional world. Heh-heh." It chuckled; or rather, Matson Glazer-Holliday chuckled. Rachmael still found it difficult, if not impossible, to recall that the pulpy, massive heap of organic tissue confronting him was Matson.

And—why this shape? Had the creditor balloon been right? Merely to evade the balloon . . . it seemed an overly extreme ruse to escape. Frankly Rachmael was not convinced; he sensed that more, much more, lay below the surface of apparent meaning.

Below the surface. Did nothing actual lie at hand? Did everything have to turn out, eventually, to consist of something else entirely? He felt weary—and resigned. Evidently this remained so. Whether he liked it or not. Delusional as this might be, obviously it was not acting in conformity to *his* wishes. Not in the slightest.

"What can you tell me," he said, "about Freya?" He set himself, braced against the possibility of horrible final news; he waited with cold stoic anticipation.

"Chrissake, she's fine," the eye-eater answered. "Nobody got her; it was me they got. Blew me to bits, they did."

"But," Rachmael pointed out, "you're alive."

"Somewhat." The eye-eater sounded disenchanted. "You call this being alive? Well, I guess technically it's being alive; I can move around, eat food, breathe; maybe, for all I know, I can reproduce myself. Okay, I admit it; I'm alive. Are you satisfied?"

Rachmael said hoarsely, "You're a Mazdast."

"Hell I am."

"But my paraworld," Rachmael said bluntly, "is Paraworld Blue. I've seen the Aquatic Horror-shape, Matson; I know from firsthand experience what it looks like." He plunged on, then, ruthlessly. "And you're it."

"Almost." The eye-eater sounded placid; he had not disturbed its potent calm. "But you yourself noticed crucial differences, son. For example, I possess a multitude of compound eyes; high in protein, they often provide me—in time of dire want—an ample diet. As I recently demonstrated. Shall I display this neat faculty once more?" It reached, then, two pseudopodia toward its recently regrown optic organs. "Very tasty," it intoned, now apparently engrossed in furthering its meal.

"Wait a moment," Rachmael said thickly. "I find your appetite offensive; for god's sake, wait!"

"Anything," the eye-eater said obligingly, "to please a fellow human being. We both are, you realize. I am, certainly. After all, I'm the quondam owner of Lies, Incorporated; correct? No, I am not a Mazdast; not one of the primordial *Ur*-inhabitants of Fomalhaut IX. They constitute a low order of organism; I spit on them." It spat, decisively. In its mind there was no doubt; it detested the Mazdasts. "What I am," it continued, "is the living embodiment of humanity and not some alien creep-thing that nature was inclined to spawn on this far-flung, rather degenerate crypto-colony planet. Well, when Computer Day arrives, all that will be taken care of. You included, you odd life-form, you. Heh-heh." It giggled once more. "Now, that book I loaned you. Dr. Bloode's book. It seems to me that if you want to catch up on the very vital facts pertaining to Newcolonizedland, you really ought to con it thoroughly. What you want to learn undoubtedly lies within. Read it! Go on! Heh-heh." Its voice trailed off stickily into an indistinct torrent of mumbled amusement, and Rachmael felt a surge of doubt, overwhelming doubt, that this was—at least now—the man he had known as Matson Glazer-Holliday. He sensed its innate alienness. It was, beyond doubt, nonhuman. To say the least.

With dignity, he answered, "I'll read it when I have time."

"But you'll enjoy it, Mr. ben Applebaum. Not only is the volume educational, but also highly amusing. Let me quote one of Dr. Bloode's quite singular Thingisms."

"'Thingisms'?" Rachmael felt baffled—and wary. He had a deep intuition that the Thingism, whatever it was, would *not* be amusing. Not to him, anyhow, or to any human.

"I always enjoyed this one," the eye-eater intoned, its saliva spilling from its mouth as it writhed with glee. "Consider: since you are about to read the book, here is Thingism Number Twenty, dealing with books.

"Ahem. 'The book business is hidebound.'"

After a pause, Rachmael said, "That's it?"

"Perhaps you failed to understand. I'll give you another gem, one more particular favorite of mine. And if *that* fails to move you . . . Oooohhh! That's a Thingism! Listen! 'The representative of the drayage firm failed to move me.' Oooohhh! How was that?" It waited hopefully.

Baffled, Rachmael said, "I don't get it."

"All right." The eye-eater's tone was now harsh. "Read the book purely for educational purposes, then. So be it. You want to know the origin of this form which I have taken. Well, everyone will take it, sooner or later. We all do; this is how we become after we die."

He stared at it.

"While you ponder," the eye-eater continued, "I'll delight you with a few more Thingisms of Dr. Bloode's. This one I always enjoy. 'The vidphone company let me off the hook.' How was that? Or this one: 'The highway construction truck tore up the street at forty miles an hour.' Or this: 'I am not in a position to enjoy sexual relations.' Or—"

Shutting his ears, ignoring the prolix eye-eater, Rachmael examined the book, finding a page at dead-random. The text swam, then set into clear focus for him.

A zygote formed between the indigenous inhabitants of Fomalhaut IX and Homo sapiens gives us evidence of the dominant aspect of the so-called 'Mazdast' genetic inheritance. From the twin radically opposing strains arises what nominally appears to be a pure 'Mazdast,' with the exceptional reorganization of the organs of sight, the cephalopodic entity otherwise manifesting itself intact and in its customary fashion.

"You mean," Rachmael said, glancing up from the book, stunned, "that when you say you're Matson Glazer-Holliday you mean you're an offspring of his and a—"

"And of a female Mazdast," the eye-eater said calmly. "Read on, Mr. ben Applebaum. There's much more there to interest you. You'll find that each of the paraworlds is explained; the structure of each is displayed so that the logic constituting each is clearly revealed. Look in the index. Select the paraworld which most interests you."

He turned at once to *Paraworld Blue.*

"And Freya Holm," the eye-eater said, as Rachmael leafed shakily through the volume for the cited page. "You wish to find her; this is your primary motive for coming here to Fomalhaut IX. Possibly there's an entry regarding Miss Holm; had you thought of that, sir?"

Huskily, with disbelief, Rachmael said, "You're kidding." It was impossible.

"Merely test out what I say. Look under Holm comma Freya."

He did so.

The index informed him that there existed two entries regarding Freya. One on page fifty. The second further in, deep into the book: on page two-hundred-and-ten.

He chose the earlier one first.

Freya saw, then, into the grave and screamed; she ran and as she ran, struggled to get away, she knew it for what it was: a refined form of nerve gas that—and then her coherent thoughts ceased and she simply ran.

"It details," the eye-eater informed him, "Miss Holm's actions on this side of the Telpor gate. Up to the present. If you want to know what became of her, simply read on. And," it added sourly, "what became of me."

His hands shaking, Rachmael read on. He had now swiftly turned to the later citation on page two-hundred-and-ten; before his eyes danced the black bug-like words, details of Freya's fate here at Newcolonizedland. He held, read, understood what he had come for; this, as the eye-eater said, contained what he wanted.

Facing the deformed entity which she had once known as the human 'wash psychiatrist Dr. Lupov, Freya whispered ashenly, "So the transformation is arranged by means of your techniques and all of those damned gadgets you use to keep people thinking along the exact lines you want. And I thought it was a biological sport; I was so completely convinced." She shut her eyes in deep, overpowering fatigue. And realized that this was the

end; she would go the way of Mat, of Rachmael ben Applebaum, of

"What way?" Rachmael demanded, lifting his eyes from the
page and confronting the creature before him. "You mean become
like you?" His body cringed; he retreated physically from even the
notion of it, let alone its presence here before him.

"All flesh must die," the eye-eater said, and giggled.

Almost unable to hold onto Dr. Bloode's volume, Rachmael
once more turned to the index. This time he selected the entry:

ben Applebaum, Rachmael

And again read on. Grimly.

To the sharp-featured, intent young man beside him, Lupov said, "I
think we can consider Reconstruct Method Three to be successful.
At least in its initial phase."

Jaimé Weiss nodded. "I agree. And you have the alternate versions of the text available? As the other persons are brought in?"
He did not take his eyes from the vid screen; he missed nothing of the
activity that at slowed-velocity passed before the magnetic scanning-
heads of the replay deck for his and Dr. Lupov's scrutiny.

"Several are ready." It did not seem urgent to Lupov to have all
alternates of the text which Rachmael ben Applebaum now read
available at the same time; after all . . . certain changes in the other
versions might be indicated, depending on which way ben Applebaum jumped. His reaction to this text—in particular the part dealing with his own "death"—would come in any moment, now.

On the small screen Rachmael ben Applebaum slowly closed
the book, stood uncertainly, and then said to the creature facing
him, "So that's how I'm going to get knocked off. Like that. Just like
that."

"More or less," the eye-eater answered, carelessly.

"It's a good job," Jaimé Weiss commented with approval.

"Yes," Lupov nodded. "It will probably function satisfactorily with this ben Applebaum person, anyhow." But the girl, he thought. Miss Holm . . . so far it had failed with her. *So far.* But that did not indicate for a certainty that it would continue to fail. She had put up a protracted expert struggle—but of course she was a pro. And ben Applebaum was not. Like the pilot Dosker, Miss Holm knew her business; it would not be easy—was not at this moment easy, in fact—to recon her mentality by means of a variety of (as she had asserted in the pseudo-spurious text) "damned gadgets you use to keep people thinking along the exact lines you want."

A good description of our instrumentalities, Lupov reflected. This Weiss person has ability. His composition, this initial variant of the so-called Dr. Bloode Text—masterful. A powerful weapon in this final vast conflict.

Of most interest would be a later response to one of the versions of the text. The reaction by Theodoric Ferry.

It was this that both Jaimé Weiss and Dr. Lupov looked toward.

And—it would not be long, now. Theodoric Ferry would soon be located where the text could be presented to him. At this moment, Ferry loitered on Terra. But—

At six-thirty, three hours from now, Ferry would make a secret trip to Newcolonizedland, one of many; like Sepp von Einem, he crossed back and forth at will.

This time, however, he would make a one-way crossing.

Theodoric Ferry would never return to Terra.

At least not sane.

THIRTEEN

In the darkness of gathering fright Freya Holm wandered, trying to escape insight, the awareness of absolute nonbeing which the intricate weapon manned by the two veteran police of Lies, Incorporated had thrust onto her—how long ago? She could not tell; her time sense, in the face of the field emanating from the weapon, had like so much else that constituted objective reality totally vanished.

At her waist a delicate detection meter clicked on, registered a measured passage of high-frequency current; she halted, and the gravity of this new configuration slapped her into abrupt alertness. The meter had been built to record one sole subvariety of electrical activity. The flux emanating from—

A functioning Telpor station.

She peered. And, gathering in the dense haze that occluded her sight, she made out what normally would have passed for—and beyond any doubt had been designed deliberately to pass for—a mediocre construct: a peripatetic bathroom. It appeared to have landed nearby, undoubtedly to give aid and comfort to some passerby; its gay, bright neon sign winked on and off invitingly, displaying the relief-providing slogan:

UNCLE JOHN'S LI'L HUT-SUT

An ordinary sight. And yet, according to the meter at her belt, not a peripatetic bathroom at all but one end of a von Einem entity, set down here at Newcolonizedland and working away full blast; the recorded line-surge appeared to be maximum, not minimum. The station could not be more fully in operation.

Warily, she made her way toward it. Heavy gray haze, a diffuse mass of drifting airborne debris, surrounded her as she entered

Uncle John's Li'l Hut-Sut station, passed down the quaintly archaic wrought-iron staircase and into the cool, dimly lit chamber marked LADIES.

"Five cents, please," a mechanical voice said pleasantly.

In a reflexive gesture she handed the nonexistent attendant a dime; her change rolled down a slot to her and she pocketed it with absolutely no interest. Because, ahead of her, two bald women sat in adjoining stalls, conversing in deep, guttural German.

She drew her sidearm and said to them as she pointed the pistol at them, *"Hände hoch, bitte."*

Instantly one of the two figures yanked at the handle nearest her—or more accurately his—right hand; a roar of rushing water thundered up and lashed at Freya in a sonic torrent which shook her and caused her vision to blur, to become disfigured; the two shapes wavered and blended, and she found it virtually impossible to keep her weapon pointed at them.

"Fräulein," a masculine voice said tautly, *"gib uns augenblicklich dein—"*

She fired.

One of the twin indistinct shapes atomized silently. But the alternate Telpor technician hopped, floundered, to one side; he sprang to his feet and bolted off. She followed him with the barrel of her gun, fired once more—and missed. *The last shot I'm entitled to,* she thought to herself wanly. I missed my chance; I missed getting both of them. And now it's me.

A current of hot, lashing air burst at her from the automatic wet-hands dryer; she ducked, half-blinded, attempted to fire her small weapon once more—and then, from behind her, something of steel, something not alive but alert and active, closed around her middle. She gasped in fear as it swept her from her feet; twisting, she managed a meager glimpse of it; grotesquely, it was the vanity-table assembly—or rather a homotropic device cammed as a vanity table. Its legs, six of them, had fitted one into the next, like old-fashioned curtain rods; the joint appendage had extended itself expertly, groped until it encountered her, and then, without the need or assistance of life, had embraced her in a grip of crushing death.

The remaining Telpor technician ceased to duck and weave; he drew himself upright, irritably tossed aside the female garments which he had worn, walked a few steps toward her to watch her destruction. Face twitching eagerly, he surveyed the rapid closure of the vanity-table defense system, oh-ing with satisfaction, his thin, pinched face marred with sadistic delight—pleasure at a well-functioning instrument of murder.

"Please," she gasped, as the appendage drew her back toward the crypto-vanity table, which now displayed a wide maw in which to engulf her; within it she would be converted to ergs: energy to power the assembly for future use.

"*Es tut mir furchtbar leid,*" the Telpor technician said, licking his mildly hairy lips with near-erotic delight, "*aber—*"

"Can't you do anything for me?" she managed to say, or rather made an attempt to say; no breath remained in her, now, by which to speak. The end, she realized, was close by; it would not be long.

"*So schön, doch,*" the German intoned, his eyes fixed on her; crooning to himself, he approached closer and closer, swaying in a hypnotic dance of physiological sympathy—physical but not emotional correspondence, his body—but not his mentality—responding to what was rapidly happening to her as the tapered extension of the vanity table drew her back to engulf her.

No one, she realized. Nothing. Rachmael, she thought; why is it that—and then her thoughts dimmed. Over. Done. She shut her eyes, and, with her fingers, groped for the destruct-trigger which would set off a high-yield charge implanted subdermally; better to die by means of a merciful Lies, Incorporated *Selbstmort* instrument placed within her body for her protection than by the cruel THL thing devouring her piecemeal . . . as the final remnant of awareness departed from her, she touched the trigger—

"Oh no, miss," a reprimanding voice said, from a distance away.

"Not in the presence of a guided tour." Sounds, the near-presence of people—she opened her eyes, saw descending the stairs of the women's room a gang of miscellaneous persons: men and women and children, all dressed well, all solemnly scrutinizing her and the remaining Telpor technician, the vanity table with its metal arm engaged in dragging her to her death . . . my god, she realized. I've seen this on TV, on transmissions from Whale's Mouth!

It can't be, Freya Holm said to herself. This is part of the ersatz reality superimposed for our benefit. Years of this hoax—*still*? This is impossible!

Yet—here it was, before her eyes. Not on TV but in actuality.

The tour guide, with armband, in carefully pressed suit, continued to eye her reprovingly. Being killed before the eyes of a guided tour; it's wrong, she realized. True; she agreed. You're absolutely correct. Thinking that, she found herself sobbing hysterically; unable to cease she shut her eyes, took a deep, unsteady breath.

"I am required to inform you, miss," the guide stated, his voice now wooden and correct, "that you are under arrest. For causing a disturbance interfering with the orderly unfolding of an official, licensed White House tour. I am also required to inform you that you are in custody as of this moment, without written notice, and you are to be held without bail until a Colony Municipal Court can, at a later date, deal with you." He eyed the Telpor technician coldly and with massive suspicion. "Sir, you appear to be involved in this matter to some extent."

"In no way whatsoever," the Telpor technician said at once.

"Then," the guide said, as his herded group of sightseers gawked, "how do you explain your unauthorized presence here in the ladies' section of this Uncle John's Li'l Hut-Sut station?"

The Telpor technician shrugged, flushing crimson.

"A Thingism," the guide said in an aside to Freya. "He flushes at his presence in a comfort station." He sniggered, and the group of sightseers laughed to various degrees. "I hold this job," the guide informed Freya as he expertly unfastened her from the manual extension of the pseudo vanity table, "for good reason; my wit delights the multitude."

The Telpor technician said sullenly, "Thingismtry is degenerate."

"Perhaps," the guide admitted. He steadied Freya as the vanity table reluctantly released her; in a gentlemanly way he assisted her away from the feral device and over to his throng. "But it helps pass the dull hours away; does it not?" He addressed his tame collection of sightseers.

They nodded obediently, the men eyeing Freya with interest; she saw, now, that her blouse had been neatly shredded by the arm of the vanity table, and, with numb fingers, she gathered it about her.

"No need of that," the guide said softly in her ear. "A bit of exposed female bosom also helps pass the dull hours." He grinned at her. "Hmm," he added, half to himself. "I wouldn't be surprised if President Jones wanted to interview you personally. He takes a grave interest in matters of this sort, these civil disturbances which upset the orderly—"

"Please just get me out of here," Freya said tightly.

"Of course." The guide led her to the stairs. Behind them, the Telpor technician was ignored. "But I don't think you can avoid spending a few moments with the august President of Whale's Mouth, in view of—or perhaps I should say because of—the anatomy which you reveal so—"

"President Omar Jones," Freya said, "does not exist."

"Oh?" The guide glanced at her mockingly. "Are you certain, miss? Are you truly ready to invite a little of Dr. Lupov's S.A.T. to remedy a rather disordered little feminine mental imbalance? Eh?"

She groaned. And allowed the guide to escort her and the group of sightseers up the stairs, out of Uncle John's Li'l Hut-Sut comfort station and onto the surface of—Newcolonizedland.

"I'd like to have your complete, legal name, miss," the guide was murmuring to her; he now held a book of forms in his left hand and a pen in his right. "Last name first, please. And if you have any i.d. on you I'd be much obliged to see that, too. Ah, Miss Freya Holm."

He glanced at her wallet, then at her face, with a totally new expression. I wonder what that means, Freya wondered.

She had an intuition that she would soon know.

And it would not be pleasant.

At the top of the stairs two agents of Trails of Hoffman Limited met her and the guide, expertly relieved the guide of his self-assumed responsibilities.

"We'll take her from here on in," the taller of the two THL agents explained curtly to the guide; he took Freya by the shoulder and led her, with his companion, toward a parked official-looking oversize flapple.

The guide, perplexed, looking after them, murmured, "Gracious." And then returned to his customary duties; he herded his group off in the other direction, circumspectly minding his own business; the expression on his face showed all too well that he recognized that somehow he had strayed out of his depth. His discomfort at unexpectedly encountering the two THL agents seemed to Freya almost as great as her own . . . and her awareness of the lethal aspect of THL grew with this recognition—in fact burgeoned into overwhelming immensity.

Even here, on Fomalhaut IX—the power, the dull, metallic size of THL was matched by nothing else; the great entity stood alone, without a real antagonist. And here the UN failed to manifest its own authority. Or so, she reflected somberly, it would seem.

The contest between Horst Bertold and Theo Ferry seemed to have resolved itself before genuinely getting underway; fundamentally it was no contest at all. And Theo Ferry, more than anyone else, knew it.

Beyond any doubt.

"Your operations here," she told the two THL agents, "are absolutely illegal." And, having announced this, she felt the utter futility of mere words. How could an empty statement abolish

THL, or for that matter, even these two minor instruments of its authority? The futility of the struggle seemed to her, at this instant, beyond compare; she felt her verve, her energy quotient, wither.

Meanwhile, the two THL agents led her rapidly toward their parked motor-on flapple.

When the flapple had achieved reasonable altitude, one of the THL agents produced a large hardbound volume, examined it, then passed it to his companion, who, after an interval, then abruptly handed it to Freya.

"What's this?" she demanded. "And where are we going?"

"You may be interested in this," the taller agent informed her. "I think you'll find it well worth your time. Go ahead; open it."

With almost occult suspicion, Freya studied the cover. "An economic history of Newcolonizedland," she said, with distaste. More of the propaganda, lurid and false, of the irreal president's regnancy, she realized, and started to hand it back. The agent, however, refused to accept the book; he shook his head curtly. And so, with reluctance, she opened to the back, glanced with distaste over the index.

And saw her own name.

"That's right," the tall THL agent said with a smirk. "You're in it, Miss Holm. So's that fathead, ben Applebaum."

She turned pages and saw that it was so. Will this tell me, she wondered, what's happened to Rachmael? Finding the page reference, she at once turned to it. Her hands shook as she read the startling passage.

"What way?" Rachmael demanded, lifting his eyes from the page and confronting the creature before him. "You mean become like you?" His body cringed; he retreated physically from even the notion of it, let alone its presence here before him.

"Good lord," Freya said. And read intently on.

"All flesh must die," the eye-eater said, and giggled.

Aloud, Freya said, " 'The eye-eater.' " Chilled, she said to the two THL agents, "What's that? In the name of god—"

"Is that in there?" the shorter of the two agents asked his companion; he appeared displeased. Reaching out, he suddenly retrieved the book; at once he put it away out of sight. "It was a mistake to let her see it," he told his companion. "She knows too much now."

"She doesn't know a damn thing," his companion said.

Freya said, "Tell me. What is the 'eye-eater'? I have to know." Her breath caught in her throat; raggedly, she managed to breathe, but with difficulty.

"A fungiform," the taller of the THL agents said briefly. "One that resides here." He said nothing further.

"Is Rachmael alive?" she demanded. At least she knew one thing. Rachmael was here at Whale's Mouth, and that she had not, up until this instant, realized.

The shorter agent was correct. She had learned too much. At least, too much for their purpose. But for hers—hardly enough.

"Yeah," the taller agent conceded. "He came looking for you."

"And found it," the other said.

For a time there was silence. The flapple droned on—heaven only knew where.

"If you don't tell me where you're taking me," Freya said levelly, "I'm going to destruct myself." Her fingers already touched the trigger at her waist; she waited, eyes fixed on the two men with her in the oversize flapple. Several moments passed. "The UN," she said, "equipped me with this—"

"*Get her,*" the taller THL agent rasped; instantly he and his companion leaped toward her, clawing.

"Let me go," she choked; her fingers, torn from the trigger, dug into their clutching hands. I couldn't do it, she realized; I couldn't activate the darn mechanism. Weariness filled her as she felt their hands rip loose the destruct mechanism, tear it apart, then drop it into the waste slot of the flapple.

"It would have destroyed all of us," the taller agent gasped as he and his companion confronted her accusingly, with indignation mixed with apprehension; she had genuinely frightened them by her near-suicide. As far as they knew, it had been close, very close. But actually she could not have done it at all.

The man's companion muttered, "We better consult the book. See what it says; assuming of course it says anything." Together the two of them pored over the book, ignoring her; Freya, with trembling fingers, lit a cigarette, stared sightlessly through the window at the ground below.

Trees . . . houses. Exactly as the TV screen had promised. Jolted, she thought, Where's the garrison state? Where's the war I saw? The battle I was a part of, only a little while ago?

It made no sense.

"We were fighting," she said at last.

Startled, the THL agents glanced at her, then at one another. "She must have gotten into one of the paraworlds," one said presently to his companion; they both nodded in attentive agreement. "Silver? White? I forget which Lupov calls it. Not The Clock, though."

"And not Blue," the other agent murmured. Again the two of them returned to the large hardbound book; again they ignored her.

Strange, Freya thought. It made no sense. And yet the two THL agents appeared to understand. Will I ever know? she asked herself. And if so, *will it be in time?*

Several worlds, she realized. And each of them different. And—if they're looking in that book, not to see what has happened but to see what will happen . . . then it must have something to do with time.

Time-travel. The UN's time-warpage weapon.

Evidently Sepp von Einem had gotten hold of it. The senile old genius and his disturbed proleptic protégé Gloch had altered it, god only knew how. But effectively; that much was obvious.

The flapple began to descend.

Glancing, she saw below them a large ship moored by its tail, in flight position, poised to ascend at any moment; in fact, wisps of fuel-vapor trickled from its rear. A big one, she decided; it belonged to someone of importance. Possibly President Omar Jones. Or—

Or worse.

She had a good idea that it was *not* Omar Jones' ship—even if such a person existed. Undoubtedly the ship belonged to Theo Ferry. And, as she watched the ship grow, a bizarre idea occurred to her. What if the *Omphalos* had been beaten, years ago, in its flight from the Sol system to Fomalhaut? This ship, huge and menacing, with its pitted gray hull . . . certainly it did have the sullied, darkened appearance of a much-utilized vessel; had it, at some earlier time, crossed deep space between the two star systems?

The ultimate irony. Theo Ferry had made the journey before Rachmael ben Applebaum. Or rather possibly had; she could of course not be sure. But she felt intuitively that Ferry had, all this time, been capable of doing it. So whatever could be learned had long ago—perhaps decades ago—been learned . . . and by the very man whom they had, at all costs, to defeat.

"Better brush your hair," the taller of the two THL agents announced to her; he then winked—lewdly, it seemed to her—to his companion. "I'm giving you fair warning; you're going to have an important visitor here in your room in a few minutes."

Almost unable to speak, Freya said. "This isn't my room!"

"Bedroom?" Both THL agents laughed in unison, and this time there was no mistaking it; the tone was one of rancid, enormous licentiousness. And, clearly, this appeared to the two men an old story; they both knew precisely what would be happening—not to them but for them to witness; she was overtly conscious of the mood already in progress. They knew what would soon be expected of them . . . and of her. And yet it did not seem to her so much concerned with Theo Ferry as it did with the environment here as a whole; she sensed an underlying *wrongness,* and sensed further that in some way which she did not comprehend, Ferry was as much a victim of it as she.

Paraworlds, she thought to herself. They, the two THL agents, had said that. Silver, White, The Clock . . . and finally Blue.

Am I in a paraworld now? she wondered. Whatever they are. Perhaps that would explain the twisted, strained wrongness which the world around her now seemed to possess throughout. She shivered. Which one is this? she asked herself, assuming it's any of them? But even if it is, she realized, that still doesn't tell me what they are, or how I got into this one, or—how I manage to scramble back. Again she shivered.

"We'll be touching ships with Mr. Ferry at 003.5," the taller of the two THL agents informed her conventionally; he seemed amused, now, as if her discomfort were quaint and charming. "So be prepared," he added. "Last chance to—"

"May I see that book again?" she blurted. "The one you have there; the book about me and Rachmael."

The taller of the two agents passed her the volume; at once she turned to the index and sought out her own name. Two citations in the first part of the book; three later on. She selected the next to last one, on page two-ninety-eight; a moment later she had begun rapidly to read.

No doubt could exist in her mind, now; it had been abundantly demonstrated. With renewed courage Freya faced Theodoric Ferry, the most powerful man in either the Sol or the Fomalhaut system and perhaps even beyond, and said,

"I'm sorry, Mr. Ferry." Her voice, in her own ears, was cool, as calm as she might have hoped for. "I failed to realize what you are. You'll have to excuse my hysteria on that basis." With a slight—but unnoticed—tremor she adjusted the right strap of her half-bra, drawing it back up onto her smooth, bare, slightly tanned shoulder. "I now—"

"Yes, Miss Holm?" Ferry's tone was dark, mocking. "Exactly what do you realize about me, now? Say it." He chuckled.

Freya said, "You're an aquatic cephalopod, a Mazdast. And you've always been. A long time ago, when Telpor first linked the Sol system with the Fomalhaut system, when the first Terran field-team crossed over *and returned*—"

"That's correct," Theodoric Ferry agreed, and once more chuckled . . . although now his—or rather its—tone consisted of a wet, wailing hiss. "I infiltrated your race decades ago. I've been in your midst

"Better get the book back from her again," the smaller of the two THL agents said warningly to his companion. "I still think she's reading too damn much." He then, without further consultation, snatched the book back from her numbed hands, this time put it away in a locked briefcase which, after an indecisive pause he then laboriously chained to his wrist—just in case.

"Yes," the other agent agreed absently; he had become completely involved in landing the flapple on the flattened roof-indentation of Theo Ferry's huge ship. "She probably read too much. But—" He spun the unusually elaborate controls "—it doesn't much matter, at this point; I fail to see what effective difference it makes." From beneath them a low scraping noise sounded; the flapple jiggled.

They had landed.

Doesn't it matter? she thought, dazed. That Theo Ferry is another life-form entirely, not human at all? That has invaded our System a long time back? *Don't you two men care?*

Did you know it all this time?

Our enemy, she realized, is far more ominous than any of us had at any time glimpsed. Ironic, she thought; one of the sales pitches they gave us—THL gave us—was the need to fight with and subdue the hostile native life-forms of the Fomalhaut system . . . and it turns out to be true after all, true in the most awful sense. I wonder, she thought, how many of THL's employees know it? I wonder—

She thought, I wonder how many more of these monsters exist on Terra. Imitating human life-forms. Is Theodoric Ferry the only one? Probably not; probably most of THL is staffed by them, including Sepp von Einem.

The ability to mingle with human beings, to appear like them . . . undoubtedly it's due to a device compounded either by von Einem or that hideous thing who works with him, that Greg Gloch.

Of all of them, she thought, none is really less human than Gloch.

The door of the flapple swung open; the two THL agents at once stood at attention. Reluctantly, she turned her unwilling eyes toward the now fully open door.

In the entrance way stood Theodoric Ferry.

She screamed.

"I beg your pardon," Ferry said, and lifted an eyebrow archly. He turned questioningly to the two THL agents. "What's the matter with Miss Holm? She seems out of control."

"Sorry, Mr. Ferry," the taller of the two agents said briskly. "I would guess that she's not well; she appears to have hallucinated one or more of what is called 'paraworlds.' On her arrival here she experienced the particular delusional world dealing with the garrison state . . . although now, from what she's told us, that delusion seems to have evaporated."

"But something," Ferry said with a frown, "has replaced it. Perhaps an alternate paraworld . . . possibly even a more severe one. Well, Miss Holm has turned out as predicted." He chuckled, walked several cautious steps toward Freya, who stood frozen and trembling, unable even to retreat. "As with her paramour, Rachmael von Applebaum—"

"Ben," the taller of the two THL agents corrected tactfully.

"Ah yes." Ferry nodded amiably. "I am more accustomed to the prefix designating a high-born German than the rather—" He grimaced offensively "—low-class name-structure employed by, ah, individuals of Mr. Applebaum's shall I say *type*." He grimaced distastefully, then once more moved toward Freya Holm.

They didn't search me, she said to herself. A spasm of fierceness filled her as she realized that—realized, too, its meaning. Within the tied tails of superior fabric caught in a bun at her midsection lay a tiny but effective self-defense instrument, provided by the wep-x people at Lies, Incorporated. Now, if ever, the time had come to employ it. True, it had a limited range; only one person could be taken out by it, and if she moved to take out Theo Ferry both of the THL agents—armed and furious—would remain. She could readily picture the following moments, once she had managed to wound or destroy Ferry. But—it appeared well worth it. Even if she had not learned of Ferry's actual physiological origin . . .

Her fingers touched the bun of cloth at her midriff; an instant later she had found the safety of the weapon, had switched it to off.

"Drot," Ferry said, regarding her uneasily.

" 'Drat,' sir," the taller of the two agents corrected him, as if routinely accustomed to doing so. " 'Drat' is the Terran ejaculative term of dismay, if I may call your attention at a time like this to something so trivial. Still, we all know how important it is—how vital you rightly feel it to be—to maintain strict verisimilitude and accuracy in your speech patterns."

"Thank you, Frank," Theo Ferry agreed; he did not take his eyes from Freya. "Was this woman searched?"

"Well, sir," the THL agent named Frank said uncomfortably, "we had in mind your overweening desire to obtain a female of this—"

"Blurb!" Theodoric Ferry quivered in agitation. "She has on some variety of—"

"Sorry sir," the agent named Frank broke in with utter tact. "The term of immediate and dismayed concern which you're reaching for is the word 'blast.' The term you've employed, 'blurb,' deals with a sensational ad for some form of entertainment; generally a notice on a book cover or flap as to—"

All at once Freya became aware, shockingly, of the meaning of the THL agent's remarks; everything which she suspected, everything which she had read in Dr. Bloode's book, now had been validated.

Theodoric Ferry had to be reminded, constantly, of the most commonplace Terran linguistic patterns. Of course; these patterns were to him a totally alien structure. So it was true. And, because of what had up to this instant seemed an absurd, pointless exchange of remarks, no doubt could exist in her mind, now; it had been abundantly demonstrated. With renewed courage Freya faced Theodoric Ferry, the most powerful man in either the Sol or the Fomalhaut system and perhaps even beyond, and said,

"I'm sorry, Mr. Ferry." Her voice, in her own ears, was cool, as calm as she might have hoped for. "I failed to realize what you are. You'll have to excuse my hysteria on that basis." With a slight—but unnoticed—tremor she adjusted the right strap of her half-bra, drawing it back up onto her smooth, bare, slightly tanned shoulder. "I now—"

"Yes, Miss Holm?" Ferry's tone was dark, mocking. "Exactly what do you realize about me, now? Say it." He chuckled.

Freya said, "You're an aquatic cephalopod, a Mazdast. And you've always been. A long time ago, when Telpor first linked the Sol system with the Fomalhaut system, when the first Terran fieldteam crossed over *and returned*—"

"That's correct," Theodoric Ferry agreed, and once more chuckled . . . although now his—or rather its—tone consisted of a wet, wailing hiss. "I infiltrated your race decades ago. I've been in your midst before Lies, Incorporated was founded; I've been with your people before you, Miss Holm, were even born." Studying her intently he smiled; his eyes shone bleakly, and then, to her horror, the eyes began to migrate. Faster and faster they moved toward the center of the forehead; there they joined, fused, became one vast compound eye whose many lenses reflected her own image back at her, as in a thousand warped black mirrors, again and again.

Within the bun of cloth slightly beneath her ribcase, Freya Holm compressed the activating assembly of the defense-gun.

"Shloonk," Theodoric Ferry wheezed. His single eye rattled and spun as his body rocked back and forth; then, without warning, the great dark orb popped from his bulging forehead and hung dangling from a spring of steel. At the same time his entire head burst; screaming, Freya ducked as bits of gears, rods, wiring, components of power systems, cogs, amplifying surge-gates, all failing to remain within the shattered structure, bounced here and there in the flapple. The two THL agents ducked, grunted and then retreated as the rain of hot, destroyed metal pieces condensed about them both. She, too, reflexively drew back; staring, she saw a mainshaft and an intricate cog mechanism . . . like a clock, she thought dazedly. He's *not* a deformed, non-Terran water-creature; he's a mechanical assembly— I don't understand. She shut her eyes, moaned in despair, the flapple, now, had faded momentarily into obscurity, so intense was the hailstorm of metal and plastic parts from the bursting entity which had posed as Theodoric Ferry just a moment before—had posed, more accurately, as an aquatic horror masquerading *as* Theodoric Ferry.

"One of those damn simulacrums," the THL agent who was not Frank said in disgust.

" 'Simulacra,' " Frank corrected, his teeth grinding in outrage as a major transformer from the power-supply struck him on the temple and sent him flailing backward, off-balance; he fell against the wall of the flapple, groaned and then slid to a sitting position, where he remained, his eyes empty. The other THL agent, arms windmilling, fought his way through the still-exploding debris of the simulacrum toward Freya; his fingers groped for her ineffectually— and then he gave up, abandoned whatever he had had in his mind; turning, he hunched forward, lurched blindly off, in the general direction of the entrance hatch of the flapple. And then, with a clatter, disappeared. She remained with the disintegrating simulacrum and the unconscious THL agent Frank; the only sound was the metallic thump of components as they continued to pelt against the walls and floor of the flapple.

Good lord, she thought indistinctly, her mind in a state of almost deranged confusion. That book they showed me—*it was wrong!* Or else I failed to read far enough . . .

Desperately, she searched about in the rubbish-heaped flapple for the book; then all at once she remembered what had happened to it. The smaller THL agent had escaped with it locked in a brief-case chained to his wrist; the book had, so to speak, departed with him—in any case, both the agent and the volume were gone, now. So she would never know what had come next in the printed text; had it corrected its own evident misperception, as she had hers? Or—did the text of Dr. Bloode's book continue on, manfully declaring that Theodoric Ferry was an aquatic—what was the term it—and she—had used? Mazdast; that was it. She wondered, now, precisely what it meant; until she had read the word in the text she had never before encountered it. But there was something else. Something at the rim of consciousness, crowding forward, attempting to enter her mind; it could not be thrust back, odious as it was.

The Clock. That term, referring to one of the so-called para-worlds. Had this been—The Clock? And if so—

Then the original encounter between the black space-pilot, Rachmael ben Applebaum and the sim of Theodoric Ferry—that, back in the Sol system, had been a manifestation—not a Ferry-simulacrum at all—but, like this, of the paraworld called The Clock.

The delusional worlds somehow active here at Whale's Mouth had already spread to and penetrated Terra. It had already been experienced—experienced, yes; but not recognized.

She shuddered.

FOURTEEN

For more than thirty minutes nothing had emanated from the anti-prolepsis chamber of Gregory Gloch, and by now Sepp von Einem realized with full acuity that something dreadful had gone wrong.

Taking a calculated risk—Gloch in the past had ranted against this as an illegal invasion of his privacy, of his very psyche, in fact—Dr. von Einem clicked to *on* the audio monitoring mechanism which tapped the input circuit of the chamber. Shortly, he found himself receiving via a three-inch speaker mounted on the wall the same signals which passed to his protégé.

The first rush of impulses almost unhinged him.

"Pun, there," a jovial masculine—somewhat elderly—voice was in the process of intoning. "Life of you, life lived over . . . see?" It then chuckled loudly in a comical but distinctly vulgar fashion. "Heh-heh," it gloated. "How you doin', ol' boy, Gloch there, ol' fella?"

"Fine," Greg Gloch's retort came. But to von Einem it had a very distinctive weak quality about it, a vivid loss of surgency which chilled him deeply, caused him to hang on each following word of the exchange. Who was this person addressing Gloch? he asked himself. And got no response; the voice was new to him. And yet—

At the same time it acutely resembled a voice he knew. A voice he could however not identify, to save his life. He had the intuition, then, that this voice had deliberately been disguised; he would need a video breakdown by which to identify it. And that would take time, precious time which no one, at this moment in the struggle over Whale's Mouth, could afford to spare—least of all he.

Pressing a command key, von Einem said, "Emergency call. I want an immediate trace put on the audio signal reaching Herr Gloch. Notify me of the origin-point, then if you must, obtain a video pic of the voice-pattern and inform me of the caller's identity." He paused, pondering; it was, to say the least, a decision of gravity which he now entertained. "Once you have the locus detailed," he said slowly, "run a homotropic foil along the line. We can obtain the voice-indent afterwards."

The microscopic feedback circuit within his ear spluttered, "Herr Doktor—you mean take out the caller *before* identification? *Das ist gar unmöglich—gar!*"

Von Einem rasped, "It is distinctly not out of the question; in fact it is essential." For, underneath, he had an intuition as to who the disguised voice consisted of. It could only be one person.

Jaimé Weiss. The *enfant terrible* of the UN, probably operating in conjunction with his brother-in-law, the 'wash psychiatrist Lupov. Thinking that, von Einem felt nausea rise like a gray tide within him. Them, he reflected bitingly; the worst pair extant. Probably in orbit in a sealed sat at Whale's Mouth . . . transmitting either at faster-than-light directly to our system or worse still: feeding their lines during routine traffic through one of our town Telpor stations.

Savagely, he said to the technician brought into contact by means of the command key at his disposal, "There is an exceedingly meager latitude for the performance of successful action against this party, mein Herr; or don't you believe me? You suppose I am mistaken? I *know* who has infiltrated the anti-prolepsis tank of poor Herr Gloch; *mach' snell!*" And you had damn well better be successful, he said to himself as he released his command key and walked moodily to the chamber to look directly at his protégé, to discern Gloch's difficulty with his own eyes.

I wonder, he thought to himself as he watched the youth's face twist with discomfort, if I shouldn't obliterate the alien audio signal that's so successfully jamming the orderly process within the chamber. Or at least reroute it so that I receive it but Gloch does not.

However, it appeared to von Einem that the interloping audio transmission had already done its job; Greg Gloch's face was a mass of confusion and turbulence. Whatever ideas Gloch had entertained for a counter-weapon against Bertold had long since evaporated. *Zum Teufel,* von Einem said to himself in a near-frenzied spasm of disappointment—as well as an ever-expanding sense that the *Augenblick,* the essential instant, had somehow managed to elude him. Somehow? Again he listened to the disruptive voice plaguing Gregory Gloch. Here it was; this was the malefactionary disturbance. This: Jaimé Weiss himself, wherever in the galaxy he had now located himself and his fawning sycophantic retinue.

Can Gloch hear me now? he wondered. Can he hear anything beyond that damned voice?

As an experiment, he cautiously addressed Gloch—by means of the customary time-rephasing constructs built into the chamber. "Greg! *Kannst hör'?*" He listened, waited; after a time he heard his words reeled off to the man within the chamber at appropriate veloc-ity. Then the lips of the man moved, and then, to his relief, a sentence by Gloch was spewed out by the transmitter of the chamber.

"Oh. Yes, Herr von Einem." The voice had a vague quality about it, a preoccupation; Greg Gloch heard, but did not really seem able to focus his faculties. "I was . . . um . . . daydreaming or . . . some darn thing. Ummp!" Gloch noisily cleared his throat. "What, ah, can I, eh, do for you, sir? Um?"

"Who's that constantly addressing you, Greg? That irritating voice which impedes every attempt you make to perform your assigned tasks?"

"Oh. Well. I believe—" For almost an entire minute Gloch remained silent; then, at last, like a rewound toy, he managed to continue. "Seems to me he identified himself as Charley Falks' little boy Martha. Yes; I'm certain of it. Ol' Charley Falks' little boy—"

"Das kann nicht sein," von Einem snarled. "It simply can't be! No one's little boy is named Martha; *das weis' Ich ja."* He lapsed into brooding, introverted contemplation, then. A conspiracy, he decided. And one that's working. Our only recourse is the homotropic weapon released to follow the carrier wave of this deceptive trans-mission back to its source; I hope it is already in motion.

Grimly, he strode back to the command key, punched it down.

"Yes, Herr Doktor."

"The homotropic foil; has it—"

"On its way, sir," the technician informed him brightly. "As you instructed; released before indent." The technician added in a half-aside, "I do hope, sir, that it's not someone you have positive inclinations toward."

"It can't be," von Einem said, and released the key with an abiding sense of satisfaction. But then an alternate—and not so pleasing—thought came to him. The homotropic foil, until it reached its target, could act as a dead giveaway regarding its *own* origin. If the proper monitoring equipment were put in use—or already had been put in functioning condition—then the foil would accomplish a handy, quick task for the enemy: it would tell him—or both of them—where the disruptive signal entitling itself "ol' Charley Falks' little boy Martha" et cetera had gone . . . gone and accomplished vast damage in respect to von Einem and THL in general.

I wish Herr Ferry were immediately here, von Einem growled to himself gloomily; he picked at a poison-impregnated false tooth mounted in his upper left molars, wondering if the time might come when he would be required by obtaining conditions to do away with himself.

But Theodoric Ferry busied himself at this moment preparing for a long-projected trip via Telpor to Whale's Mouth. A most important journey, too, inasmuch as there he would complete the formulation of contemplated final schemes: this was the moment in which the vise of history would clamp shut on the unmen such as Rachmael ben Applebaum and his doxie Miss Holm—not to mention Herr Glazer-Holliday, who might in fact well already be now dead . . . or however it was phrased.

"There," von Einem mused, "is a no-good individual, that Matson person, that slobbering hyphenater." His disgust—and satisfaction at either the already-accomplished or proposed taking-out of Glazer-Holliday—knew no limit; both emotions expanded like a warm, unclouded sun.

On the other hand, what if Weiss and Lupov managed to obtain the reverse trace on the homotropic foil now dispatched themwards? An unease-manufacturing thought, and one which he still did not enjoy. Nor would he until the manifold success of the foil had been proclaimed.

He could do nothing but wait. And meanwhile, hope that Herr Ferry's journey to Whale's Mouth would accomplish all that it entertained. Because the import of that sally remained uncommonly vast—to say the least.

In his ear the monitor covering aud transmissions entering Gloch's anti-prolepsis tank whined, "Say, you know? An interesting sort of game showed up among us kids the other day; might interest you. Thingisms, it's called. Ever hear of it?"

"No," Gloch answered, briefly; his retort, too, reached the listening Herr von Einem.

"Works like this. I'll give you this example; then maybe you can think up a few of your own. Get this: 'The hopes of the woolen industry are threadbare.' Haw haw haw! You get it? Woolen, threadbare—see?"

"Umm," Gloch said irritably.

"And now, little ol' Greg," the voice intoned, "how 'bout a Thingism from you'all? Eh?"

"Keerist," Gloch protested, and then was silent. Obviously he had directed his thoughts along the requested direction.

This must stop, von Einem realized. And soon.

Or Theo Ferry's trip to Whale's Mouth is in jeopardy.

But why—he did not know; it was an unconscious insight, nothing more. As yet. Even so, however, he appreciated its certitude: beyond any doubt his appraisal of the danger surging over them all was accurate.

To the exceedingly well-groomed young receptionist wearing the topless formal dress, a gaggle of dark red Star of Holland roses entwined in her heavy, attractive blonde hair, Theodoric Ferry said brusquely,

"You know who I am, miss. Also, you know that by UN law this Telpor station is inoperative; however, we know better, do we not?" He kept his eyes fixed on her; nothing could be permitted to go wrong. Not at this late date, with each side fully committed to the fracas on the far side of the teleportation gates. Neither he nor the UN had much left to offer; he was aware of this, and he hoped that his analysis of the UN's resources was not inadequate.

Anyhow—no other direction lay ahead except that of continuation of this, his original program. He could scarcely withdraw now; it would be an immediate undoing of everything so far accomplished.

"Yes, Mr. Ferry," the attractive, full-breasted—with enlarged gaily lit pasties—young woman responded. "But to my knowledge there's no cause for alarm. Why don't you seat yourself and allow the sim-attendant to pour you a warm cup of catnip tea?"

"Thank you," Ferry said, and made his way to a soft, comfortable style of sofa at the far end of the station's waiting room.

As he sipped the invigorating tea (actually a Martian import with stimulant properties, not to mention aphrodisiac) Theo Ferry unwillingly made out the complex series of required forms, wondering sullenly to himself why it was that he, even he!, had to do so . . . after all, he owned the entire plant, lock, stock et al. Nevertheless he followed protocol; possibly it had a purpose, and in any case he would be traveling, as usual, under a code name—he had been called "Mr. Ferry" for the last time. Anyhow for a while.

"Your shots, Mr. Hennen." A THL nurse, middle-aged and severe, stood nearby with ugly needles poised. "Kindly remove your outer garments, please. And put away that cup of insipid catnip tea." Obviously she did not recognize him; she, a typical bureaucrat, had become engrossed in the cover projected by the filled-out forms. He felt amiable, realizing this. A good omen, he said to himself.

Presently he lay unclothed, feeling conspicuous, now, while three owlish Telpor technicians puttered about.

"Mr. Mike Hennen, Herr," one of the technicians informed him with a heavy German accent, "please if you will reduce your gaze not to notice the hostile field-emanations; there is a severe retinal risk. Understand?"

"Yes, yes," he answered angrily.

The ram-head of energy that tore him into shreds obliterated any sense of indignation that he might have felt at being treated as one more common mortal; back and forth it surged, making him shrill with pain—it could not be called attractive, the process of teleportation; he gritted his teeth, cursed, spat, waited for the field to diminish . . . and hated each moment that the force held him. Hardly worth it, he said to himself in a mixture of suffering and outrage. And then—

The terminal surge dwindled and he succeeded in opening his left eye. He blinked. Strained to see.

All three Telpor technicians had vanished. He lay now in a vastly smaller chamber. A pretty girl, wearing a pale blue transparent smock, busied herself strolling back and forth past the entrance-doorway, a hulking hand-weapon at ready. Patrolling in case of UN seizure or attempted seizure, he understood. And sat up, grunting.

"Good morning!" the girl said blithely, glancing at him with an expression of amusement. "Your clothing, Mr. Hennen, can be found in one of our little metal baskets; in your case, marked 136552. Now, if you should by any chance find yourself becoming unsteady—"

"Okay," he said roughly. "Help me to my goddamn feet."

A moment later, in a side alcove, he had dressed; he gathered together his portable possessions, examined his reflection in a rather dim-with-dust mirror, then strolled out, feeling much better, to confront the prowling girl in the lacy smock.

"What's a good hotel?" he demanded—as if he did not know.

But the pose of being an ordinary neocolonist had to be maintained, even toward this loyal employee.

"The Simpy Cat," the girl answered; she now studied him intently. "I think I've seen you before," she decided. "Mr. Hennen. Hmm. No, the name is new to me. An odd name; is it Irish?"

"Who knows," he muttered as he strode toward the door. No time for chitchat, not even with a girl so pretty. Another time, perhaps . . .

"Watch out for Lies, Incorporated police, Mr. Hennen!" the girl called after him. "They're everywhere. And the fighting—it's really getting awful. Are you armed?"

"No." He paused reluctantly at the door. More details.

"THL," the girl informed him, "would be glad to sell you a small but highly useful weapon which—"

"Nuts to that," Ferry said, and plunged on outdoors, onto the dark sidewalk.

Shapes, colorless, vast and swift-moving, sailed in every layer of this world. Rooted, he gaped at the new ghastly transformation of the colony which he knew so well. The war; he remembered, then, with a jolt. Well, so it would be for a while. But, startled, he had difficulty once more orienting himself. Good god, how long would *this* last? He walked a few steps, still attempting to adjust, still finding it impossible; he seemed to sway in an alien sea, a life unanticipated by the environment; he was as strange to it as it to him.

"Yes sir!" a mechanical voice said. "Reading material to banish boredom. Newspaper or paperback book, sir?" The robot 'pape vendor coasted eagerly in his direction; with dismay he observed that its metal body had become corroded and pitted from the discharge of nearby anti-personnel weapons' fire.

"No," he said rapidly. "This damn war, here—"

"The latest 'pape will explain it entirely, sir," the vendor said in a loud braying voice as it pursued him; he peered about hopefully for a flapple-for-hire, saw none, felt keen nervousness: out here on the pavement he remained singularly exposed.

And in my own damn colony planet's own main hub, he said to himself with aggrieved indignation. Can't walk my own streets with impunity; have to put on a cammed identity—make it appear I'm some nitwit nonentity named Mike Hennen or whatever . . . he had already virtually lost contact with his false identity, by now, and the loss frankly pleased him. Damn it, he said to himself, I'm the one and only—

At that moment he caught sight of the single main item which the 'pape vendor had to offer. *The True and Complete Economic and Political History of Newcolonizedland,* he read. By who? Dr. Bloode. Strange, he thought. I haven't run across that before, and yet I'm in and out of this place all the time.

"I perceive your scrutiny of this remarkable text which I have for sale," the vendor declared. "This edition, the eighteenth, is exceptionally up-to-date, sir; possibly you'd like to glance through it. No charge for that." It whipped its copy of the huge book in his direction; reflexively, he accepted it, opened it at random, feeling restless and set-upon but not knowing precisely how to escape the 'pape vendor.

And, before his eyes, a passage dealing with him; his own name leaped up to stun him, to hold and transmute his faculties of attention.

"You, too," the 'pape vendor announced, "can play a vital role in the development of this fine virgin colonial world with its near-infinite promise of cultural and spiritual reward. In fact, it is a distinct possibility that you are already mentioned; why not consult the index and thereby scout out your own name? Take a chance, Mr.—"

"Hennen," he murmured. "Or Hendren; whichever it is." Automatically obeying the firm promptings of the vendor he turned to the index, glanced up and down the H's, then realized with a start that he had already been doing exactly that: reading about himself, but under his real name. With a grunt of irritation he swept the useless pages aside, sought his actual, correct name in the index.

After the entry Ferry, Theodoric, he found virtually unending citations; the page he had formerly been reading consisted of but one out of many.

On impulse he chose the first entry, that with the lowest page number.

Early in the morning Theodoric Ferry, chief of the vast economic and political entity Trails of Hoffman Limited, got out of bed, put on his clothes and walked into the living room.

Damned dull stuff, he decided in bewilderment. Is this book full of *everything* about me? Even the most trivial details? For some strange and obscure reason, this rubbed him the wrong way; once more he sought the index and this time selected a much later entry.

That early evening when Theo Ferry entered the Telpor station under the false code-indent, that of one Mike Hennen, he little glimpsed the fateful events which would in only a short time transpire in his already baroque and twisted

"For godsake," he complained hoarsely. They already knew; already had hold of his cover name—in fact had had time to print it up and run off this weird book concerning him. Slander! "Listen," he said severely to the alert 'pape vendor, "my private life is my own business; there's no valid reason in the galaxy why my doings should be listed here." I ought to bust this outfit, he decided. Whoever these people are who put together this miserable book. Eighteenth edition? Good lord, he realized; it must have to lack this entry if for no other reason than that I just may be lacking some of these entries about me. In fact it would have to lack this entry if for no other reason than that I just within the last day or so hit on my name-cover.

"One poscred, sir," the vendor said politely. "And the book becomes yours to keep."

Gruffly, he handed over the money; the vendor, pleased, wheeled off into the clouds of debris created by the warfare taking place a few blocks off. The book carefully gripped, Theo Ferry sprinted surefootedly for the security of a nearby semi-ruined housing structure;

there, crouched down among the fragmented blocks of building-plastic, he once more resumed his intent reading. Fully absorbed in the peculiar text he became totally oblivious to the noises and movements around him; all that existed for him now was the printed page held motionless before his intense scrutiny.

I'm damn near the main character in this tract, he realized. Myself, Matson, that Rachmael ben Applebaum, this girl named Freya something and of course Lupov—naturally Lupov. On impulse he looked up a citation regarding Dr. Lupov; a moment later he found himself engrossed in that particular section of the text, even though admittedly it did not deal with himself at all.

Peering tautly into the small vid screen, Dr. Lupov said to the sharp-featured young man beside him, "Now, is the time, Jaimé. Either Theo Ferry examines the Bloode text or else he never does. If he turns to page one-forty-nine, then we have a real chance of—"

"He won't," Jaimé Weiss said fatalistically. "The chances are against it. In my opinion he must somehow be maneuvered very clearly and directly into turning to that one particular page; somehow an instrument or method must be employed which will first of all provide him with that page number out of all possible page numbers, and, when that's done, somehow his curiosity must

Hands shaking, Theo Ferry leafed through the book to page one hundred and forty-nine. And, compulsively, unblinkingly, studied the text before him.

With a snort of exultation, Jaimé Weiss said, "*He did it.* Dr. Lupov—I was absolutely right." Gleefully, he slapped at the series of meters, switches and dials before the two of them. But of course the ploy had succeeded because of the 'wash psychiatrist's accurate diagnosis of all the passive factors constellating in Theo Ferry's psyche. Inability to resist danger . . . the suggestion that it constituted a hazard, his turning to that one page: the very notion that an extreme risk was involved had caused Ferry to thumb frantically in that direction.

He had gone unresistingly to that page—and he would not be coming back out.

"Sir," one of Lupov's assistants said suddenly, startling both Weiss and the psychiatrist, "we've just picked up something deadly on the scope. A detonation-foil tropic to both of you has passed through the Telpor gate that we made use of to reach Greg Gloch in his chamber." The man's face shone pale and damp with fright.

Jaimé Weiss and Dr. Lupov looked at each other wordlessly.

"I would say," Lupov said presently, his voice shaking, "that everything now depends on how rapidly the foil moves, how accurate it is, and—" He gestured convulsively at the microscreen before them, "—and how long it takes Mr. Ferry to succumb to the 'wash instructions on the page."

"How long," Jaimé said carefully, "would you estimate it would take for a man of Ferry's caliber to succumb?"

After briefly calculating, Lupov said huskily, "At least an hour."

"Too long," Jaimé said.

Lupov, woodenly, nodded slowly, up and down.

"If the foil reaches us first," Jaimé said then, "and takes both of us out, will Ferry's pattern be altered?" What a waste, he thought; what a dreadful, impossible waste, if not. Everything we set up: the pseudo-worlds, the fake class of "weevils," everything—with no result. And to be so close, so incredibly close! Again he turned his attention to the small screen; he deliberately forgot everything else. Why not? he asked himself bitterly. After all, there was nothing they could do, now that the defense-foil from von Einem's lab had passed through the gate and had come here to Fomalhaut IX.

"I can't predict," Lupov said, half to himself in a drab mutter, "what Ferry will do, if you and I are—"

The back of the bunker burst in a shower of murdering white and green sparks. Jaimé Weiss shut his eyes.

Studying the page before him, Theo Ferry, engrossed, failed to hear the buzzer at his neck-com the first time. At last, however, he became aware of it, grasped the fact that von Einem was attempting to reach him.

"Yes," he said brusquely. "What is it, Sepp?"

"You are in extreme danger," the distant faded voice came to him, a tinny, gnat-like dancing whisper from many light-years off. "Throw away that thing you have, whatever it is; it's a Lupov invention—the 'wash technique structured for you, sir! Hurry!"

With unbelievable effort Theo Ferry managed to close the book. The page of print vanished . . . and as soon as it did so he felt strength return to his arms; volition flooded back and he at once jumped up, dropping the book. It tumbled wildly to the ground, pages fluttering; Theo Ferry at once jumped on it, ground his heel into the thing—hideously, it emitted a shrill living cry, and then became silent.

Alive, he thought. An alien life-form; no wonder it could deal with my recent activities; the page actually contained nothing—it was no book at all, only one of those awful Ganymede life-mirrors that Lupov was supposed to use. That entity that reflects back to you your own thoughts. Ugh. He winced with aversion. And it almost got me, he said to himself. Close.

"The report back by the foil," von Einem's far-off voice came to him, "indicates that Lupov and Weiss built up over a long period of time, perhaps even years, an intricate structure of subworlds of a hypnotic, delusional type, to trap you when you made your crucial trip to Whale's Mouth. Had they fully concentrated on that and left Greg Gloch alone they might very well have been successful. This way—"

"Did you get Weiss and Lupov?" he demanded.

Von Einem said, "Yes. As near as I can determine. I'm still waiting for the certified results, but it seems hopeful. If I may explain about these mutually exclusive delusional worlds—"

"Forget it," Ferry broke in harshly. "I have to get out of here." If they could come this close, then he was hardly safe, even now; they had spotted him, prepared for him—Lupov and Weiss might be gone, but that still left others. Rachmael ben Applebaum, he thought. We didn't get you, I suppose. And you have done us a good deal of harm already, harm that we know of. Theoretically you could do much, much more.

Except, he thought as he groped in his clothing for the variety of miniaturized weapons he knew were there, *we're not going to let you.* Too much is at stake; too many lives are involved. You will not succeed, even if you have outlasted Mat Glazer-Holliday, Lupov and Weiss and possibly even that Freya girl, the one who was Mat's mistress and now is yours—you still don't stand a chance.

Thinly, he smiled. This part I will enjoy, he realized. My taking you out of action, ben Applebaum. For this I will operate out of my own ship, *Apteryx Nil.* When I'm finally there, I'll be safe. Even from you.

And you, he said to himself, have no place equal to it; even if the *Omphalos* were here at Whale's Mouth it would not be enough.

Nothing, ben Applebaum, he thought harshly, will be enough. Not when I've reached *Apteryx Nil.* As I enter it your tiny life fades out.

Forever.

FIFTEEN

To Freya Holm the flapple repeated in high-pitched anxiety, "Sir or madam, you must evacuate at once; all living humans must leave me, as my meta-battery is about to deteriorate. Due to various punctures in my hull, which punctures having been caused by the demolition of the simulacrum of Mr. Ferry, or rather because of which—in any case I am no longer able to maintain homeostasis, or whatever the phrase is. Please, sir or madam; do heed me: your life, sir or madam, is being risked each moment!"

Furiously, Freya grated, "And go where, once I leave here?"

"Down to the surface of the planet," the flapple said, in a tone of voice suggesting ultimate mechanical smugness; as far as the flapple was concerned it had solved everything.

"Jump?" she demanded. "Two thousand feet?"

"Well, I suppose your point is well-taken," the flapple said in a disgruntled tone; it evidently was displeased to have its solution dealt with so readily. "But the enormous inter-plan and -system ship which I am now attached to; why not hie yourself there? Or however the expression goes."

"It's Ferry's!"

"Ferry's, Schmerry's," the flapple said. "This way you'll perish when I do. You want THAT?"

"All right," she snarled, and made her way unsteadily toward the entrance hatch of the flapple, the link between it and the huge ship blowing its ceaseless wisps of fuel vapor, obviously ready to take off at an instant's command.

"My meta-battery has nowwwaaaa fooooof," the flapple intoned hazily; its expiration had accelerated by leaps and bounds.

"Goodbye," Freya said, and passed out through the entrance hatch, cautiously following the shorter of the two THL agents.

Behind her the flapple murmured in its dim fashion, "Tttturnnn uppp yrrrr hearing aaaaaaiddddd, missssszzzz." And drifted into oblivion.

Good riddance, she decided.

A moment later she had entered the great ship—Theo Ferry's post from which he—obviously—operated when on Fomalhaut IX.

"Kill her," a voice said.

She ducked. A laser beam cut past her head; instantly she rolled, spun to one side, thinking, They did it to Mat, but not to me; they can't do it to me. A second last try for us, she thought desperately; if Rachmael can do anything. I can't. "Ferry," she gasped. "Please!"

The prayer proved worthless. Four THL agents, in military brown, deployed strategically at several compass points of the ship's central cabin, aimed at her emotionlessly, while at the controls, his face a dull mask of almost indifferent concentration, sat Theodoric Ferry. And, she realized, this was the man himself; this did not constitute a simulacrum.

"Do you know," Ferry said to her quietly, "where Rachmael ben Applebaum is at this moment?"

"No," she gasped. Truthfully.

At that Ferry nodded toward the four THL agents; the man to his immediate right caustically grimaced—and squeezed the button that controlled his laser tube.

I made a mistake, Freya realized. The flapple tricked me; it deliberately made me come here—it's a THL flapple and it knew who I was and what I wanted to do. It was my enemy . . . and I failed to identify it as such—in time. Now it was too late, far too late.

The laser beam came once more, narrow and alit with strength; it scraped past her, created its own escape-hole in the wall behind her.

"I'm very much interested in this Rachmael individual," Ferry informed her. "If you could possibly recall where he might be—"

"I told you," she said in a tight, almost inaudible whisper. "I have no idea."

Again Ferry nodded at his employee, an expression of resignation on his face. The laser beam howled, then, in Freya's direction.

Once more she prayed. And this time not to Theodoric Ferry.

The eye-eater said pleasantly, "Mr. ben Applebaum, reach inside me and you will find a slightly different edition of Dr. Bloode's Text. A copy of the twentieth edition, which I ingested some time ago . . . but as far as I can determine, not already dissolved by my gastric juices." The idea seemed to amuse it; the lower portion of its face split apart in a peal of excruciatingly penetrating laughter.

"You're serious?" Rachmael said, feeling disorganized. And yet the eye-eater was correct; if it did possess a later edition of the text he most certainly had reason to seek it out—wherever it lay, even within the body of the offensive eye-eater.

"Look, look," the eye-eater exclaimed; it held in one of its longer pseudopodia several remaining unchewed eyes, and these it had placed close to its stomach in order to see properly. "Yes, it's still in there—and you can have it, free! No, but seriously, folks, the twentieth edition is worth a lot more to a collector than the seventeenth; get it while the getting's good or this free money-back offer expires forever."

After a pause Rachmael shut his eyes and reached his hand gropingly into the midsection of the cephalopodic life-form.

"Fine, fine," the eye-eater chortled. "That feels really cool, as the ancients said. Got hold of it yet? Reach deeper, and don't mind if the digestive juices destroy your sleeve; that's show biz, or whatever it was they formerly said. Tee-hee!"

His fingers touched something firm within the gelatinous, oozing mass. The edge of the book? Or—something else. It felt very much as if—incredibly—it consisted of the crisp, starched, lower edge of a woman's bra.

"For god's sake!" a female voice declared furiously. And at the same instant a small but wildly intent hand grabbed his, forced it back toward him.

Immediately he opened his eyes. The eye-eater glowered at him in indignation. But—it had changed. From it long strands of women's hair grew; the eye-eater had a distinctly female appearance. Even its pawful of eyes had altered; they now appeared elongated, graceful, with heavy lashes. A woman's eyes, he realized with a thrill of terror.

"Who are you?" he demanded, almost unable to speak; he jerked his hand back in revulsion and the pseudopodium released him.

The pseudopodia of the eye-eater, all of them, terminated in small, delicate hands. Like the hair and the eyes, distinctly female.

The eye-eater had become a woman. And, near the center of its body, it wore—ludicrously—the stiff white bra.

The eye-eater said, in a high-pitched voice, almost a squeal of indignation, "I'm Gretch Borbman, of course. And I frankly don't believe it's very funny to—do what you did just now." Breathing hotly, the eye-eater glowered even more darkly.

"I'm—sorry," he managed to say. "But I'm lost in damn para-world; it's not my fault. So don't condemn me."

"Which paraworld is it this time?" the eye-eater demanded. "The same one as before?"

He started to answer . . . and then noticed something which froze him into silence where he stood. Other eye-eaters had begun to appear, slowly undulating toward him and Gretch Borbman. Some had the distinct cast of masculinity; some obviously were, like Gretch, female.

The class. Assembling together in response to what Gretch had said.

"He attempted to reach inside me," the eye-eater calling itself Gretchen Borbman explained to the rest of them. "I wonder which paraworld that would indicate."

"Mr. ben Applebaum," one of the other eye-eaters, almost certainly Sheila Quam by the sound of her voice, said. "In view of what Miss Borbman says, I think it is virtually mandatory for me to declare a special emergency Computer Day; I would say that beyond a reasonable doubt this situation which you've created calls for it."

"True," the eye-eater named Gretch agreed; the others, to varying degrees, also nodded in unison. "Have his paraworld gestalt fed in so it can be examined and compared. Personally I don't think it's like *anyone* else's, but of course that's up to the computer to determine. Myself, I feel perfectly safe; I know that whatever he saw, or rather sees, bears absolutely no resemblance to anything *I* ever perceived."

"What did he do just now," an eye-eater which reminded him of Hank Szantho said, "that made you yip like that?"

The Gretch Borbman thing said in a low, sullen voice, "He attempted to diddle me."

"Well," the Hank Szantho eye-eater said mildly, "I don't see where that alone indicates anything; I might even attempt that myself, some day. Anyhow, as long as Sheila feels it's called for—"

"I've already got the forms ready," the one whom he had identified as Sheila Quam said. To Rachmael she said, "Here is 47-B; I've already signed it. Now, if you'll come with me—" She glanced toward the Gretchen Borbman eye-eater. "Miss Borbman already knows her paraworld . . . I hope her confidence is vindicated; I hope that what you perceive, Mr. ben Applebaum, is not congruent with hers."

"I hope so, too," the Gretchen Borbman thing agreed faintly.

"As I recall," the Sheila Quam eye-eating entity declared, "Mr. ben Applebaum's initial delusional experience, set off by the LSD dart, consisted of involvement with the garrison state. Do you remember clearly enough to voluntarily testify to that, Mr. ben Applebaum?"

"Yes," he said huskily. "And then the aquatic—"

"But before that," Sheila interrupted. "When you first crossed by Telpor. Before the dart—before the LSD."

Hazily, he said, "It's a blur to me, now." Reality, for him, had slipped and floundered too much; he could not be absolutely sure of the sequence of events. With a vast final effort he summoned his waning attention, focussed on his past—it seemed a billion light-years ago, and yet in actuality the experience with the garrison state had been reasonably recent. "It was before," he said, then. "I perceived the garrison state, the fighting; *then* a THL soldier shot me. So the experience with the garrison state came first; then, after the LSD, the aquatic nightmare-shape."

Hank Szantho said thoughtfully, "You may be interested to know, Mr. ben Applebaum, that you are not the first person among us to live with that hallucination—I refer to the prior one, that of the garrison state. If your delusional gestalt, when you present it to the computer, comes out on those lines, I can assure you that a true bi-personal view of a paraworld will have been established . . . and this, of course, is what we fear, as you well know. Do you want to see the garrison state world established as the authentic reality?" His voice lifted harshly. "Consider."

"The choice," Sheila Quam said, "is not his; it's mine. I therefore officially declare this late Wednesday afternoon and Computer Day, and I order Mr. ben Applebaum to accept this form I hold here, to fill it out, and then return it to me, as Control, to sign. You understand, Mr. ben Applebaum? Can you think clearly enough to follow what I'm saying?"

Reflexively, he accepted the form from her. "A pen?" he asked.

"A pen." Sheila Quam, plus all the other eye-eating quasi-forms, began to search about their bulb-like bodies—to no avail.

"Chrissake," Rachmael said irritably, and searched his own pockets. Not only to be compelled to fill out the 47-B form, but to come up with his own pencil—

In his pocket his fingers touched something: a flat, small tin. Puzzled, he lifted it out, examined it. The eye-eaters around him did so, as well. In particular the Gretchen Borbman one.

MORE FUN
AFTER DONE!

"How disgusting," Gretchen Borbman said. To the others she said, "A tin of Yucatán prophoz. The worst kind possible—fully automated, helium-battery powered, good for a five-year life span . . . is this what you had in mind, Mr. ben Applebaum, when you diddled me a moment ago?"

"No," he said. "I forgot I had these." Chilled, he thought, Have I had this all along? The cammed, hyperminned UN weapon: the personnel variation of the time-warping construct which constituted the major device in Horst Bertold's arsenal. Naturally he retained it; the effectiveness of the camouflage lay beyond dispute—and had now been tested and ratified in practice . . . it had even seemed to him, during the first moment of discovery, that this was exactly as it appeared to be: a box of prophoz and nothing more.

"Out of respect for decency and the women present here," the Hank Szantho eye-eater said, "I believe you should put that obnoxiously specific tin away, Mr. ben Applebaum; don't you, on second thought, agree?"

"I suppose so," he said. And opened the tin.

Acrid smoke billowed about him, stinging his nostrils. He halted, dropped into an instinctive crouch of self-defense. Matson saw gray barracks.

Beside him. Freya appeared. The air was cold; she shivered and he, too, quaked, drew against her, stared and stared at the barracks; he saw row after row of them, and—charged, twelve-foot-high wire fences with four strands of barbed wire at the top. And signs. The posted restrictive notices; he did not even need to read them.

Freya said, "Mat, have you ever heard of a town called Sparta?"

"'Sparta,'" he echoed, standing holding his two suitcases.

"Here." She released his fingers, set the suitcases down. A few people, drably dressed, slunk by, silently, carefully paying no attention to them. "I was wrong," Freya said. "And the message of course to you, the all-clear, was spurious. Mat, I thought—"

"You thought," he said, "it was going to be—ovens."

She said, with quiet calmness, tossing her heavy dark mane of hair back and raising her chin to meet his gaze, look at him face-to-face, "It's work camps. The Soviet, not the Third Reich, model. Forced labor."

"Doing what? Clearing the planet? But the original authentic monitoring satellites reported that—"

"They seem," she said, "to be forming the nucleus of an army. First starting everyone out in labor gangs. To get them accustomed to discipline. The young males go into basic training at once; the rest of us—we'll probably serve in *that*." She pointed and he saw the ramp of a subsurface structure; he saw the descent mechanism and he knew, remembered from his youth, what it meant, this pre-war configuration.

A multi-level autofac. On continuous schedule, hence not entirely homeo. For round-the-clock operations, machines would not do, could not survive. Only shifts, alternating, of humans, could keep the belts moving; they had learned that in '92.

"Your police vets," Freya said, "are too old for immediate induction; most of them. So they'll be assigned to barracks, as we will be. I have the number they gave you and the one they gave me."

"Different quarters? We're not even *together*?"

Freya said, "I also have the mandatory forms for us to fill out; we list all our skills. So we can be useful."

"I'm old," he said.

"Then, Freya said, "you'll have to die. Unless you can conjure up a skill."

"I have one skill." In the suitcase resting on the pavement beside him he had a transmitter which, small as it was, would send out a signal which, in six months, would reach Terra.

Bending, he brought out the key, turned the lock of the suitcase. All he had to do was open the suitcase, feed an inch of punched data-tape into the orifice of the transmitter's encoder; the rest was automatic. He switched the power on; every electronic item mimicked clothing, especially shoes; it appeared as if he had come to Whale's Mouth to walk his life away, and elegantly at that.

"Why?" he asked Freya as he programmed, with a tiny scholarly construct, the inch of tape. "An army for what?"

"I don't know, Mat. It's all Theodoric Ferry. I think Ferry is going to try to outspit the army on Terra that Horst Bertold commands. In the short time I've been here I've talked to a few people, but—they're so afraid. One man thought there'd been a non-humanoid sentient race found, and we're preparing to strike for its colony-planets; maybe after a while and we've been here—"

Matson peered up and said, "I've encoded the tape to read, *Garrison state. Sound out Bertold.* It'll go to our top pilot, Al Dosker, repeated over and over again, because at this distance the noise-factor—"

A laser beam removed the back of his head.

Freya shut her eyes.

A second beam from the laser rifle with the telescopic sight destroyed first one suitcase and then its companion. And then a shiny, spic-and-span young soldier walked up, leisurely, the rifle held loosely; he glanced at her, up and down, carnally but with no particular passion, then looked down at the dead man, at Matson. "We caught your conversation on an aud rec." He pointed, and Freya saw, then, on the overhang of the roof of the Telpor terminal building, a netlike interwoven mesh. "That man"—the soldier kicked—actually physically kicked with his toe—the corpse of Matson Glazer-Holliday—"said something about 'our top pilot.' You're an organization, then. Friends of a United People? That it?"

She said nothing; she was unable to.

"Come along, honey," the soldier said to her. "For your psych-interrogation. We held it off because you were kind enough—dumb enough—to inform us that your husband was following you. But we never—"

He died, because, by means of her "watch" she had released the low-velocity cephalotropic cyanide dart; it moved slowly, but still he had not been able to evade it; he batted at it, childishly, with his hand, not quite alarmed, not quite wise and frightened enough, and its tip penetrated a vein near his wrist. And death came as swiftly and soundlessly as it had for Matson. The soldier swiveled and unwound and unwound in his descent to the pavement, and Freya, then, turned and ran—

At a corner she went to the right, and, as she ran down a narrow, rubbish-heaped alley, reached into her cloak, touched the aud transmitter which sent out an all-points, planet-wide alarm signal-alert; every Lies, Incorporated employee here at Whale's Mouth would be picking it up, if this was not already apparent to him: if the alarm signal added anything to his knowledge, that which had probably come, crushingly, within the first five minutes here on this side—this one-way side—of the Telpor apparatuses. Well, anyhow she had done that; she had officially, through technical channels, alerted them, and that was all—*all* she could do.

She had no long-range inter-system transmitter as Matson had had; she could not send out a macrowave signal which would be picked up by Al Dosker at the Sol system six months hence. In fact none of the two thousand police agents of Lies, Incorporated did. But they had weapons. She was, she realized with dread and disbelief, automatically now in charge of those of the organization who survived; months ago Matson had set her up legally so that on his death she assumed his chair, and this was not private: this had been circulated, memo-wise, throughout the organization.

What could she tell the police agents who had gotten through—tell them, of course, that Matson was dead, but what would be of use to them? What, she asked herself, *can we do*?

Eighteen years, she thought; do we have to wait for the *Omphalos,* for Rachmael ben Applebaum to arrive and see? Because by then it won't matter. For us, anyhow; nor for this generation.

Two men ran toward her and one bleated, "Moon and cow," shrilly, his face contorted with fear.

"Jack Horner," she said numbly. "I don't know what to do," she said to them. "Matson is dead and his big transmitter is destroyed. They were waiting for him; I led them right to him. I'm sorry." She could not face the two field reps of the organization; she stared rigidly past them. "Even if we put our weapons into use," she said, "they can take all of us out."

"But we can do some damage," one of the two police, middle-aged, with that fat spare tire at his middle, a tough old vet of the '92 war, said.

His companion, clasping a valise, said, "Yes, we can try, Miss Holm. Send out that signal; you have it?"

"No," she said, but she was lying and they knew it. "It's hopeless," she said. "Let's try to pass as authentic emigrants. Let them draft us, put us into the barracks."

The seasoned, hard-eyed paunchy one said, "Miss Holm, when they get into the luggage, *they'll know.*" To his companion he said, "Bring it out."

Together, as she watched, the two experienced field reps of Lies, Incorporated assembled a small intricate weapon of a type she had never seen before; evidently it was from their advanced weapons archives.

To her the younger man said quietly, "Send the signal. For a fight. As soon as our people come through; keep the signal going so they'll pick it up as they emerge. We'll fight at this spot, not later, not when they have us cut down into individuals, one here, one there."

She. Touched. The. Signal-tab.

And then she said, quietly, "I'll try to get a message-unit back to Terra via Telpor. Maybe in the confusion—" Because there was going to be a lot of confusion as the Lies, Incorporated men emerged and immediately picked up the fracas-in-progress signal "—maybe it'll slip by."

"It won't," the hard-eyed old tomcat of a fighter said to her. He glanced at his companion. "But if we focus on a transmission station maybe we can take and keep control long enough to run a vid track through. Pass it back through the Telpor gate. Even if all two thous of us were to—" He turned to Freya. "Can you direct the reps to make it to this point?"

"I have no more microwave patterns," she said, this time truthfully. "Just those two."

"Okay, Miss Holm." The vet considered. "Vid transmissions through Telpor are accomplished over there." He pointed and she saw an isolated multi-story structure, windowless, with a guarded entrance; in the gray sun of midday she caught a glint of metal, or armed sentries. "You have the code for back home you can transmit?"

"Yes," she said. "One of fifty. Mat and I both had them; committed to memory. I could transmit it by aud in ten seconds."

"I want," the wary, half-crouching veteran policeman said, "a *vid* track of this." He swung his hand at the landscape. "Something that can be spliced into the central coaxial cable and run on TV. Not just that we know but that they know." *They.* The people back home—the innocents who lay beyond the one-way gate; forever, she thought, because eighteen years is, really, forever.

"What's the code?" the younger field rep asked her.

Freya said. "'Forgot to pack my Irish linen handkerchiefs. Please transmit via Telpor.'" She explained, "We, Mat and I, worked out all logical possibilities. This comes the closest. Sparta."

"Yep," the older vet said. "The warrior state. The troublemaker. Well, it is close geographically to Athens, although not quite close enough." To his companion he said, "Can we get in there and transmit the aud signal?" He picked up the weapon which they had assembled.

"Sure," his younger companion said, nodding.

The older man clicked the weapon on.

Freya saw, then, into the grave and screamed; she ran and as she ran, struggled to get away, she knew it for what it was: a refined form of nerve gas that—and then her coherent thoughts ceased and she simply ran.

The armed sentry-soldiers guarding the windowless building ran, too.

And, unaffected, their metabolisms insulated by preinjective antidotal hormones, the two field reps of Lies, Incorporated dogtrotted toward the windowless structure, and, as they trotted, brought out small, long-range laser pistols with telescopic sights.

That was her final view of them; at that point panic and flight swallowed her and it was only darkness. And a darkness into which people of all sorts—she glimpsed, felt, them dimly—ran alongside in company with her; she was not alone: the future radiated.

Mat, she thought. You will not have your police state here at Whale's Mouth, and I warned you; I told you. But, she thought, maybe now *they* won't either. If that encoded message can be put through. *If.*

And if, on the Terran side, there is someone smart enough to know what to do with it.

SIXTEEN

In his ship near the orbit of Pluto, Al Dosker received, routinely, the message transmitted from Freya Holm at Whale's Mouth to the New New York office of Lies, Incorporated.

FORGOT TO PACK MY IRISH LINEN HANDKERCHIEFS. PLEASE
TRANSMIT VIA TELPOR. FREYA.

He walked to the rear of the ship, leisurely, because at this distance from the sun everything seemed entropic, slowed down; it was as if, out here, there was a slower beat of the sidereal clock.

Opening the code box he ran his finger down the Fs. Then found the key. He then took the message and fed it directly into the computer which held the spools that comprised the contents of the box.

Out came a paper ribbon with typed words. He read them.

MILITARY DICTATORSHIP. BARRACKS LIFE ON SPARTAN BASIS.
PREPARATION FOR WAR AGAINST UNKNOWN FOE.

Dosker stood for a moment, then, taking the original encoded message, as handled by Vidphone Corporation, ran it through the computer once again. And, once again, he read the message in clear and once again it said what it had to say—could not be denied from saying. And there was no doubt, because Matson Glazer-Holliday himself had programmed the computer-box.

This, Dosker thought. Out of fifty possibilities ranging from the Elysium field to—hell.

Roughly, this lay halfway on the hell side. By a gross count of ten. It ranked about as bad as he had expected.

So, he thought, now we know.

We know . . . *and we can't validate it.*

The scrap of ribbon, the encoded message, was, incredible as it seemed, completely, utterly worthless.

Because, he asked himself, *whom do we take it to?*

Their own organization, Lies, Incorporated, had been truncated by Mat's action, by the sending of their best men to Whale's Mouth; all which remained was the staff of bureaucrats in New New York—and himself.

And, of course, Rachmael ben Applebaum out in 'tween space in the *Omphalos.* Busily learning Attic Greek.

Now, from the New New York office, a second message, encoded, arrived; this, too, he fed to the computer, more quickly, this time. It came out drearily and he read it with futile shame—shame because he had tried and failed to stop what Matson planned; he felt the moral weight on himself.

WE CANNOT HOLD OUT. VIVISECTION IN PROGRESS.

Can I help you? he wondered, suffering in his impotent rage. Goddamn you, Matson, he thought, you had to do it; you were greedy. And you took two thousand men and Freya Holm with you, to be slaughtered over there where we can't do anything because "we" consist of nothing.

However, he could perform one final act—his effort, not connected with the effort to save the multitude of Terran citizens who, within the following days, weeks, would be filing through Telpor gates to Whale's Mouth, but to save someone who deserved a reprieve from a self-imposed burden; a burden which these two encoded messages via Telpor and the Vidphone Corp had rendered obsolete.

Taking the risk that a UN monitor might pick up his signal, Al Dosker sent out a u.h.f. beamed radio signal to the *Omphalos* and Rachmael ben Applebaum.

When he raised the *Omphalos,* now at hyper-see velocity and beyond the Sol system, Dosker asked brutally, "How's the odes of Pindar coming?"

"Just simple fables so far," Rachmael's voice came, distantly, mixed with the background of static, of inter-system interference as the signal-gathering cone aboard Dosker's ship rotated, tried to gather the weak, far-distant impulse. "But you weren't supposed to contact me," Rachmael said, "unless—"

"Unless," Dosker said, "this happened. We have, at Lies, Incorporated, an encoding method that can't be broken. Because the data are not in what's transmitted. Listen carefully, Rachmael." And, amplified by his ship's transmitter, his words—he hoped— were reaching the *Omphalos;* a segment of his equipment recorded his words and broadcast them several times: a multiplication of the signal to counter, on a statistical basis, the high background; by utilizing the principle of repetition he expected to get his message through to Rachmael. "You know the joke about the prison inmate," Dosker said, "who stands up and yells, 'Three.' And everyone laughs."

"Yes," Rachmael said alertly. "Because 'three' refers to an entire multi-part joke. Which all the inmates know; they've been confined together so long."

"By that method," Dosker said, "our transmission from Whale's Mouth operated today. We have a binary computer as the decoder. Originally, we started out by flipping a coin for each letter of the alphabet. Tails made it zero or gate-shut; heads means one or gate-open. It's either zero or one; that's the binary computer's modus operandi. Then we invented fifty message-units which describe possible conditions on the other side; the messages were constructed in such a way that each consisted of a unique sequence of ones and zeros. I—" His voice came out ragged, hoarse. "I have just now received a message, which when reduced to the elements of the binary system consists of a sequence reading: 11101001100111 0101100000100110101001110000100111110100000111. There is nothing intrinsic in this binary sequence that can be decoded, because it simply acts as one of the fifty unique signals known to our box—here on my ship—and it trips one particular tape. But its length—it gives a spurious impression to cryptographers of an *intrinsic* message."

"And your tape—" Rachmael said, "that was tripped—"

"I'll paraphrase," Dosker said. "The operational word is— Sparta." He was silent then.

"A garrison state?" Rachmael's voice came.

"Yes."

"Against whom?"

"They didn't say. A second message came, but it added relatively little. Except that it came through in clear and it told us that they can't hold out. They're being decimated by the military, over there."

"And you're sure this is authentic data?" Rachmael asked.

"Only Freya Holm, Matson and I," Dosker said, "have the decode boxes into which the messages can be fed as a binary tripping-sequence. It came from Freya, evidently; anyhow she signed the first." He added, "They didn't even try to sign the second one."

"Well," Rachmael said, "then I will turn back. There's no point to my trip, now."

"That's up to you to decide." He waited, wondering what Rachmael ben Applebaum's decision would be; but, he thought, as you say, it really doesn't matter, because the real tragedy is twenty-four light-years away, and not the destruct, the taking-out, of Lies, Incorporated's two thousand best people, but—the forty million who've gone before. And the eighty million or more who will follow, since, though we have this knowledge on *this* side of the teleport gates, there's no means by which we can communicate it over the mass info media to the population—

He was thinking that when the UN pursuit ships, three of them like black sliding fish, closed noiselessly in on him, reached a.-to-a. missile range; their missiles fired, and Dosker's Lies, Incorporated ship was cut into fragments.

Stunned, passive, he floated in his self-contained suit with its own air, heat, water, transmitter, waste-disposal deposit box, squeeze-tubes of food . . . he drifted on and on, seemingly for eternity, thinking about vague and even happy things, about a planet of green forests and of women and the tinkling noise of get-togethers, and yet knowing dully that he could live only a short time like this, and wondering, too, if the UN had gotten the *Omphalos* as they had gotten him; obviously their vigilant switchboard of monitors had picked up his radio carrier-wave, but whether they had picked up Rachmael's too, which operated on another band . . . god, he thought, I hope not; I hope it's just me.

He was still hoping when the UN pursuit ship moved up beside him, sent out a robot-like construct which fished at him until it had with great care grappled him without puncturing his suit. Amazed, he thought, Why don't they just dig a little hole in the suit-fabric, let out the air and heat, let me float here and meanwhile die?

It bewildered him. And now a hatch of the UN pursuit ship was opening; he was reeled in, like an enmeshed quarry; the hatch slammed shut and he felt the artificial gravity which prevailed within the expensive, ultra-modern vessel; he lay prone and then, wearily, got to his feet, stood.

Facing him, a uniformed UN senior officer, armed, said, "Take off your suit. Your emergency suit. Understand?" He spoke with a heavy accent; Dosker saw, by his armband, that he was from the Nordic League.

Piece by piece, Dosker shed his emergency suit.

"You Goths," Dosker said, "seem to be running things." At the UN, anyhow. He wondered about Whale's Mouth.

The UN officer, still pointing the laser pistol at him, said, "Sit down. We are returning to Terra. *Nach* Terra; *versteh'n?*" Behind him a second UN employee, not armed, sat at the control console; the ship was on a high-velocity course directed toward the third planet and Dosker guessed that only an hour's travel lay ahead. "The Secretary General," the UN officer said, "has asked to speak to you personally. Meanwhile, compose yourself and wait. Would you like a magazine to read? We have *UN Back-peop Assist.* Or an entertain-spool to watch?"

"No," Dosker said, and sat staring straight ahead, blindly.

The UN officer said, "We tracked the *Omphalos* by her carrier-wave transmission, also. As we did your ship."

"Good bit," Dosker said sardonically.

"However, due to the distance involved, it will take several days to reach her."

Dosker said. "But you will, though."

"That is a certainty," the UN officer said, with his heavy Swedish accent, nodding. He had no doubts. Nor did Dosker.

The only issue was the time-factor. As the officer said, some few days; no more.

He stared ahead, sat, waited, as the high-velocity UN pursuit ship hurried toward Terra, New New York and Horst Bertold.

At the UN Headquarters in New New York he was given a thorough physical examination; the doctors and nurses attached one testing apparatus after another, checked their readings, located no grafted-in subdermal devices.

"You survived your ordeal amazingly well," the doctor in charge informed him, at last, as he was given his clothing and allowed once more to dress.

"And now what?" Dosker asked.

"The Secretary General is ready to see you," the doctor said briefly, marking his chart; he nodded his head toward a door.

Having dressed, Dosker walked step by step to the door, opened it.

"Please hurry it up," Horst Bertold said.

Shutting the door after him Dosker said, "Why?"

Seated at his large antique oak desk, the UN Secretary General glanced up; he was a heavy man, red-haired, with a pinched, elongated nose and almost colorless small lips. His features were small but his shoulders, his arms and his ribcage, bulged, as if from countless steam baths and from handball; his legs, his feet, showed the tonus of great childhood walking trips and miles of bike riding; this was an outdoor man, confined by his job to a desk, but longing for open spaces which did not now exist. A thoroughly healthy man, physically speaking, Dosker thought. Strange, he thought, and, in spite of himself, received a good impression.

"We picked up your radio communication with the *Omphalos*," Bertold said, his English perfect—in fact overly perfect; it had a tape-like quality, and probably it had been so learned. The impression here was not so good. "Thereby as you know we located both ships. We also understand that you are now the ranking executive of Lies, Incorporated, Miss Holm and Mr. Glazer-Holliday having crossed via Telpor—under cover names, of course—to Whale's Mouth."

Dosker shrugged, said nothing, imparted no free information; waited.

"However—" Horst Bertold tapped his pen against the top document on his desk, frowned. "This is a transcript, verbatim, of the interchange between you and the fanatic, Rachmael ben Applebaum. You initiated the radio exchange; *you* raised the *Omphalos*." Bertold glanced up and his blue, light eyes were sharp. "We have put our cryptographers on the sequence in code which you transmitted . . . the same which you previously received from the Vidphone

Corp. Intrinsically it means nothing. But in the wreckage of your ship we located your decoding computer, the intact box with its fifty tapes. We therefore matched the transmission and recorded binary sequence to the proper tape. And it was as you informed ben Applebaum."

"Did that surprise you?"

"Of course not," Bertold said swiftly. "Why should you deceive your own client? And at the risk—a risk which should not have been taken, as it so turned out—of revealing the location of your own vessel? Anyhow—" Bertold's voice sank to an introspective murmur. "We still were not satisfied. We therefore checked over our monitoring—"

"They're being wiped out, over there," Dosker said. "The two thousand field reps and Mat and Freya." His voice was toneless; he told this because he knew they would get it by a 'wash anyhow—they could get anything that was there, any memory, any motives, plans, projects; after all, his own organization, far smaller than the UN, could do so—had done so, over many years, and to many persons, by means of psychiatrists and their techniques.

Bertold said, "Trails of Hoffman Limited and Theodoric Ferry entirely control Newcolonizedland. The UN has no staff at Whale's Mouth. All we know is what we have received, as a courtesy, in aud and vid form. The info signals through the Telpors, over these years of colonization; our original monitoring satellites have been inoperative ever since THL auspical jurisdiction began."

There was silence and then Dosker said incredulously, "Then this is as much news to you as it is to—"

"We believed the fifteen years of aud and vid tapes; we saw no reason to check for ourselves. THL had volunteered to underwrite the colonization economically; they picked up the tab and we gave them the franchise *because they owned the Telpor patent and equipment.* Dr. von Einem's patents are possessed exclusively by THL; he had the legal right to so arrange that. And this—" Bertold picked up the top document from his desk, showed it to Dosker; it was a typed transcript, in its entirety, of his own conversation by radio with Rachmael. "This," Horst Bertold said, "is the result."

Dosker said, "Tell me what it means." Because, he thought, I don't know. I saw the original messages when they arrived; I understand the literal meaning of the words. But that's all.

The UN Secretary General said, "Out of the forty million colonists Ferry has conscripted an army and provided it with modern, sophisticated weapons. There is no 'non-humanoid race,' no non-Terran culture to encounter. Had there been our unmanned monitors would have detected them; by now we've touched every star system in our galaxy." He stared at Dosker. "It's us," he said. "The UN. That's what Theodoric Ferry is proposing to engage. When enough colonists have gone across. Then the up-to-then 'one-way' aspect of the teleportation equipment will suddenly reveal that the so-called Theorem One was false."

"Here?" Dosker said, then. "They'll reenter through their own Telpor outlets?"

"And take us on," Bertold said. "But not now. At this point they're not quite large enough." To himself he said, "At least so we estimate; we studied samples of groups who had emigrated; he can't have more than one million men actually under arms. But weapons—they may have u.s.h.: ultra sophisticated hardware; after all, they've got von Einem working for them."

Dosker said. "Where is von Einem? At Whale's Mouth?"

"We put a tail on him instantly." Bertold's fingers convulsed, crushed the document. "And proved already—*ganz genug!*—that we were correct. Von Einem has been all these years passing back and forth between Terra and Whale's Mouth; he has always used—they have always—operated the Telpor instruments for two-way travel—*so it's verified*, Dosker. Verified!" He stared at Dosker.

SEVENTEEN

When Rachmael ben Applebaum made out the dim, shadowy shapes of the UN pursuit ships as they approached to escort the *Omphalos* he knew that, whatever else was a cover, at least this much was true: the UN had traced him, had him and no doubt Dosker as well. So—he clicked on the microwave transmitter and raised, after an interval, the UN pursuit ships' local commanding officer.

"I'll believe you," Rachmael said, "when I hear Al Dosker say it." And when I look him over, he said to himself, for signs of a cephalic 'wash. But—why would they say it if it wasn't true? They had him; he and the *Omphalos,* detected, were now booty captured by the armed inter-system vessels of the great UN structure that spanned from planet to planet. Why make up a cover when there was no force to influence, no force able to provide any resistance?

God above, he thought. If it's true, then we can rely on Horst Bertold. We let our prejudices blind us . . . von Einem is German and Horst Bertold is German. But that does not any more prove they are working together, are secret collaborators, than, say, any two Ubangis or any two Jews. Adolf Hitler was not even a German . . . so our own thinking, he realized, has betrayed us. But— maybe now we can believe this. We can see. New Whole Germany has produced Dr. Sepp von Einem and Trails of Hoffman Limited . . . but it may also have produced something else when it created Horst Bertold.

We will see, Rachmael said to himself.

—Will wait until we are in New New York at UN Headquarters; face Horst Bertold and see the evidence of the assertion given by relayed macroradio signal.

The assertion that as of six a.m. New New York time this morning, UN troops had entered all retail outlets of Trails of Hoffman Limited, had seized the Telpor instruments—had, throughout Terra, arbitrarily and without warning of any kind, halted emigration to Whale's Mouth.

Twelve hours later Rachmael was led by a worried overworked female secretary into the UN Secretary General's office.

"The fanatic," Horst Bertold said, surveying him. "The idealist who sparked the hankering in Matson Glazer-Holliday that caused him to attempt his *coup d'etat* at Whale's Mouth." He turned to an aide. "Bring in the Telpor *Apparat.*"

Seconds later the familiar bipolar mechanism was noisily carted into the UN leader's office, along with a thoroughly unnerved-looking technician; minus his goggles he looked frightened and—small.

To the Telpor technician, Horst Bertold said, "Does this operate to permit teleportation two ways? Or only one? *Zwei oder ein? Antworte.*"

"Just outward, mein Herr Sekretär General," the technician quavered. "As Theorem One demonstrates, the recession of matter toward—"

Horst Bertold said to his aide, "Bring in our 'wash psychiatrists. Have them start with their EEG machines."

At that, the Telpor technician said, in a voice that broke with dismayed intimidation, *"Dass brauchen Sie nicht."*

"He's saying," Bertold said to Rachmael, "that he will cooperate; we don't need to employ our psychiatrists with him. So ask him." He jerked his head fiercely toward the cowering THL employee, this man in his white smock who had assisted in the emigration of literally millions of innocent human beings. "Ask him whether the Telpors work both ways."

The technician said, virtually inaudibly, *"Beide.* Both ways."

"There never was any 'Theorem One,'" Bertold snapped.

"Sie haben Recht," the technician agreed, nodding.

"Bring in Dosker," Bertold said to his overworked female secretary.

When Dosker appeared he said to Rachmael at once, "Freya is still alive over there." He indicated the Telpor instrument. "We've been in contact through this. But—" He hesitated.

Horst Bertold said, "Matson Glazer-Holliday is dead. They murdered him immediately. But nearly half of Lies, Incorporated's field personnel remain alive at various installations at Newcolonizedland, and we're beginning to supply them on a strategic basis. With weapons of types which they instantly need. And presently we will, at tactical spots, try commando teams; we can do a lot, I think, with our commando teams."

"What can I do?" Rachmael said. He felt overwhelming impotence; it was going on—had been going on—without him. While he journeyed—pointlessly—through 'tween, utterly empty, space.

This, the UN Secretary General seemed to read on his face. "You awakened Matson," he pointed out. "Which caused Matson to attempt his aborted coup. And the relayed message from Freya Holm to Dosker and then to the *Omphalos* informed us of the reality hidden under Theodoric Ferry's cover; a cover which we carry the moral stigma for accepting all these fifteen years. Everything based on the one fundamental hoax that teleportation could be achieved in only one direction . . ." He grimaced. "However, Trails of Hoffman Limited made an error as great as their cover when they did not impede your two thousand Lies, Incorporated veterans from crossing over." To Dosker he said, *"But even so, that would not have been enough.* However, with our tactical support—"

"It wasn't enough even at the start," Dosker said, "since they took out Matson right away." Half to himself, half to Rachmael, he said, "We never had a chance. Probably Matson never knew; he probably didn't even live that long. Anyhow, maybe you can retrieve Freya. Do you want to?"

Instantly Rachmael said, "Yes." To Horst Bertold he said, "Can I get equipment out of you? Defensive screens, if not offensive hardware? And I'll go alone." They would not, in the confusion, notice him, perhaps. Whale's Mouth had become a battlefield, and too many participants were involved; one lone man was a cypher, a mote; he would enter inconspicuously and if he found her at all it would be that way, as an entity too trifling to be considered by the vast warring entities. Within the context of the power struggle which had already truncated Lies, Incorporated; one contender had been abolished at the start, and now only the two monoliths existed in the field to slug it out, THL on one hand, the UN as its wise old antagonist, its roots of victory deep in the last century. The UN, he reflected, had a head start, that of fifty years.

But Trails of Hoffman Limited had the inventive genius of half-senile but still crafty old Dr. Sepp von Einem. And—the inventor of the Telpor instrument might not have ceased with that construct.

He wondered if Horst Bertold had considered this.

It didn't matter, because if von Einem had produced something else of equal—or of merely significant—value, *it would show up now.*

In the streets of Newcolonizedland, whatever Dr. Sepp von Einem and THL had over the years developed would be at this moment in full use. Because this was, for all participants, the Dies Irae, the Day of Wrath; now they were, like beasts in the field, being tried. And God help, Rachmael thought, the contender who was found wanting. Because out of this only one participant would live; there would be extended to the loser no partial, no half, life. Not in *this* arena.

He himself—he had only one task, as he saw it. That of getting Freya Holm out of Whale's Mouth and back safely to Terra.

The eighteen-year journey, the odyssey aboard the *Omphalos,* learning Attic Greek so that he could read the *Bacchae* in the original—that childlike fantasy had withered at the press of the iron glove of the reality-situation, the struggle going on—not eighteen years from now—but at this instant, at the Whale's Mouth terminals of six thousand Telpor stations.

"*'Sein Herz voll Hass geladen,'*" Horst Bertold said to Rachmael. "You speak Yiddish? You understand?"

"I speak a little Yiddish," Rachmael said, "but that's German. 'His heart heavy with hate.' What's that from?"

"From the Civil War in Spain," Bertold said. "From a song of the International Brigade. Germans, mostly, who had left the Third Reich to fight in Spain against Franco, in the 1930s. They were, I suppose, Communists. But—they were fighting Fascism, and very early; *and they were Germans.* So they were always 'good' Germans . . . what that man, Hans Beimler, hated was Nazism and Fascism, in all its stages and states and manifestations." After a pause he said. "We fought the Nazis, too, we 'good' Germans; *verges' uns nie.*" Forget us never, Bertold had said, quietly, calmly. Because we did not merely join the fight late, in the 1950s or '60s, but from the start. The first human beings to fight to the death, to kill and be killed by the Nazis, were—

Germans.

"And Terra," Bertold said to Rachmael, "ought not to forget that. As I hope they will not forget who at this moment is taking out Dr. Sepp von Einem and creatures allied with him. Theodoric Ferry, his boss . . . who, by the way, is an American." He smiled at Rachmael. "But there are 'good' Americans. Despite the A-bomb dropped on those Japanese women and children and elderly."

Rachmael was silent, he could not answer this.

"All right," Bertold said, then. "We will put you together with a wep-x, a weapon expert. To see what gear you should have. And then good luck. I hope you bring back Miss Holm." He smiled—fleetingly. And turned at once to other matters.

A minor UN official plucked at Rachmael's sleeve. "I'm to take charge of your problem," he explained. "I will be handling it from now on. Tell me, Mr. ben Applebaum; precisely what contemporary—and I do not mean last month's or last year's—weapons of war you are accustomed to operating, if any? And how recently you have been exposed to the neurological and bacterial—"

"I've had absolutely no military training," Rachmael said. "Or antineuro or -bac modulation."

"We can still assist you," the minor UN official said. "There is certain equipment requiring no prior experience. However—" He made a mark on the sheet attached to his clipboard. "This does make a difference; eighty percent of the hardware available would be useless to you." He smiled encouragingly. "We must not let it get us down, Mr. ben Applebaum."

"I won't," Rachmael said grimly. "So I'll be teleported to Whale's Mouth after all."

"Yes, within a matter of an hour."

"The unteleported man," Rachmael murmured. "Will be teleported." Instead of enduring the eighteen years aboard the *Omphalos*. Ironic.

"Are you capable morally," the UN official inquired, "of employing a nerve gas, or would you prefer to—"

"Anything," Rachmael said, "that'll bring back Freya. Anything except the phosphorus weapons, the jellied petroleum products; I won't use any of those, and also the bone-marrow destroyers—leave those out. But lead slugs, the old-fashioned muzzle-expelled shells; I'll accept them, as well as the laser-beam artifacts." He wondered what variety of weapon had gotten Matson Glazer-Holliday, the most professional of men in this area.

"We have something new," the UN official said, consulting his clipboard, "and according to the Defense Department people very promising. It's a time-warping construct that sets up a field which coagulates the—"

"Just equip me," Rachmael said. "And get me over there. To her."

"Right away," the UN official promised, and led him rapidly

down a side hall to a hi-speed descent ramp. To the UN Advance-weapons Archives.

At the retail outlet of Trails of Hoffman Limited, Jack and Ruth McElhatten and their two children emerged from a flapple taxi; a robot-like organism carted their luggage, all seven overstuffed seedy—borrowed for the most part—suitcases, as they entered the modern, small building which for them was to be the last stopping-point on Terra.

Going up to the counter, Jack McElhatten searched about for a clerk to wait on them. Jeez, he thought; just when you decide to make the Big Move *they* decide to step out for a coffee break.

A smartly uniformed armed UN soldier, with an arm-band identifying him as a member of the crack UAR division, approached him. "What did you wish?"

Jack McElhatten said, "Hell, we came here to emigrate. I've got the poscreds." He reached for his wallet. "Where are the forms to fill out, and then I know we got to take shots and—"

The UN soldier politely said, "Sir, have you watched your info media during the last forty-eight hours?"

"We've been packing." Ruth McElhatten spoke up. "Why, what is it? Has something happened?"

And then, through an open rear door, Jack McElhatten saw *it*. The Telpor. And his heart bent with mingled dread and anticipation. What an admirably large move this was, this true migration; seeing the twin wall-like polar surfaces of the Telpor was to see—the frontier itself. In his mind he recalled the years of TV scenes of grasslands, of miles of green, lush—

"Sir," the UN soldier said, "read this notice." He pointed to a square white with words so dark, so unglamorous, that Jack McElhatten, even without reading them, felt the glow, the wonder of what for him was a long-held inner vision, depart.

"Oh good lord," Ruth said, from beside him as she read the

notice. "The UN—it's closed down all the Telpor agencies. Emigration has been suspended." She glanced in dismay at her husband. "Jack, it's now illegal for us to emigrate, it says."

The UN soldier said, "Later on, madam. Emigration will resume. When the situation is resolved." He turned away, then, to halt a second couple, who, with four children, had entered the Trails of Hoffman office.

Through the still-open rear door, McElhatten saw, to his dumb disbelief, four work-garbed laborers; they were busily, sweatily, efficiently torch-cutting into sections the Telpor equipment.

He then forced himself to read the notice.

After he had read it the UN soldier tapped him—not unkindly—on the shoulder, pointed out a nearby TV set, which, turned on, was being watched by the second couple and their four children. "These are Newcolonizedland," the UN soldier said. "You see?" His English was not too good, but he was attempting to explain; he wanted the McElhattens to understand *why*.

Approaching the TV set, Jack McElhatten saw gray, barracks-like structures with tiny, slotted windows like raptor eyes. And—high fences. He stared, uncomprehendingly . . . and yet, underneath, comprehending completely; he did not even have to listen to the aud track, to the UN announcer.

Ruth whispered, "My god. It's a—concentration camp."

A puff of smoke and the top floors of the gray cement building disappeared; dwarfed dark shapes scampered, and rapid-fire weapons clattered in the background of the announcer's British-type voice; the calm, reasonable commentary explained what did not need to be explained.

At least not after this sight.

"Is that," Ruth said to her husband, "how we would have lived over there?"

Presently he said, to her and their two children, "Come on. Let's go home." He signaled the robot-organism to pick their luggage up once more.

"But," Ruth protested, "couldn't the UN have helped us? They have all those welfare agencies—"

Jack McElhatten said, "The UN is protecting us now. And not with welfare agencies." He indicated the work-garbed laborers busy dismantling the Telpor unit.

"But so late—"

"Not," he said, "too late." He signaled the robot-thing to carry their seven bulging suitcases back outside onto the sidewalk; avoiding the many passing people, the dense, always dense, sidewalk traffic, he searched for a flapple taxi to take himself and his family home again to their miserable cramped, hated conapt.

A man, distributing leaflets, approached him, held out a broadsheet; McElhatten reflexively accepted it. The Friends of a United People outfit, he saw. Glaring banner:

UN VERIFIES COLONY TYRANNY

He said, aloud, "They were right. The cranks. The lunatics, like that guy who wanted to make the eighteen-year trip by interstellar ship." He carefully folded the broadsheet, put it into his pocket to read later; right now he felt too numbed. "I hope," he said aloud, "that my boss will take me back."

"They're *fighting*," Ruth said. "You could see on the TV screen; they showed UN soldiers and then others in funny uniforms I never saw before in all my—"

"You think," Jack McElhatten asked his wife, "you could sit in the taxi with the kids while I find a bar and get one good stiff drink?"

She said, "Yes. I could." Now a flapple taxi was swooping down, attracted; it headed for the curb, and the four of them and their mound of fat luggage enticing its tropism.

"Because," Jack McElhatten said, "I can use for instance a bourbon and water. A double." And then, he said to himself, I'm heading for UN recruiting headquarters and volunteer.

He did not know for what—not yet. But they would tell him.

His help was needed; he felt it in his blood. A war had to be won, and then, years from now but not eighteen as it had been for that nut written up in the 'papes, they could do it, could emigrate. But before that—the fighting. The winning of Whale's Mouth all over again. Actually, for the first time.

But even before that: the two drinks.

As soon as the luggage was loaded he got with his family into the flapple taxi and gave it the name of the bar where he often stopped after work. Obligingly the taxi spouted up into the overcrowded, me-first, nose-to-nose density of supra-surface Terran unending traffic.

And as the taxi rose Jack McElhatten dreamed again of tall, windtouched grasses and froglike creatures and open plains meandered over by quaint animals that were not afraid because no one intended to hurt them. But his awareness of the reality remained and ran parallel to the dream; he saw both at once and he put his arm around his wife and hugged her and was silent.

The taxi, expertly maneuvering among all the other vehicles, directed itself toward the bar on the east side of town; it knew its way, too. It, also, knew its task.

AFTERWORD
TO THE VINTAGE EDITION

by Paul Williams
LITERARY EXECUTOR
OF THE ESTATE OF PHILIP K. DICK,
1983–1992

This novel has an unusual history. Philip K. Dick wrote it during his very prolific mid-1960s period (he wrote ten novels in two years, 1963 and 1964). In a 1977 letter, Dick recalled: "Part Two of *The Unteleported Man* was written in 1964, a number of years after Part One was written—for *Amazing-Fantastic*, by the way, in response to a cover they had gotten and wanted to use. They needed a story to go with the cover, so they sent me a photo of the cover [painting] and I came up with forty thousand words, which was the maximum number they'd accept. Don Wollheim at Ace [Ace Books, Dick's primary paperback publisher at the time] said he'd like an expansion to use as a novel, rather than a forty-thousand-word novelette; however, Part Two did not please him, so he published the forty-thousand-word Part One as one half of an Ace double."

The records at the Scott Meredith Literary Agency show that the manuscript for "The Unteleported Man" (evidently the title was Dick's) was received by the agency on August 26, 1964, and that the manuscript of the requested expansion material was received on May 5, 1965. The short novel was first published in the December 1964 issue of *Fantastic* (one of two science fiction magazines produced by the same editor and publisher) and then the same short novel (without the rejected expansion material) was published as a paperback book by Ace in 1966. It was published in their "double book" format, with another short novel by another author (the back cover of each book was actually the cover of the other book, so the two novels were printed upside down to each other in the same volume; Dick's first published novel, *Solar Lottery*, in 1955, had been such a "double book" and he'd had other novels published by Ace in the same format over the years).

Ace reissued *The Unteleported Man*, again as half of a "double book," in 1972. The novel was published under the same title, but with the previously unpublished expansion material added, by Berkley Books in 1983. This was because Dick, in 1979, had gotten his editor at Berkley to agree to publish the novel with the rejected 1965 expansion added on. The Ace edition was out of print, so Dick had the rights back, and he knew he had a copy of the rejected expansion material in the collection of his manuscripts that he'd given to the library at California State University, Fullerton. The cover of the 1983 paperback says, "now uncensored for the first time," which is dramatic and somewhat misleading, since the previous editions contained every word of what had been published in *Fantastic* and originally submitted to and bought by Ace. Dick, of course, still unhappy that his expansion had been rejected in 1965, and eager to justify this new edition of the novel, had himself promoted this slightly misleading idea that the book would now be uncut for the first time.

When Dick obtained a copy of his 1965 expansion material from the Fullerton library, he found he had a problem. Four pages were missing from three different places in the manuscript, creating three gaps in the text that he now had to write new connective material to fill in. He also realized that this expansion wasn't exactly a "part two" that could be placed immediately after the rest of the book with no explanation. In the course of dealing with these matters, he got the idea of "reframing" the book by writing new opening pages and perhaps various bits of new connective material.

So, probably in a single day or a few hours, he wrote a brand new Chapter One, and rewrote the original Chapter One extensively to make a new Chapter Two, and found himself giving the book a new title (*Lies, Inc.*), and made a few other small changes here and there for consistency with the elements introduced in the new opening pages. He also made the big decision as to where in the existing novel to place the large chunk of 1965 expansion material. He inserted it almost three-fourths of the way through the original short novel, in the middle of the original Chapter Seven. But he didn't write the connective material to fill in those annoying gaps. That, and possibly some other thoughts he had about new material he should write to make the new book flow together properly, kept him from calling the job done and sending the rewrite off to his editor (Mark Hurst) in New York.

So it came to pass that in July 1983, sixteen months after Philip K. Dick's death in March 1982, Berkley Books published an edition of *The Unteleported Man* that was twice as long as the 1966 Ace edition but did not use the new title or the recently written pages and did have the anomaly of three gaps in the text of the second half of the novel.

This was not the end of the saga, however. Dick's U.K. publisher, Gollancz, had a contract to publish a British edition of the expanded *Unteleported Man*, and before the end of 1983, I, as PKD's literary executor, came across the revised and retitled 1979 typescript of the book and had it sent to Gollancz. There was still the matter of those missing manuscript pages, and so Gollancz, with the permission of Dick's estate, hired science fiction writer John Sladek to write short connective material to fill in the gaps (only two gaps now, because Dick's revisions deleted the last six pages of expansion material, which was the location of the third gap). So the book was published by Gollancz in 1984 with the 1965 expansion and Dick's 1979 revisions and Sladek's connective material, under the title *Lies, Inc.*

Then in 1985, while doing some research in the PKD papers at

Cal State University's Fullerton Library, I found the missing pages from the 1965 *Unteleported Man* expansion (they had found their way into a box containing manuscript material for *Do Androids Dream of Electric Sheep?*). Those pages were then published in the eighth issue of *The Philip K. Dick Society Newsletter* . . . and they are included in this (first American) edition of *Lies, Inc.*

So this is *The Unteleported Man*, take two, as the author intended it in 1979, but necessarily without any further revisions he may have thought about making but never got around to. For the curious, the 1965 expansion material begins several pages into Chapter Eight of the current edition with the words "Acrid smoke billowed about him," and ends halfway through Chapter Fifteen just before the paragraph (added by Dick in 1979) that starts, "Acrid smoke billowed about him." Because the 1965 material was inserted into the original novel at a different place in the 1983 Berkley edition (Berkley at the time had no way of knowing where, in 1979, Dick had intended for it to go), this present edition gives the novel a very different resolution than the 1983 edition does. So what you are holding is the first American edition of this novel as Philip K. Dick intended it in 1979 when he prepared this "Lies, Inc." version of *The Unteleported Man*.

Paul Williams
Encinitas, California
April 2003